D1568329

Finding the Moon in Sugar

Gint Aras

Copyright © 2009 by Karolis Gintaras Žukauskas

ISBN 0-7414-5093-3

Published by:

PUBLISHING.COM

1094 New DeHaven Street, Suite 100
West Conshohocken, PA 19428-2713
Info@buybooksontheweb.com
www.buybooksontheweb.com
Toll-free (877) BUY BOOK
Local Phone (610) 941-9999
Fax (610) 941-9959

Printed in the United States of America

Printed on Recycled Paper

Published January 2009

for Taiyda

That Fateful Saturday

I swear right now that everything your gonna read in here happened 100% true. Cauze when I used to look back at all this crap that went down with me, sometimes I wouldn't even believe it myself. I used to trip a lot on shrooms and acid, plus get high off weed or hash in weird places which can mess up how your ass remembers shit. (Though shrooms can help you with other stuff, but I'll tell you about that later.) The thing is, when you start writin' down a story from your life, it totally makes you sort shit out, so I'll admit I'm doin' this to understand what the fuck happened myself. Still, for anybody who wants to read it, it's a real good story even though there's parts in here that get kinda wigged.

The whole thing started way earlier than that fateful Saturday on April 1, 2006. But I'm scared all the stuff about my dad and the hometown where I'm from is gonna bore your ass. Unless you live around there, probably you never even heard of Berwyn frickin' Illinois. Cauze there's people from Chicago who never even heard of it, though on sunny days you can see the Sears Tower clean off Ogden Avenue. Berwyn has some nice streets with good houses, though also the town is trashy, like corner bars and train tracks and dudes walkin' around with their jeans fallin' down. If you lost your beer gut, probably someone in Berwyn picked it up and never even noticed.

Back in '06 I was tryin' to get my life improved, cauze my job at the stupid Buona Beef wasn't workin' out like I planned. I was takin' some classes by this community college called Sterling which is over in Cicero, like the town right next door by Berwyn where some parts get ghetto. My first class started in January, though by March already I was dropped out and flunked. It got way too hard, frickin' *English 086* and *Intermediate Algebra*. You gotta study all day for them classes, only you don't got all day when you crash a car and end up owin' a guy lots of cash.

I knew this dude Diego. By accident I smashed up his uncle's Buick with more than two grand in damage. And Diego needed it fast cauze his uncle was gonna come home from Mexico in like a month or six weeks without no warning. The only way I could get that cash was sellin' weed, which I promised after high school I wouldn't do no more. But Buona Beef wasn't gonna pay for no Buick.

One buyer I knew was this landlord (not mine) with some properties all around Oak Park and Berwyn and Cicero...he was real rich cauze he inherited maybe a dozen houses when his old man died. The thing is, this dude was a SMOKER...a frickin' Deadhead, Phishhead and Radiohead, all his clocks 4:20 all the time and every day. His beard was real big, like three gallons of hair on his face. So in my story I'm gonna call him Big Beard.

I would meet him by Oak Park in this laundrymat right near the Green Line el stop on Oak Park Avenue. We would make the deal in my car cauze he never wanted to show where he lived. So that's where it started on April 1st, 2006 when I was waitin' for Big Beard in the frickin' laundry and mindin' my own business. He was usually dead on time, though now he was maybe ten minutes late. But I stayed cool, busted out some Cypress Hill on my headphones. I had a yellow pillow case with three jeans in there so I could throw them in a dryer, pretend I'm an official laundry user. And I just watched my jeans go round and round and sat chillin' with Cypress.

Now I'm gonna change another name. Cauze this story is really about a lady who came in the laundry that day...I'm gonna call her Audra. She was from this country called Lithuania, which is totally a real place and you can google it if you want. Over there they talk Lithuanian, a real messed up language with longass names like *Aušrainė, Ventvaitė* and *Šišvaiška,* so Audra's more easy for you to read. When I first seen her, she was maybe 32 or 34. Though also she could of been 29 or 30 since I never got her real age pinned down exact. Back then I was just 20, so when she first came in I didn't think too much about it. I mean, she was real beautiful. But big deal. Tall blonde women walk around Oak Park all the time cauze they get married with all them rich assholes who live there.

Big Beard wasn't coming. I called with my cell but he didn't pick up. Then I went out to roll some Drum and have a smoke, look up and down the street for his ass. Frickin' I didn't see him noplace and went back in to wait real annoyed about it.

From the place where I sat down I could see Audra's reflection in a dryer. After this one thin dude left with his laundry basket, it was only me and Audra in there. She didn't have no load to wash, just kept messin' with her phone, readin' some messages and textin' somebody. I thought I was real smooth lookin' at her reflection so she didn't know about it, but then we had one of them moments where the chick catches you starin' at her. Real quick I looked at some "important shit" like the trash can. But I was nailed red handed and dumb, especially since my dryer was already finished for like five minutes.

I'm one of them dudes who gets like a moron if a hot chick is gonna talk with me. It's all this buzzing on my back, plus my tongue goes dry like a brick. She was comin' over...totally knew how to click her heels so damn evil. I figured I'll get my dry clothes, act like everything's regular, though I got paranoid cauze maybe she's a cop. She knows that's *my* Plymouth Horizon outside, the one with an ounce of weed in the glove.

Audra said, "Can I ask you something?"

"Um." I was trying to button some jeans. "Sure."

"Would you like to make a thousand dollars?"

That question didn't really make it all the way to my brain. Audra sighed. "Earth to Nate," she said. "Can you answer? Stoner boy?"

"What? Sorry." It was kinda smooth how I took off my earphones and put the whole CD player in the pillowcase. "I'm Nate, yeah. You mean, like dollars?"

"One thousand dollars, Nate? Do you want to make that much?" Right there I heard how she talked with a little accent, only it was real small. "Won't take long."

I think I shrugged. Or maybe I scratched my chin or something. "Sure. I'll make that much." I kinda went auto pilot and followed her to a shiny ass Lincoln Navigator. To hide my boner I kept the pillow case in my lap when she was drivin' me around.

Dude, my name ain't Nate. That's just the name I used to give weed customers like Big Beard. I guess I should of known right there Audra had something to do with him, probably she knew him and got the name from him. But I was seein' her legs up close and could smell her perfume like sleeping potion. I said, "My name's Andrew. Though that's like the long version. Cauze people call me Andy mostly. Or Drew...they call me Drew. Frickin' Cicero boys, they just turn it into D. But that's kinda ghetto."

I could of been named Larry Hick Dominick or Michael Jeffrey Jordan, she didn't care about it at all. Audra just drove that huge car with her blue eyes on the road. I looked at them eyes real careful cauze I seen a rainy day in there like something was sad. Also her one eye was kinda red, a little swelled when I had a better look.

I grew up in my life with some real depressed women. Pill poppers and boozers, my older sister, my mom, my alcoholic grandma, all three filled up with hurt inside where they wouldn't tell nobody. My dad left my mom with a whole pile of crap, kids and bills, stuff that's real hard to handle by yourself, and lookin' at Audra I could see that kind of thing in her. If you know it, it's a real special quiet, though under the quiet they got lots of loudness tied up with real tight knots. I knew for sure she had it cauze it was strong from deep inside. Not no make up or fancy clothes can cover it up.

She pulled that Navigator in a garage where I seen a boat. On the walls it was lots of fishing stuff, like poles that you could catch a shark or a whale, plus posters with dudes wearin' them green rubber pants and stupid hats. The garage went to the house and I followed Audra through some rooms, like four or five. The kitchen had a shandeleer in there and I seen crystal bowls and some dishes on small tables. A Mexican lady was cleanin' the place and I almost stepped on the mophead dog cauze the little shit was the exact same color like the carpet.

One room smelled like clay and wet paint...it was filled up with paintings and statues, some of 'em leaned up by the walls. One painting was a dude fishing, then another one showed this cabin by a river and some people sittin' by a bonfire. But in the middle of the room was this clay thing. It wasn't finished yet, but I could tell it was frickin' Big Beard's head! He was makin' his own face...the same way how sometimes you see a dude's head on a piano, only bigger. Further down one hallway I seen a picture of him shaved trim with Audra in her wedding clothes. She wasn't that much younger then.

Audra made me go in a bedroom. Before I could ask what the hell's goin' on or where the fuck is Big Beard, she was takin' off her clothes. "Andy? Or Drew?" It took like ten seconds and she was standin' butt naked like we're in porno. "You don't mind, do you?" Audra touched my face real gentle and I went shiverin'. I was tryin' to hide behind the pillow case but she dumped that stupid thing in a corner. Then she fell back on the bed and spread her legs. "I want you to eat me out," she said. "Please. You'll do it, won't you?"

Dude, I laughed, I think, cauze Audra also started laughin'. One thousand dollars? When I seen her laid down like that and feelin' herself I forgot about money. I was just happy this one girl gave me all them pussy eating lessons my junior year. Thanks to her, I totally got in there real confident.

It's amazing how much wacko shit you can think while you go down on a strange older woman. Am I breakin' some laws? What if Big Beard comes home? He'll hook me up with them fishing hooks. The Mexican lady was closin' some doors and slidin' shit way deep in the house. We could hear all that with the bedroom door wide open, but I wasn't gonna stand up to close it now.

In the beginning it was kinda fun. But pretty soon shit got complicated. She started howlin' loud like someone's stabbin' her, totally makin' extra noise. I thought we were done, but she wanted more. She kept makin' my hands go all over her body, made me pinch her and told me to do it harder. She wouldn't let me take no break, would just grab my head and hold my ears. Pretty soon she was moanin' like her family died and her face turned sunburn red. Then Audra told me, "Just wait a moment," and right there she busted out her cocaine stuff.

Dude, it wasn't cool. Cauze when a real gorgeous woman cokes up naked in front of you, it ain't hot, just tweaked and wigged...she rubbed her eyes and some mascara got smeared. I started wantin' to get the hell outta there, and when my cell rang I thought I had a chance. But she knocked it outta my hand and made me do it again. I did just cauze I couldn't know what she's got next, maybe a knife stashed under a pillow or a gun. She was totally jacked up and crazy, like she wanted an orgasm to kill her.

The phone kept ringin'. The Mexican lady fired up a blender in the kitchen. Then somebody started a lawn mower outside and a helicopter flew over pretty low. "Turn that shit off," she said, but she had her hands tight around my head and was pressin' me down. "Turn it off!" She held me tighter...I didn't know what the fuck to do...Audra was so damn strong and her nails went diggin' real hard in my neck. I didn't know why, but pretty soon she started beatin' her hands on the bed with real hard slaps, then she pushed me with her feet so I fell off the bed. I think she was cryin' now or freakin' out, or just makin' a scene to scare me. She yelled, "Don't you touch that phone."

"Hey, it's cool." I tried to stay chill. "It's okay. I ain't gonna call nobody. It's cool." I kinda sat down next to her real gentle and pet her real light. After a couple seconds, she freaked. "Just take money and get out!" Audra rolled over by a little drawer where it was loads of cash in one envelope, totally crisp bills. She counted the money, shoved it in my hand and told me to get the fuck out.

The Mexican lady was still in the kitchen with a blender. I walked past with my shirt torn and my neck all ripped up, my face barely even wiped off. But the lady just kept cuttin' mangoes, kinda rubbin' her forehead with the back of her hand. I got lost in that house for a minute, but then found my way out some side door. I was already on the corner of LeMoyne and Oak Park Avenue when I checked my pocket, figured out I left my phone in Big Beard's house.

Now it was no way to remember his number. And from LeMoyne the walk back to the laundry was like twelve long blocks past Augusta and Chicago Avenue and then Lake Street. But Big Beard must of been hard up for weed cauze he was still waitin' in a restaurant across the street from my car. That dude came out when he seen me pissed from a parking ticket stuck on my window. "Nate. What the hell happened to you?"

"Nothing. Where the fuck were you? Called your ass, you were late first."

"Had some issues, sorry." He was lookin' me over real good when I was messin' with my car keys. "That's blood on your back? You get into a fight?"

"Don't worry about it." We made the deal. I thought he might smell his wife's perfume on me, so I rushed him out, said I'm late for all kinds of shit. Then I frickin' left Oak Park with more cash in my pocket than I ever even seen in my whole damn life.

Sugar Mama

Here's the thing...money sucks. I think it's way more fucked up than drugs, mostly cauze you need money to get drugs. But also money can mess with your ass in lots more different ways, though most of 'em you can't even predict. Right here's a good example...let's say *boom!* you end up with twelve hundred bones in your pants. For real, you start seein' shit totally different, and it's kinda like hallucination or when your dreamin' off weed. On one side you kinda know your a hooker, though you don't even know how the fuck it happened. But then you drive by a store where they got good turn tables and some amps in the window and it gets you thinkin' *screw Diego's Buick.* I came home and the wind went blowin' used motorbike ads on my front stairs totally on purpose. On the tube they put one of them Southwest commercials where you can go someplace way better than Berwyn, like Miami or Florida where it's warm and you can live outside if you want.

But here's the real bullshit with money. The only time you give drugs to somebody else is when they're buyin' from you...or it can happen with friends when your tryin' to be cool and share. But when you get twelve hundred bones in your pants, right away you have to give most of it to the bastards. Like Audra just gave it to me, but right there the parking ticket already subtracted fifty. Then the landlord down the street needed $585 (a rip off for livin' in a frickin' basement near the Burlington Northern where freight trains shaked the ground all night). I gave Diego only $465 so I could keep a hondo for myself and have somethin' to feel good about.

But it didn't work. Two days after payin' all my bills, I was sittin' on my couch and lookin' at Ben Franklin's fat head. And I was thinkin' maybe I should call a bank to see if a hundred bones is good to open up for savings. I swear I used to *think* about puttin' money away all the time, like savin' up to get another class at Sterling. Or enough just to get the hell outta Berwyn...go frickin' *anywhere* but Berwyn, even a short trip to Normal, IL where two of my buddies were livin' with total freedom. But anytime I had extra cash, some shit would come up where I would have to pay for stuff I couldn't even predict. A frickin' new cell phone since I lost it. Or somebody from my family would need me to help them from a fix.

Like my mom. She always had this damn radar in her head...*beep, beep, beep, Drew's come up with cash. Drew's come up with cash.* I was totally gettin' ready to spark one up so I could go down by the mall and check out some phones. But then I heard my mom's knock rattle the screen door real loud since she never used the doorbell.

My mom's kinda fat. She smokes around two packs of Basic 100's a day so her face is wrinkled from them cigs. The thing is, she's real young compared with most moms, had my sister at 16, then me two years later. When she came in my place, I seen she was kinda drunk...if my mom has just one Bud Light, she starts wipin' her mouth with a closed hand, plus her forehead gets pink spots. A little more booze and her thin hair flies all over the place like a bunch of flags, which it was doin' right now. She kinda mumbled, "Hi," and had a look around my place. A *High Times* poster was hangin' by the door and she stood over there for a while. "Your hangin' up junk again, Andrew?"

"No."

"How come it's a weed poster?" She wiped her mouth. "Your dealin' again?"

"No way."

She stared me down. Even if she's hammered, still her eyes can go straight in the middle of your blood and boil a couple bubbles. "Know what it cost me last time, Andrew?" Mom kinda fell on my couch and sighed real hard with all her mom stress. "How come your not pickin' up your phone? Turned off for three days now? Or four?"

"The phone. Yeah, cauze it fell in water. By accident."

"What water?"

"Like water."

"Bullshit, Andrew. You lost your phone. Or it's turned off. Where's your phone?" I was gonna come up with some story about a puddle, but I couldn't even say one word cauze mom started rantin' up a speech. Right now I won't tell the whole thing...she got talkin' how she bought me a phone when she never bought me no phone. And she didn't pay no phone bill, though mom kept sayin' it costs her bad when I keep losin' *phones*, lots of 'em, like I dumped frickin' the whole company Nokia in Lake Michigan. And it was real expensive the last time I got busted for dealin' (though it was only *possession*, like when I was seventeen) so she couldn't count on me. Especially since grandma broke her elbow now and nobody's gonna help with the bill.

"Gram broke her elbow? Where?"

"Here!" Mom pointed. "That's the elbow right there, Andrew."

"But she can't barely walk."

"Tried gettin' up." Mom wiped her mouth again. "Don't look at me. Nobody *made* her get up. She got up by her own, so don't make no eyes." Mom took a drag where I thought she was done talkin'. But she still had more stuff to bitch about cauze the roof had a leak and squirrels were havin' babies in the garage. And my sister took the last money for an oil change, though probably it was to spend on dudes. Mom said somebody stole shit from the back yard, like the garden hose and a couple lawn chairs.

Right there the doorbell rang. This was a pretty good surprise for me...I seen mom get real annoyed since she don't like no interruption. "Who's that? Dope customers?" I figured it was the

Jehovahs or maybe kids sellin' candy. But when I seen Audra standin' there I almost shit a brick.

She was dressed like one of them Michigan Avenue ladies with big sunglasses and hair cut straight so it was real high class. Her outfit was one of them dark blue business suits with a skirt, only real advanced with a fluffy blouse. By her side she had that stupid yellow pillowcase. Audra said, "Andy? I'm sorry. You've got company?"

Mom said, "Not company. Just his ma." She took a while to stand from the couch, hard to get up. When she seen Audra come in the room, for her it could of been Sharon Stone or Maria Sharapova...mom's face turned like wet cement, her cheeks hangin' real heavy. Audra said, "Are you sure...I can come back later?"

"Sit down, dearie." Mom pointed to a chair with her smoke. "You want somethin' to drink? Drew, you probably got some Chivas Regal in here."

Audra said, "No, no. I can't stay very long."

We all kinda sat around awkward, one of them horrible moments when nobody frickin' knows what to say or where the hell they should look. I could smell Audra's swanko perfume, like nobody in Berwyn smelled stuff like that before. And I seen what a serious pig I am, dirtyass cups everywhere, a pizza box with crumpled aluminum, plus a bottle of flat RC. But the real shock was to see how hardcore different Audra was actin' now. She was sittin' like a regular lady with a job, maybe like a bank person or one of them ladies from a skyscraper, the ones you see waitin' for the Metra trains real early in the morning. I guess mom wanted me to make some introduction, but I was rememberin' Audra naked. Out from nowhere I said, "I got half a fridge in the burrito."

Audra only whispered, "No, thank you." She put the pillow case down by the table.

Mom said, "That's *my* pillow case." She blew some smoke at it. "Drew, how come this dearie has my pillow case?" That was the first time in my life when my mom gave this look like she's *sure* this is somebody I'm screwin'...her eyes went accusin' me like *oho ho.* Audra said, "Andrew left this pillowcase at my place."

"*Really*? At *your* place?" Mom ashed in a cup. "If you don't mind it blunt, who're you anyway?"

"This must be an awkward moment for you, Mrs. Nowak."

I had no idea how the hell Audra got my last name. Mom got real annoyed, "Not no Nowak to you. Not even close, dearie. That's my ex-husband's name, and *this* one here," she pointed at me. "It's Andrew's name, but it ain't mine."

"Well, I'm sorry. It was rude of me to guess."

"You bet your sweet ass." Mom kinda crossed her fat arms. "You an immigrant? Cauze I hear some kinda accent in there."

"I'm Lithuanian."

"Oh, a Lugan? That's why you think your shit don't stink." Mom coughed a little. "My husband was Polish."

"Oh, great." said Audra. She kinda pulled her skirt down. "I've never been to Poland. But I hear it's very nice."

"Real nice. So nice all them Pollacks come live by Midway airport."

Audra nodded and shrugged some.

Mom said, "Your gonna say who you are?"

"I don't know if Andy wants me to tell you. But if it will help you relax...I'm...yes, I'm his sponsor."

"Sponsor?" Mom's face went more wrinkled. "Sponsor for what?"

I said, "Cauze I'm tryin' to quit drugs, mom. And go back to school." That kinda confused her so she had to think it through real good. She went, "What the hell's a sponsor got my pillow case for?"

Audra said, "It's just a sack." She took out the CD player and popped it open. "These items helped discussions. This music, for example." Audra handed me the Cypress Hill CD. It had my name *Andy Nowak* written on there with a Sharpie. Audra said, "Also, you left your phone at the last meeting."

"Aha!" mom shouted. "Cauze bullshit, Drew, your a liar! There it is, Drew. There it is! A liar." She stood up, wheezin' hardcore, "Water, my ass. Water *my ass*, Drew! That's your phone right there. He lies regular all the time, *all* the time since he's a little shit. But he won't even give his ma no dime to help out. Just lies straight to my face! Straight with them puppy eyes." She took her purse. "We got bills. The doctor and a roof. And your visitin' your Lugan missy here. She ain't no sponsor. What you buyin' from him?"

"Mom..."

"Your good for nothin'! Just like your old man, good for shit, only even more dumb. If I didn't have no kids, you know what my life would be right now? Kids who can't get no job. Just freeload, that's all. If I didn't have none..."

"Your son isn't a bad person, Mrs. Nowak."

"Drop the bit. And I ain't no Nowak to you, missy fitness. Who'd you marry to get over here? Probably the fuckin' green card lottery, which is good for *your* ass. Cauze nobody makes no lottery when your born in America. Not no Lugans, not *nobody*."

Mom took the pillowcase to dump it. Them three jeans fell out so she kinda looked at me with her face disgusted. Then she stuffed that case in her purse real dramatic, totally worked up so it was givin' me a guilt trip.

Right now your gonna think I'm a tool. But I need to admit it, how mom's guilt trips always worked on me and made me feel real down. I would feel sorry for her since it was kinda true...nobody never helped her out. I knew her whole thing was show and drama, but it didn't matter. I ended up takin' that hondo...it was folded in my fist so Audra couldn't see how much when I handed it to mom. At first she pushed my hand away, but then she seen it's cash. "This?"

"For gram."

"How'd you get it?"

I shrugged. Mom kinda shaked her head, but then she put the money in her pocket. Goin' out, she pushed my screen door so the spring squeaked and the door slammed hard. I could hear her muffler rumble up outside and then her old Ford drove away.

For a second me and Audra just stared at each other. She wasn't shocked or surprised, not annoyed or nothing like that. Just said, "I didn't mean to cause that, Andy." Then she was quiet with her knees pressed together real tight...maybe she could tell I felt real stupid, though also I was pissed off. I said, "It don't matter." "I stayed. I saw what was happening. I'm sorry."

I rolled my Drum with my fingers kinda shakin'. It was totally weird and wigged for me to sit with her now cauze she was actin' shy and uncomfortable, frickin' completely different from Big Beard's house. For real, I thought maybe she's one of them bipolars, like which part is real and which one fake? Or it could be from cocaine, like she's come down to act regular. I said, "Is it all you wanted? To give my stuff back?"

"Oh..." She got real awkward. "Yes. Not only...but also to tell you...and to ask...to see."

"You get to see how I live real dirtbag."

"Oh no." She looked around. "No, it's refreshing. I like it."

"That's bullshit, dude."

She kinda smiled, though not in a happy way. "Dude?"

I was quiet for a while, kinda lookin' at her to figure her out. "Well...what I'm supposed to call you? You got two names for me. But I don't know even one for you."

I never expected it when she blushed. Maybe it was fake, though how can you fake a blush? She told me her name. Then she was havin' a hard time tryin' to say more stuff. "Do you want me to leave you alone? Tell me honestly."

"I didn't expect nobody. Just bad timing with my mom."

Audra stood up kinda sudden so she was right by the door. "Well...I'm sorry." Then she went lookin' through her purse for car keys, takin' way too long to find 'em. "If you want, Andy. Have you eaten today?"

"No."

"We could eat someplace. Is there a place around here that you like? But they need to have drinks. Because I'd like a drink."

"I ain't twenty one."

"That's okay. I am."

Dude, half of me (or maybe like 48%) wanted to say, "No, sorry. Cauze I'm real busy." And probably if *anybody* else would of come in my apartment to act like a Jack and Hide, I totally would of said some excuse. But I gotta explain it right here...Audra was one of them people where you can't tell her *I gotta check my phone messages* or *I'm datin' somebody*. She would give real bad vibes so you would think about it for a longass time and feel dumb, like you missed out on something. For real, with Audra you could love her or hate her, understand her clean or feel totally confused from stuff she did, but *still* you would do anything she said, frickin' follow her ass down the street. So I told about a booze diner down Windsor, like not even four blocks from my house. And I went outside to her car, this silver ass Quattro.

Audra said nobody's gonna card my ass if I went with her. And it was true...we got Long Island Iced Teas, the first time I ever tried one of 'em, like four shots of booze. She bought me baby backs with roasted potatoes and soup and salad, plus some salmon and veggies so we both ate like pigs. At first we only talked about food, then her bad ass car and my neighborhood. But after we got lubed up it started feelin' normal to sit with her, like I knew her for a long time.

She had lots of questions for me, almost like an interview. How did I grow up and who were my parents? It was weird how she wanted to know and I could tell she was comparin' me with somebody from her life. I ended up tellin' lots of stories, especially about dad cauze that seemed real important for her. Especially when I said he was a wood maker, like a carpenter who made nice doors with designs, or trimming for the floor. Audra had lots of questions about him and I told her everything free. "When was he happiest?"

"If the Bears would win. Cauze he would pick me up and throw me up and down. Then we would go to Proksa Park...that's down the street over here. Just to throw the football around and get tackled in leaves."

Me and Audra kept drinkin' them Long Islands and pretty soon stuff got more heavy. Cauze I said stories how my dad could act real dirtbag. He would call mom a bitch and a cunt or a whore, do it real loud in stores or in the back yard so neighbors could hear. One of his favorite things was to bake meat in the kitchen, but then my sister Jen would have to clean up the whole mess. But anytime Jen made a mess, like if she left her dolls all around the floor or something then dad would yell real loud, "You wanna grow up like your ma?" Lots of people thought he hit us, though that never happened and I ain't lyin'.

Dude, Audra was listenin' to me real deep when I talked. She never yawned or spaced out...except for gram, nobody never listened to me like that in my whole life. It helped Audra get lots of stuff out of me that day.

I told about the problem I had when I was a kid, mostly till 4th grade. I never really knew how come it used to happen to me, but weird stuff that wasn't even important would make me cry and get real sloppy, like if I seen a dead bird on the sidewalk, or if a dog barked at me loud in the alley. I was the only kid in the neighborhood who got sloppy like that, and if dad was around he would jerk me. "Are you my son? Whose son is this? Whose? Be a man, Andrew."

That was his main thing, "My son is a man." Especially since the other problem I had was wettin' the bed...like I did it all the way till 3rd grade. It was so bad I had to sleep with plastic on the mattress sometimes. And almost every morning before goin' to work dad would come real early to wake me up and check. If the bed was dry he would get real happy and shake my hand or give me a dollar. But if I peed, he would poke the bed. "You need diapers. Do you want your mother to put diapers?" One time he yanked me out and went shoutin', "Look what you did. Look! When will you be a man?"

The *man* thing wasn't too bad, cauze I guess I knew I was still a kid. The worst thing I hated was, "You can't be my son," since he said that a lot. It was like rules...you can't get scared from nothing like dogs or bigass spiders that would make webs in the tomatoes he had growin' in the yard. I would go to help pick the tomatoes, though anytime I seen them spiders I would get frozed up and stand still.

It's the last thing I remember about him. One time I was standin' frozed up and he said, "Who's afraid of bugs?" Dad totally went over and grabbed a spider to smush it hard in his fist. Then he washed the hand with the garden hose right in front of my face. "Now you do it, Andrew. Here's another one, go ahead. It's nothing, just little bugs." But I stood there all frozed up and bitin' down inside my mouth to make sure I don't get sloppy. He grabbed one spider and held it with his fingers, tellin' me "Take it. It's small. Your so much bigger. Take it." But he seen me real scared and knew I'm hopeless, I won't never do it. So dad just got disappointed, threw the spider on the cement and stepped on it real light.

Audra asked me, "When did he leave?"

I was already kinda hammered. "I was ten."

"Where is he now?"

"It was Monday Night Football. Dad said he was gonna go watch in the bar. But then he never came home. Gram says he's dead, like his body's in the I & M Canal or the Desplaines. But mom said he found somebody else. Cauze they looked for him with cops and shit. After that, mom didn't want to talk about it too much."

Audra said, "But you don't hate him. I can tell...you don't hate him."

"Sometimes yeah. Since it ain't fair...if your gonna go, then don't have no kids. Or who gives a shit, move down the street with your new woman if you got one younger or more pretty. Don't leave everybody alone. My mom don't even have no GED."

Audra thought about it, kinda stirrin' in her drink. "Andy, no...you don't hate him. Because I know hatred...I can hate deeply, completely. My husband, for example. In case you couldn't tell."

I guess I nodded. "If Big Beard would of found me over there, what would he do?"

   Audra ordered some coffee. Then she kept stirrin' the ice in
her glass, suckin' a little through a straw. She said, "Andy, I
thought I'd find a *drug dealer* in the laundrymat. Not a sweet and
handsome boy. With his name on a compact disc. And his address
in the phone book."
   They brought the coffee. She ripped the most small hole in
one of them *half and half* cups, just dripped a few drops to mix.
"Andy, I'm sorry for treating you that way. Because I thought you
were...anyone. *Anyone*, some piece of trash." She looked up at me.
"It was sweet how you tried to calm me down so gently. If you
think I'm trash or a coke head, I want you to know that I'm not."
She put her hand on my fingers real light. "What I did wasn't fair.
It wasn't as dangerous as you think, but it wasn't fair. So I wanted
to find you, and I'm glad I did. I hope you won't think anything
sick about me. And I hope you'll accept my apology."

Passport

Here's what a tool I used to be. She was real good to me like that, paid for the whole dinner and talked so many nice things. And when I got a ride home in her swanko car, Audra gave me a soft one on the cheek. She looked at me like *now you have to ask*, but I didn't have no guts to ask her number or if we're gonna see each other again. For real, I got kinda unsure...probably it's just in my head, no way she wants to see me again. I went, "Good night then, Audra. Thanks for dinner and everything like that." She said, "Okay, good night." Two minutes later I was alone in my place and knew I screwed it up real bad. Like I got stoned on the couch listenin' to live Dave Matthews, frickin' *Gray Street* and *Stay or Leave*. Crashed right there and woke up kinda early the next day.

Here's the thing, I didn't have too much time to think about her or wonder what anything means. Cauze when I plugged my phone to charge up I seen all the missed calls in there, like more than twenty. I figured most of them would be buyers, but I only got a couple calls from dudes lookin' to score. Diego called to see what's up with me and my mom left some messages. But most of the stuff in there was from Jen, my sister.

Usually she would only call when shit hit the fan, or if she knew about a party and needed shrooms or weed. For the last two months she was tryin' real hard to get me to do crystal meth with her...it was her brand new thing and she totally wanted me to know all about it. But meth would wig me out...lots of her friends

19

were tweakers and Jen used to go nuts with them, stay up for two days straight without eating no food. So I frickin' got ready to hear some weird shit in her messages.

The first one sounded pretty much like this. The computer went, *Next message sent Saturday, April 1ˢᵗ at blah blah blah PM.* "Drew, holy shit, you gotta help me out. I don't know how the hell I'm gonna tell ma cauze I just got married. Totally married. This ain't no April Fool's neither, okay, so call me back. Just call me back."

Dude, every next message after that got more and more insane. I knew she was tweakin', callin' me at weird times like 5:02 in the morning. Sometimes she just went babblin' a million miles, but also she got real pissed at me. "You ain't callin' back on purpose! I shoulda known. You don't even care how I'm gonna tell ma. But it don't even matter what you think, Drew, cauze I'm married to a sweet guy, if you even knew him a little. Though you don't even know. He don't care if your my brother or what, and we won't need nobody else, just us. *Just us*, Drew, if you wanna know. Do you even wanna know?"

Here's what happened...Jen was 22. Pretty much overnight she went and eloped with this dude from Berwyn. He looked pretty good on paper cauze his family owned some businesses in Lyons and Brookfield, like a patio store and a car wash, though their most famous store was a gun shop. Jen's husband mostly worked over there sellin' guns, so in my story I'm gonna call him Gunther Bullets. I had no idea Jen even had a boyfriend, definitely not no honcho almost the same age like our mom, maybe 35. Gunther had a pornstar mustash on his face and his best friend was a taxidermist with mullet hair and a *Git-r-done* shirt.

Gunther was way different from Jen. You won't believe me, but Jen wasn't nothing like him. Even though she had trouble showin' it, she was real smart. All the time when we were little she would do homework in the kitchen and give me all my math answers. In 4ᵗʰ grade she won the spelling contest against older kids, plus she got some awards and certificates for readin' a bunch of books. Before dad left, Jen was this nerd and four-eyes, but things kinda started goin' apeshit for her right around junior high. She would get stoned in school or drop acid. It didn't help too much when mom told her, "You keep this shit up, you'll be dropped out." So just like mom predicted it, Jen dropped out. Just wouldn't go to school no more.

When I finally called her back, she was in a honeymoon cabin in the middle of frickin' Door County, Wisconsin. Gunther was there with some tweakers and a girl named Wilma. Jen was down from meth and sounded real sick, totally wiped out. She just kept askin' me, "What we tell ma, Drew? How you think we should do it?"

"Who cares, Jen. Big deal...you married a dude. Call and say it straight since there ain't no other story. No way around it."

"No, Drew. Cauze you gotta tell her first so she's totally ready for it. Say he's like a nice guy with a job. And tell where his house is at...the real nice one on Euclid that you seen before."

"Dude, is he a tweaker?"

"Fuck you, don't *say* that, Drew. Just cauze you do some meth don't make you no tweaker. It's just cauze your *pissed*. That's the thing...all the time your *pissed* no matter what. You don't even know Gunther yet, so you can't talk shit."

"How come I gotta do it?"

She sighed real hard. "She'll freak if I do it, Drew. When you say stuff to her she just sits quiet." That was kinda true, though also it was kinda bullshit. Jen said, "Make it real easy. So it ain't no surprise for her when we talk."

I had two frickin' choices. I could get the crap over with in the next couple days...or I could deal with Jen callin' me five times a day till it was done. So I picked a time when I knew mom was gonna be home for sure. Didn't call or nothing like that, just drove over.

The front door was open cauze gram was sittin' like usual and watchin' *MeTV*, drinkin' her favorite hot tea with sugar and a thimble of Clan McGreggor. My grandma wasn't super old, just 54. But back in the day she fell off a motorbike and busted up her back real bad, though it never healed right. She had pain in her body pretty much all the time, plus she would get some my grains, real bad ones where you had to pull all the shades and give her Motrin. But she never bitched about nothing except if we ran outta Clan or the TV was broke. She wasn't divorced and her husband didn't leave her...my grandad died in Vietnam where he was a soldier. It made gram real private, but I got along better with her than anybody else in the family.

"Hey, Andrew," she said. "Heard you got older women comin' over your house."

I seen her elbow. "Yeah, gram. Also I heard you broke your elbow."

"Broke?" She kinda puffed this laugh. "Not in hell, ain't broke, just a bump." Gram put some sugar in her tea. "Wrapped it up and rubbed Icy Hot. But anyhow that's old news, already it's almost healed."

"Where's mom?"

"Kitchen. Just come home, maybe ten minutes."

Mom was at the table havin' a bourbon and ginger, and still wearin' the apron from the Italian bakery where she worked on Cermak Road. I didn't waste no time. "I got some weird news, mom."

"Can't believe that, Andrew."

I kinda sat down with her. "Yeah, cauze you ever seen that house on Euclid? Like blue with a white roof? Above ground pool in the back, takes pretty much the whole yard?"

She put a chubby hand on her cheek and just shaked her head.

"You seen it for sure. Cauze you talked about it one time, said it's nice."

"What the hell are you talkin' about?"

"That house. It's kinda cool. Real nice, especially since now Jen married the guy livin' in there." Mom's eyebrows kinda went up, frickin' hardcore wrinkles in her forehead. For a while she just stirred her bourbon with a fat pinky. I said, "It's maybe a week now and they're in Wisconsin. Like a honeymoon."

She shrugged only one shoulder. "Well. Who's our lucky fella?"

"Gunther Bullets."

Mom knew the family I was talkin' about, though she didn't know exactly which one was Gunther. But she totally knew he was around her age. At first it wasn't no reaction, though pretty soon all that wet cement in her face dried up. The ice in her drink made tinkles and she turned like a mule, a solid rock that didn't need no love from nobody. She asked me, "That's the only reason you come by?"

"I mean. It's pretty big."

"Has to be big if your here."

I bit inside my mouth. Then I told her, "Also I wanted to see about gram's elbow."

Mom nodded real slow with her eyes spacin' out a little. "Well, you go and see. See about it, Andrew."

When I went back to sit with gram she was totally different about the whole story. I guess the Clan had her buzzed, but also it was more natural for her to be laid back. "Jen's married, Andrew? Who to? On Euclid? A car wash and a gun shop, well that's a damn good combo. Practical, lots better than a disability check, probably less work, ha ha. Yeah...Jen's gonna find out what it's all about real fast. She pregnant?"

"Don't know about that. Doubt it, though."

"Well, call me for the divorce party. Even clean up my wheel chair for it, shine it with Ajax. Hopefully the girl didn't sign none of them 'nuptual agreements. If she was smart."

I ain't gonna waste too much time tellin' how Jen came to move all her stuff and it turned in a big scene. Mom chewed Jen's ass and gave a mean guilt trip, "So now your on your own, is that it? Now your staked out?" I helped with the move mostly cauze I wanted to see Gunther up close. He was kinda thin and lifted weights so his arms had them roadmaps, though that pornstar stash looked real dirtbag, mostly cauze his hair was goin' bald. A thing that freaked me out...his old Chevy truck had a bumper sticker on it, *Guns don't kill people, Abortion clinics kill people.* And inside his house it was dead animals all over the place, like a deer head and some ducks, plus five or six stuffed fish and a picture of him holdin' a wild turkey in the woods. Even though it was weird in there, his house was cleaned up real nice, some wood patio chairs and a pool, a big garage with a snowmobile and a Harley. The basement had HDTV with frickin' 8,000 channels, plus a bar and a dartboard.

Me and Jen were sittin' down by the bar where Gunther was makin' us a drink. She said, "It's my favorite room down here." Then she was lookin' around and seen a spider in the corner, like a web by the ceiling. She told him, "Gunny, we got a spider web." The dude went over to look at it, then just grabbed the spider with his hand, crushed it and wiped with a napkin, used a little rag to clean the web off.

I remembered that for a long time. Especially back in my dump apartment where I tried to clean up, though all I did was move trash, crappy cups from the table to a frickin' cupboard. For a while I got real depressed and kinda scared for Jen. Like I seen through Gunther's CD collection, all his *Alman Brothers* and country, plus *Journey* and *Kansas*. It was real different from Jen's music...she was into *Marilyn Manson, Incubus* and *Avenged Sevenfold*. Gettin' married with him didn't make no sense to me. Also for him to get married with *her* wasn't straight...if I had a house and a job, would I marry a girl without no GED? Maybe my stoner ass was thinkin' way too much, seein' too much into shit. But watchin' him kill that spider made me wonder, should I tell Jen what I think? Cauze what happens if he dumps her or treats her like garbage? If I don't tell, then some of it would be my fault.

One night I was just sittin' around my place. And I got out my notebook to write down thoughts I was havin', plus all the stuff that happened with Audra. Havin' a notebook was a habit I kinda picked up after dad left...a teacher said I should do it sometimes, especially if I'm worried or feelin' unsure. For real, I liked writin' stuff down even though I felt ashamed and never told nobody...like I would use regular notebooks from Walgreen's so they would look like homework. I always felt better about stuff when I wrote it down, plus it helped me to remember better. That was the main thing...I always wanted to remember stuff, even stupid crap like shopping lists and White Sox scores. Or if we had a big blizzard and how many inches. Cauze I would think sometimes if I forgot then maybe something didn't happen. If you can't remember clean how stuff happens, what's the point of it happening?

The thing is, this time the notebook didn't make me feel better. I had the tube on and was smokin' some Drum when I got caught blindside real sudden, totally unexpected. It was an explosion with lots of feelings, so I got totally sloppy from it, real hardcore and heavy where I couldn't stop. Tellin' Audra about my family brought shit out, crap I had down in a box shoved deep in some drawers. For real, it was low self-esteem cauze I had to admit I'm dirtbag. On top of everything, I wasn't even good at sellin' weed, my dumbass name on the Cypress. A bad drug dealer is the worst employee, cauze even though *everybody* wants drugs, still you can't sell none. If you can't sell stuff people frickin' want, how can you be good at a normal job where you have to trick somebody, sellin' a vacuum cleaner the dude don't even need?

The tube was showin' another one of them Southwest commercials. So I turned it off and put on some tunes, got high and thought about Audra. I remembered real clean how she made that little hole in the *half and half* and dripped just a couple drops where it barely changed the color. Your gonna make fun of me, but rememberin' them white drops made me feel real sorry for myself. Cauze it's a pathetic feeling when you remember someone, but you know nobody else in the whole world remembers your ass, just maybe your grandma.

A train went by the Burlington Northern and shaked the whole house. I listened real good to the freight rhythm, like screech sounds and booms, a real power groove goin' through my whole body. Kinda spaced out, I was messin' with my phone, just flickin' through my contacts. And by accident I thought I seen Audra's name in there, so I knew I was smokin' way too much weed. But then I flicked back one more time and seen it in there

again. Audra's fuckin' name in my phone. Cauze she put it in
there herself.

Dude, that was moodswing city right there! My ass got
totally jacked and I turned on a light to see if she also put the
phone number. Then I pushed "Talk" without even thinkin' what
the hell I'm doin', almost like I wanted to see if it would work.
The phone was ringin' *prrrrrr, prrrrrr* and then the train was
over. When Audra picked up I was totally shocked to hear her
talkin' with me. "Well, *Andy*. So your calling me. How are you?"

I went, "Hello, Audra. Cauze it works."

"What works?"

"No, no. I mean. Right now I just found a girl's name in my
phone. Audra. It happened right now."

"A *girl*, Andy? Well, that's a compliment."

"Yeah, yeah." I got quiet. "I'm at home."

"Oh? I'm in my car."

"Where you goin'?"

"To celebrate."

"Cool...that's cool. Something good happened to you?"

"*Well*. I got my passport in the mail today."

"Passport?"

"Yes, my friend. Today. To...*day*!"

"Your goin' someplace? Your takin' a trip?"

"No, Andy. Not like that. I'm a *citizen* now."

"Oh...cauze you ain't illegal no more? That's real cool." I
tried makin' a joke, "Now you get to pay taxes."

"Fuck taxes, Andy. I can go *anywhere* now. I'm free...utterly
utterly free. God damn, I've been waiting years for this. So I'm
celebrating. Do you want to come?"

She frickin' picked me up in the Quattro maybe fifteen
minutes later. And we drove super fast down the Ike and Lake
Shore Drive to this Chicago neighborhood called *The Gold Coast*
where I never been before. Before I called, Audra was just gonna
have dinner by herself and drink some champagne, maybe get a
movie and go for a walk...I guess she did that a lot without Big
Beard. We ended up in this real swanko cafe called The 3rd Coast

where you can get a plate of sawed off cheese that smells like farts and costs fifteen bones. The "bowl" of soup is like one inch deep, and they don't put no lettuce in the salad, just *endive* or *arrugula.* For the price Audra got ripped off in there we could of had five burritos each. It's totally wigged to see rich people act proud when they get ripped off just cauze they can afford it.

Nobody carded my ass. We got buzzed off vodka and kinda giggled the whole night about stupid shit. I never asked no questions about her personal life even though that was all I really wanted, like would she divorce Big Beard and how come that guy didn't celebrate with her? I told Audra about my sister gettin' married and she said, "Look at the bright side. Gunther's wealthier than you. Your mom can hit him up." Me and Audra had a toast where she said this was the start to something different and new for both of us. I went along with it just cauze she said it, but now I know she was totally right.

It was weird for me to figure out how lonely she was. After that night she started callin' *me* and we hung out a bunch of times. I fixed up my place more clean so she could come over. (Like I bought some soft bed sheets at Target just in case.) A couple times I got her stoned and she told private stuff from her kid days, how her family was messed up. That's kind of a long story so I'll tell it later on. Plus, you totally need to be ready for it.

Dude, sometimes she would call me just to ask questions. "Andy, do you think I look better in red or yellow?" But also she would get hardcore moodswings, like it could happen in ten seconds. If she got coked up, hangin' out would be complicated since she would drive the car real crazy and think stupid crap. One time she thought there's a moth stuck in her hair just cauze they were flyin' around by a lamp. Another night by my house she stood in front of this express Metra train till the last second so it scared the shit out of me. Later on, she took off a silver ring and gave it to this homeless dude in Berwyn. We went to this bar called Miller's in the Loop and I came back from the pisser to see her at the bar flirting with some business dude, makin' him like silly putty just to feel her power. She said she flirted with them dipshits just cauze they were stupid. "I hate stupidity more than anything." Audra probably said it fifty times, "It's why I really want to leave America. The stupidity. If I could, I'd buy all your brother-in-law's guns just to murder all the stupid people here. Line them up and shoot off their dicks."

"But then you'd shoot my dick."

She got annoyed. "Stop it, Andy!"

"For real..."

"No, be quiet! I hate it when you talk like that. It's immature to fish for compliments. I'll get angry and leave, so don't do that with me."

Dude, when I finally sold off my grass and paid Diego for good, I felt some freedom. His uncle didn't come back from Mexico and we got some dudes to fix up the car no problem. After I made that last payment, I called Audra right away since I had some money left over. Maybe this time I could pay the frickin' dinner and eat something more normal. But when her cell picked up, I heard this message. "Hello, you've reached Audra's cell phone. I'm abroad at the moment and do not have a mobile in Vilnius. If you need to reach me, please e-mail me at audra1974@zuikis.lt. I hope to be returned by the end of the year. Thank you for calling, and take care." Then she said the same thing in Lithuanian.

It got me real welled up when I heard that message...not sloppy or nothing like that, just some unexpected feelings. For a while I was real shocked how come she didn't say good-bye. But then I seen my e-mail at the library and found a real short message. *Andy, I'm sorry to tell you like this, but I'm leaving for Vilnius...I don't know if I'll come back. I should have called but things happened in the last minute. You are very sweet and I wanted to thank you for spending so much time with me, for putting up with me sometimes. Maybe we'll see each other again someday. Please don't forget about me. Good-bye, Audra.*

Readin' that...dude, I kinda moped around Berwyn for a while. Went back to my place, smoked some bud and laid on my couch. A train went by so I felt the freight rhythm go through my whole apartment and rumble up my whole body. My room turned real small and I was tryin' to think something to do, though I didn't know a place to go, nothin' that would be fun or cool. Mom called me, but I just waited for the long ass train to be done before I heard her message. "Drew, there's a whole mess of Jen's crap you forgot. I picked this junk up and there's a bag of crack or some kinda cocaine here. If you know about this you better call me right now. How much is this crap worth? Who's givin' it to her?"

Maybe an hour later Jen left me a message. "Drew, what the fuck? You know it's me, so answer. Right now I just opened up this box where you threw my CD's in a big mess. A bunch got scratched now and they fuckin' skip. Also I'm missin' stuff. If you go by ma's, see in my room if it's a box of clothes cauze I need some important shit from there. And call me back!"

Dude, I turned off my fuckin' phone. And I didn't deal with it at all, just left that thing on a table for a couple days. It was weird cauze I felt real lonely, though I didn't want no conversation with nobody, just went wanderin' around Berwyn, smokin' weed and hearin' the same songs from Dave Matthews (*Some Devil* and *Seek Up*) on repeat.

Later on I went to check my e-mail. Like I thought maybe I should write Audra a message. But when I came up to the front door in the library, right inside there I seen this sign hangin' on one of them cork boards. Just a small ass paper left up for years even though this was the first time I seen it. *Apply for a Passport at the Berwyn Public Library. Ask for forms at the Circulation Desk.*

A Loaf of Bread and a Half Liter
of Water

Okay, so this was the situation. It was the middle of July, 2006. Mom was pissed at Jen and raggin' on her, so she didn't pay too much attention to me. And Jen had to stay low key after mom found that meth...I didn't hear all that much from her. It was kinda easy to sell my car and stuff without nobody wonderin' what the hell I had planned...and I didn't tell my plan to nobody. The only thing, I stashed all my old notebooks in mom's attic under some junk, way in the corner by this pile of old drapes. When all my shit was sold (or I just gave it away to Diego and some other people, like my CD player and some clothes), the only stuff I had to my name was a passport, a one-way ticket to Vilnius (since it was cheaper) and a small black backpack, like one of them for school. In there I put some underwear, a couple shirts, some jeans, a notebook and a pen. Then later I remembered to get toothpaste and a box of Trojans. For money I had $428.67 in cash. The only smart thing I did was to make a reservation for a hostel in Vilnius cauze I found out about it on the internet. But I didn't know about no traveler's checks, so that wasn't even part of my plan.

The day when it was time for me to go, I put on a White Sox cap, a little gray windbreaker, a black t-shirt, some jeans and dark blue Converse All-Stars. To finish up my weed, I ripped a bong in my apartment and left that plastic piece of crap in the middle of the room so my landlord could find it. The asshole wouldn't give back no deposit since I was leavin' early, so I dumped bongwater all over the rug. And that was it, I just took the bus to the Blue Line, then the Blue Line to O'Hare.

Now I got some advice for anybody goin' to the airport or takin' a plane...it's a real bad idea to rip bongs. Nobody told me O'Hare is so complicated and confused where you can't know what crazy direction your supposed to be going. For real, the place makes you paranoid and you need to pay attention to lots of signs and numbers. I seen probably eight thousand people, like Indian families, dudes in suits and psycho bible Christians with dresses buttoned all the way up. All the off-duty cops were starin' at me the whole time and I got freaked when this hardcore lady said I was "selected" for a random check...like she's totally trained to know how you look when your baked. A Homeland Security dude frickin' busted out latex gloves to make me think he was goin' private. But then he only went through my backpack, workin' good to touch my underpants and Trojans real official. That's what happens when cop school pays off for your ass, you get to rub inside somebody's Hanes.

I got the worst seat on the plane right in the frickin' middle of 5 people, for sure the seat above the gas tank that blows up first. To my right was this Sloppy Joe with love handles goin' over my arm rest, some real soft and sweaty fat. But on my left was this thin business lady with a computer. The plane was goin' to Warsaw first, but the lady was gonna fly to Vilnius just like me...she was sellin' a house over there and knew lots of stuff about the place. "Make sure you get *Vilnius in Your Pocket*. Never go any place unless you can find it on the map yourself. *Call* taxis. If you flag them down, you'll pay an arm. If you see big groups of drunk Russian men, never look at them. And *don't* talk to them. Never fall asleep in the trolley bus, especially at night." That was way more info than I had before I got on the plane. Like I didn't even know Russians lived in Vilnius or how the hell would I know what they looked like?

Dude, I didn't know the plane ride was gonna be seven hours! Frickin' we just kept flyin' and flyin' so I got wigged, like how far away is it? Don't they need to stop for gas? Sloppy Joe was elbowin' me for the whole ride, like he was eatin' barbecue beef and stickin' them elbows. Then he needed to fix his pillow about eighty times. I had this little TV in front of my face, but for the whole flight it only said *show will start in 175 minutes*, like it would be totally better just to give everyone a watch.

I was kinda passed out when the plane landed in Warsaw. Outside it was the wrong time and my eyes stung bad cauze I was zombie tired. I figured maybe I could get a Polish sausage in the Warsaw airport, though in Poland they make it totally different. You don't get no bun or nothing good on top, just a kielbasa with sauce, some weird ketchup with white dots in it. And I got coffee, only it was this real hot tar, like the plastic spoon kinda melted flimsy.

Right away in Poland everything's totally different. Everybody's talkin' *pishich ishpisht* anyplace you go. You kinda get to see what it's like for immigrants cauze they put the Polish words in big black letters, but then the English is red and small, wrong stuff like *this table not for eating*. In the bathroom there's a dude workin' to take care of the place, and the toilet paper is real different, all gray and hard. I got lucky cauze I didn't have to use it, but it was close since I drank coffee. Like I didn't even roll no smoke, frickin' scared from that toilet paper.

Dude, I was wonderin' how long we need to fly next, but the plane to Vilnius is like fifty minutes even though it's a new country. The airport over there is real small...you come up by a booth with soldiers checkin' all the passports, then behind them it's a place to get your bag. After that you go in a tall white room where you can change cash in some small windows. This dude gave a whole pile of Monopoly money with pictures of priests and guys with huge beards, plus a shitload of coins. I stuffed all that in my pocket with my passport. The business lady totally helped me out, put me on this real advanced bus with flashin' lights and a girl voice tellin' the stations that sounded like *keketeki, zinkylinky* and *shmeeshmaishmeel.*

I gotta tell you some stuff about them first couple days. Cauze what do you do when your in a new country that's totally far away and frickin' nobody even knows your there? The first thing is your too tired to freak out from all the weird shit. Even though you need a reservation in the hostel, the place is still a dump...frickin' gray walls, bunk cots and the room stinks real bad from a Spanish dude's socks. I totally slept for two days...would wake up at weird times around 5:15 in the morning and crash at 22:30[*]. Later on I had some troubles cauze the frickin' Vilnius tap water gave me the runs. So the toilet paper got revenge on my ass, though I felt better after I ate cheese and some rolls.

For real, I didn't know nothing official about Vilnius, only a couple internet pictures, plus stories from Audra, how all the people are way more smart over there and it's real pretty. That's totally true cauze when you get there you think Berwyn and Cicero is totally ugly and disgusting compared with Vilnius. Vilnius is like Lord of the Rings, a small village where everybody's sellin' jewelry and gold, plus paintings, sweaters and some real expensive pants. And it's so many beautiful girls all over the place...EVERYWHERE you go it's a supermodel with real nice clothes, and they smile real pretty, hold their smokes to be sexy on purpose. Then the buildings add a real cool thing cauze the city is old with a castle on the hill. Some of them houses got made with red rocks, though they painted others yellow, orange or light green. Downtown streets turn real narrow, like two horses would get stuck going through. And in summer the night is totally fucked up cauze it's still light out at 23:00. It only gets totally dark for maybe 2 hours, and on cloudy nights the sky glows gray like a big ass ghost.

Without no drinkin' age, I could hang out anyplace I wanted. All around town I checked out bars till I found this one called

---

[*] Lithuanians use military time cauze they're scared any moment it might be another war over there.

ŠMC. That place turned into my favorite bar and I would hang out there pretty much every day. You could get a good breakfast, like rolled up pancakes with cheese and at night they stayed open real late. Lots of people talked some English and it was easy to score good nuggs by the bar. Just hangin' around ŠMC* for a couple days, I totally bought some kind bud, like the best shit you ever even smoked. And get this...the guy who sold it was the frickin' bar manager, this bald dude named Raimis.

He was maybe 28 but almost totally bald, just some blond hair by his ears. Raimis smoked me up right on the ŠMC patio where we were sittin' by one of them umbrella tables. After havin' some laughs, me and him started hangin' out. He talked like this, "I like it practice English. But please for me speak slow. Today after work finish, we go maybe make some beers."

I got blowed away when I tried drinkin' with Raimis and his friends. With him you go 100% Vilnius style where *make some beers* means the beer just goes on the side with vodka. I figured out fast how vodka is totally important in Vilnius...for some people it's like their main food. I seen dirty old men huggin' each other for balance just to make it down the street, totally pinball off lamps and trees. A couple times the parks got full of hammered people passed out in bushes or fallin' off benches. The first time after drinkin' with Raimis, I woke up in some dude's apartment...he was puttin' ice cubes on my face to kick my ass out. I didn't even know who he was or how I got there.

I started wakin' up every day with pretty bad hangovers. Like I would get cleaned up and wash my face, then I would think, "Okay... today *for sure* I'm gonna look for Audra. Like I'll try sendin' her e-mail." Pretty much every morning I got coffee at ŠMC and wrote some stuff in my notebook like this...*Holy shit, me and Raimis and his one friend Varna got ripped last night. I paid for a room at the hostel but woke up in Varna's Volvo. Like he*

* Some guys told me it standed for *Shoodas Malimo Centras*, like "The bullshitting center". For real, *Šiolaukinio Meno Centras* is the art school next door and *ŠMC* is just the bar. (Art schools get bars in Vilnius.)

drove to work and left me in the back seat so I sweated without no
air. That kind of shit is funny for his ass.

Dude, this guy Varna is a total trip and I need to tell you
about him cauze he turns real important later. He was kinda this
key dude around ŠMC, like a regular where everybody knew him.
His job was a government tax inspector so he had to wear hardcore
gray or light blue suits every day without no tie. He had some
gypsy blood and that gave his head a bigass pile of curly black
hair, plus real small eyes that never showed no feelings, only
poker face. Anytime you seen him he was sittin' like he knew all
the frickin' secrets in the world, makin' deals on his phone and
smokin' Dunhills, like these smokes with gold wrappers. Every
day at 17:30 he would have his first joint, checkin' his watch real
careful to make sure he don't miss it.

One night me and some people kinda ended up at his place.
We smoked hash and drank this stuff Metaxa, and later a girl
picked me up. She said Raimis told about me, and next thing I
knew she was draggin' me down by her place to make sex. I kinda
remember it, though not really. She explained how come she's so
pretty...she used to be a butterfly from Argentina, but then
reincarnation made her a girl. That's what a palm reader said.

It was a weird night for me. I woke up next to her and seen
her frickin' mascara all smeared, so it reminded me about Audra.
Right there I kinda crashed, but soon she woke me up, told me to
take my backpack and leave so she could go shopping. Outside the
sun was rammin' bright even though it was only around 7:00. And
I was still kinda wasted off Metaxa and Varna's hash. I didn't
really know what direction I was goin' and ended up in this
trashed neighborhood by the train station where lots of hardcore
drunks were hangin' around some sawed off places...a couple
cafes made from plywood. There's a McDonald's where all the
trolleys stop, so I found one that would take me more close by my
hostel.

Goin' past some trashed neighborhood with old ladies
carryin' plastic bags, I felt some real big courage. "Gotta write

Audra e-mail today. No more bullshit." I figured I'd sleep off the booze, get some food and go by an internet cafe.

The youth hostel gives you this little locker by the side of your bed. I came in my dorm and went to get my toothbrush, but I found that locker wide open. Did I forgot to lock that bastard up? For real, it was wide open without no key in it. And when I looked in there I felt a real sharp buzz go up my back cauze some fucker ripped me off! My passport, all my money...they just left socks and soap and some papers in there, that's all.

You don't know what kind of panic it was! All over I felt electric shocks...my heart started poundin' and I was stone sober in like two seconds, frickin' went through my whole backpack to find what's left. Dude, that money they stole was *all* I had, just over 600 Litas (about $230) and I couldn't find my passport. All I had in my pocket was a five Litas coin, the only things on me worth cash was some kind buds and the windbreaker. Maybe my White Sox cap could get me somethin', but that was it. I was frickin' nude.

When you get in that situation, lots of shit goes through your head real fast. And Vilnius ain't no Lord of the Rings no more...now it's nasty gray and crumbled with all the gutters broken and garbage everywhere. Busted windows with cages to keep out robbers, then some dirty and thin cats runnin' around real paranoid. In front of a church I seen old ladies beggin' with their hands totally swelled up and they were kneeled down on the stones with pictures of Mary and Jesus and little cloth hats where people put coins. Real beautiful girls walked right by with Dolce and Gabana jeans and huge sunglasses. Also they walked right by me without lookin' at all.

I went by ŠMC hopin' Raimis would be around. But the waitress said he was in some town where his aunt lived, wasn't comin' back to Vilnius for a couple days. I asked if I could have coffee and pay later, but she got pissy and said no. I looked if Varna was around or if I could remember the way to that office where he worked. But then I just sat by a tree for a while and felt like a tool.

After a while I said fuck it. It cost me 1.50 Litas to write Audra at this internet cafe. *Subject: ripped off!!!! im in vilnius. got ripped off, fuckin all my moneys gone. sometimes i hang around the smc. like the art school bar. leave a message with this guy raimis the manager in there and tell where i can find you. im broke and dont got no place to stay. this aint no joke audra and i aint high.*

Then I was so fuckin' hungry. With the rest of the money, I got a loaf of bread and a half liter of water to put in my backpack.

A Safe Place

Here's what I wrote in my notebook later on...

Fuck I dont wanna sleep outside. Somethin I cant handle right now cauze theres nowhere to do it, I didnt see no good places with a roof. You remember how dad use to say if you dont act like a man then your gonna end up under the bridge? Fuckin I can already see its gonna rain...some gray clouds over there. In the train station I seen cops pokin passed out drunks with sticks. Or somebodys gonna roll my ass. I swear when I see a homeless guy from now on I wont say hes dirtbag or a garbage picker. For sure this is punishment for runnin away from home.

Dude, the rain came on purpose just to fuck with me cauze pretty soon it started to drizzle. My loaf of bread would be totally wasted if it got wet. I found this mall where I could hang around for a while, but then the security seen I ain't no customer and kicked my ass out. Down this huge main street called *Gedimino Prospektas* I found a trolley shelter and sat in there to fake like I'm waitin' for the right one. It started rainin' good and all these people came from the stores. Lots of 'em had bags full of food or they started eatin' chocolate right in front of my face and sharin' it with friends. This old dude stood extra close by me so I got to smell the baked chicken in his bag.

Pretty soon I got on a trolley. In Vilnius you don't have to pay to get on, just they bust you if a surprise *controller* comes and checks you without no ticket. My trolley was painted like *Triumph*

38

panties and took me to the bridge by the river *Neris*. I had to admit this was the best roof I could get, so I got off.

By the river I seen fishermen dressed up with raincoats and green boots. People put lots of garbage over there, some broken booze bottles, plus old newspapers and some cloth, like maybe trashed drapes. Even though the bridge had traffic goin' over, down below it was quiet so you could hear the raindrops on the river. That's a real sweet sound I don't think I heard so clean before, but now I didn't want it. I was wishin' for a small radio with the White Sox game, or the Burlington Northern freight trains. Fuck, I would of listened to elevator muzak, anything to take away them thoughts that were gettin' real loud.

I started rememberin' stuff so perfect, like somebody sprayed my brain with Windex and took a squeegee. All of it was stuff from back home...the el and the Pace bus. Diego's grandma, how she would make tamales with her sister so the whole street smelled from the food. I remembered stupid shit that didn't mean noth-ing...Berwyn sewer caps and the mailman's cart. Guys blowin' leaves off a sidewalk with blowers. It was like a slide show with stuff I never thought could be in my head like that real clean and bright.

For sure, I was rememberin' Audra super hardcore. How she would check her teeth for lipstick, or the special way she walked down Michigan Avenue to make her boobs bounce extra. I got some fantasies where I was washin' her hair, and then sittin' with her in that Vilnius trolley shelter with the rain outside. Right there I kinda thought about it...I didn't have no way to prove if Audra really came to Vilnius. Maybe that answering message was bullshit and what the hell was I gonna do then?

I was sittin' under the bridge for maybe four or five hours. Now and then I just ate real small pieces from the bread and sipped the water to save it. Later on I seen this wet dog come by to look at me...for real, it was almost like he just appeared when I turned my head. He was starin' all begged out, his eyes dark and soft and one of his ears flopped over. Your gonna think I'm a tool cauze I totally knew the old boy could pick through every trash can in the city if he wanted. But I gave that little shit a small piece of bread, seen him chew with his tail flyin' around. I didn't give him no more and figured he was gonna ditch my ass, but the boy stopped beggin' and just laid down by my leg. So right there I ended up with a little buddy.

He was totally a street mutt but a cool dog, small and gray with that floppy ear kinda goin' over one eye. When the rain mellowed out, he went followin' me every place, stayin' right near me to make sure *I* don't run away. I had to think up some name for him, though it didn't feel right to give one in English. So I looked through them trashed newspapers to get a name that was easy to say. Through all them five million words, I found *Tepti* and thought maybe that's a real name. But later I found out it means *to apply ointment*, though by that time it was already stuck.

Havin' Tepti totally worked out. I talked any stuff that went in my head to him, like the explanation how I got in this mess with only bread and all my shit ripped off. The old boy would totally sit and listen real good, sometimes liftin' that flopped ear like he didn't want to miss no important parts.

I told Tepti all the shit I knew about Audra, like her whole story. And since jack shit is gonna happen to me for damn near three days while I'm homeless around Vilnius, this is a good place also to tell the story to you. Even though this is gonna be a short version, all the most important stuff's in it. Make sure you don't skip over none of it cauze this is important for later.

You probably already guessed Audra was born in Vilnius. But back in them days Lithuania was the same parts with Russia, kinda like the USA contains New Mexico. Only Russia was called The United Soviet Society Republic and Audra said it was mostly poor people, though her grandpa was a Minister (like a government chief), so her family could steal expensive shit way more easy, sell it to all their friends for cash. A government family also got special treatments, totally the same like in the USA...regular people didn't get no ride to kindergarten in a Russian limo, but Audra got that ride from her grandpa's driver. She also got special presents, like gym shoes from Checkoslakia, a country which back then was hard to find.

Her family went like this...the dad was a history professor and the mom worked in a piano school for totally genius children. Audra had two brothers and one sister...the older sister was like five years older and the smallest brother two years younger. Here's the tripped out part... right in the middle with Audra was her twin brother, like an identical twin, just a boy! Audra showed a picture from her purse with them sittin' in a sandbox and no way could I tell which one's the girl.

For summers, the kids would hang in this farm village where Audra's grandpa was born. And she was like 9 or 10 when they had a real bad accident. This neighbor kid was takin' them for a ride in a horse wagon, like one of them from the olden days. He made it go too fast and Audra's twin brother got bounced, so he fell off the wagon real hard and it dragged him for a while. The kid broke his skull and got paralyzed neck down, so the only stuff he could do was breathe, swallow mushed food and feel pain, cauze they seen it in his face.

That situation was real intense for Audra. I totally heard about it...if your twins with someone, sometimes you can feel lots of their pain. Her back and head started hurtin' and she would get real warm or dizzy from his fevers. She dreamed lots of nightmares how her head was gettin' crushed. And sometimes she wished her bro would fall asleep and never wake up even though it made her guilty to think like that.

The mom also took it real bad. At first she was just sad and feelin' real down, but then later she started talkin' to herself. Like she would be standin' by a huge pile of dishes and mumblin' *Can't you see it's finished? Please finish it finally. What are you waiting for?* The whole family would ignore her and feel weird. Like the dad would just go on the balcony to smoke and hit sauce.

One day the kids were waitin' by the table to eat and the mom was boilin' some potatoes. Without sayin' nothing or showin' no feelings in her face, she just went real quiet in the other room. Audra felt some bad vibes so she followed her mom and seen her take a pillow from the sofa, go where the brother was layin' down on a bed. And right there mom put the pillow on the boy's face and held it down real hard till he got suffocated. Audra seen the whole thing and she knew exactly when he died cauze inside her this part had gasps and went hollow. She didn't hate mom for doin' it...said lots of pain went away kinda peaceful. But also it felt heavy like a weight, real confused and wrong.

The mom changed pretty drastic...like she stopped eatin'. Every day she would make a place at the table where Audra's brother used to sit and she would put her own food on that plate. Pretty soon the grandfather told some official dudes to put mom in a hospital, though Audra said it was more similar with jail. Anytime she visited, mom thought Audra was her brother...she talked stuff like *Finally you come to see me. Why don't you come to live with your mother?* Audra's mom died in that place some years later, like only a couple weeks after the grandfather (the mom's dad) died from cancer.

That was a real bad time for the whole family. Cauze the USSR was totally fallin' apart and goin' broke. Audra said the Soviet Republic was like welfare for the whole country and you only had to pretend to work. But all of a sudden everybody got cut off, and without the grandfather nobody got no more special deals. Audra's older sister married some dude from Germany, ditched the family and never sent no cash. Audra started college and got a job waitressin' in a bar for business dudes from USA and England. But her dad didn't do nothin', only hit the sauce everyday. And her youngest bro was like a freeloader.

I'm gonna call that dude Kovas. He was like a big secret or a special story for Audra and she didn't talk about him too much. I only got to hear about him one night when all the power went out in Berwyn. Like I'll never forget that night...even if torture perverts lock me up and erase my brain, still I won't forget it. My whole street was totally pitch black and quiet with a small drizzle kinda like a spray. We were sittin' in her Quattro with the blue and gold lights from her car radio, that's all. She wasn't on no drugs, not even a glass of wine, but Audra got real dreamy and full of memories. Totally the same how it happens when your alone and miss home real bad.

She said Kovas was real delicate and sensitive...he would get bored and confused about the family. At first he was actin' like a regular kid, goin' around town with a skateboard, maybe drinkin' some beers and ditchin' school. But then Audra didn't even know how his whole gang turned into junkies, totally into heroin. (Vilnius is full of them kids, real thin and dirty and askin' for cash around churches. You can see 'em a lot, some like only 14 or maybe even younger than that.)

Kovas started rippin' off the house to get smack. He stole a drill, the mom's old jewelry, Audra's watch...any crap he could pawn. So Audra kicked him out and changed all the locks, told him some real nasty shit. For a while Kovas was disappeared, so things got easier. Audra could finish college and land a better job.

This blew me away, cauze Audra was an English teacher for a while, frickin' exactly the same school where her mom worked. The job was pretty good...she could afford bills. And got engaged with a dude...they were almost ready to move in their own place. But then Kovas showed up one day, like he came back to steal the dad's car.

The cops found Kovas wigged out and pulled over in some ditch, a couple teeth knocked from his face and his body only skin and bones. Audra had to sell a bunch of crap to put him in special rehab where they found he had HIV. On top of that, the dad went to the hospital and they said he needed a stomach operation cauze it was life or death. All them medical bills and problems chased away Audra's boyfriend...he dumped her and moved to Ireland.

I remember how Audra was tellin' the story in the Quattro. She started babblin' to me real slow, "Andy...when you *lose*." She said *lose lose* over and over lots of times, "*Lose*, Andy. You can watch yourself losing, everything disappears like your standing and looking, can't do anything. My friends were telling me, *You need a doctor, you need a shrink*. Maybe I hated myself, I don't know. But I made a decision, and the decision paid me money. Thick clumps of the easiest, worst kind of money. When you see it come, not for teaching, not for waitressing. It comes and you see what people really value in this world."

Dude, if you walk around any main street in Vilnius, pretty soon your gonna run into a peep show. At night me and Tepti walked by a bunch, like a whole stripper mall right by this main hotel...all them pink and purple neon lights kinda makin' hypnotism on you. Audra got the best doctor she could for her dad. And she said she was gonna quit them shows once she paid the whole operation, plus her bro's rehab. Only her plan kinda backfired.

Some people from her school seen her in the show. I guess it was students who got in the bar...she didn't really know, but pretty soon she couldn't even show her face around the school. Somebody put a story in the paper, how the dead minister's family was only shame...a mom who killed her kid, a drunk professor, a sister who ran away, then a junkie and a stripper. After that newspaper came out, not even no strip club would hire Audra no more. The only move she had left was to try one of them internet bride deals, and that's how she got with Big Beard.

I finished tellin' Tepti the whole story pretty much that way, "That's how come me and you are sittin' in this park right now with all our bread finished." It was this huge and real beautiful park down *Gedimino Prospektas*, like flowers and nice benches. You can't know how I was hungry, kinda lightheaded, maybe goin' a little crazy. Lots of times I would see a blonde lady and think it's Audra. But one time it was a dude with long hair and he was maybe 6'3" with a chin beard.

It was a pretty low point for me. Tepti would go through garbage cans and I would think *maybe he'll find somethin' in there and I'll totally eat it.* Like I would watch people eat sandwiches or french fries in the park to see if they would finish it all or throw some parts away. The situation was gettin' pretty bad.

Me and Tepti were walkin' across the lawn in that park. Them lawns get cleaned real good, but by accident I seen this piece of paper in the grass. First I thought I'm seein' shit again...no way would somebody drop cash on the lawn. But I went for a closer look, bent down to check, and fuck! Totally! It was cash! A frickin' ten Litas bill, still nice and clean without even no dirt on it.

You don't know how I completely lost my shit right there and went whistlin' like a total freak. "Tepti! Dude, we scored. We scored." Tepti's tail was goin' lightspeed and we went by this Maxima grocery store to get some fresh rolls, a box of multivitamin juice and a small piece of cheese. Frickin' me and Tepti totally ate every damn ass crumb...I made my mouth like a vacuum cleaner to suck all the crumbs from the bag.

Buyin' that food, I made sure to have change left over, like two Litas for later. And I told myself, *You gotta make this last, Drew. Take better care of your shit.* No way was I gonna put that change in my pocket...a heavy coin that could fall out real easy. I had to stash it in a safe place and knew a good one in my backpack, like a secret pocket in there. So I opened that sucker up, looked inside, and let me just say hello to everybody. Let me say *oh la* my best *muchachos* and *compadres.* Cauze you better know what I seen in there. For three days I was walkin' around with my passport and a telephone card, plus Raimis' cell phone number wrote down on a piece of paper. And I had over 600 Litas folded up nice in a small brown envelope and shoved real careful in my safe place.

A Text Message

Dude, I got so excited and humiliated, so jacked and stupid that me and Tepti kinda went walkin' in some direction, sometimes almost joggin'. From all them times in my whole life when I didn't really know what to do, this was the time when I didn't know what to do even more than ever before. We went past some smart guy restaurants, this place called *Pizza Jazz* and a swanko brewery called *Avilys*. Suddenly all them places turned *real* again...we could smell the pizza sauce and it wasn't torture or dreamland. For real, all you need is a shower and you can go in there.

I was feelin' pretty good goin' across the Cathedral Square, this huge area with a massive white church and a clock tower. It was like *I'm back!* and *Everybody check me out!* Down the other side, like 200 yards in front of me, I seen this bald dude in a bright orange and yellow stripe shirt, plus big ass silver sunglasses. It was Raimis and he was totally welded, like the wind was blowin' him my way. When he came close up, at first he didn't recognize me, but then his mouth opened like a cave where I thought a bat would fly out. He went, "Crazy motherfucker? What a fuck happens to you?"

"Some crazy shit."

"You crazy shit, man. Ei...yes...good good, because you save my ass." He took car keys from his pocket. "*Blet**, you are driving my car. I'm fucking too much drunk."

His little Volkswagen truck was like three blocks away and he wouldn't shut up the whole way there. "God damn you save my ass, man. Because I think, *blet*, howwa hell I get hiss *pizda*** car home?" Sometimes he'd kick into Lithuanian *shmeeshmaishmeel*, but would snap out of it. "Ei, you have dog. What a *blet* you need some dog for, man? Hiss one have sickness."

At his place I took a super hot shower...he had one of them special bathtubs with a hose connected to the faucet. Frickin' three days of crud washed off so the water was totally gray. I could feel how my body hurt in places, my back and knees. And I had to borrow some clothes from Raimis cauze my stuff was attractin' flies. Dude, when I frickin' seen his clothes I knew we would need a laundry pretty soon. Cauze he gave some shiny gray jogging pants and this green, yellow and silver techno shirt, like more loud than a Berwyn drunk. It was super advanced Euro-cool, which is pretty bad if you never seen it.

Raimis set my ass up with some hash and a beer, then some raw bacon with black bread and I frickin' ate that shit like a dog. Tepti got to eat some old cheese with sour milk, a bone from a ham with his tail goin' all over the place. I told Raimis the whole story how I was homeless and he went holdin' the sides of his face, starin' at the table and laughin' so hard. "Safe place. Yes, crazy motherfucker, safe place." Eventually I passed out on the sofa for like a day, got up maybe one time to eat carrots with vinegar and this real salty fish called *silkay*, which is pretty good if you have black beer and bread.

When I was finally rested up and felt half-way normal, my stuff kinda organized and I gave Tepti a bath, I knew it was time

---

* They say this *blet* all the time. It means whore. But you can say it anytime just like fuck or shit.

** The way you say it is "peezda". It means cunt, though they say it all the time and write it all over the walls.

to get serious. Not homeless no more, I understood some things totally true and knew from now on I gotta concentrate on my plan. So I wrote it down in my notebook to make sure I understood it straight and could remember it clean.

#1, You can't spend money on booze and drugs, cauze 600 Litas really ain't that much if you count it. Plus, you need to find a laundry.

#2, When you find Audra, you gotta make sure she knows you ain't here to skimp from her.

#3, This is complicated, but your gonna need to get a job or something.

Then I was ready to go back down by ŠMC to see if I could check my e-mail in Raimis' office. His apartment was near this school for railroad workers and mechanics, so the back yard had old train transmissions and axles and shit, real massive engine parts. He told me on the phone, "Take right at train parts and go straight." It was true...from the rusty train engine it was pretty much a straight line to downtown Vilnius. With Tepti sorta leadin' the way, we ended up on this street called *Trakų Gatvė* and from there it was easy to figure out.

Dude, ŠMC was happenin'! The place was packed with people, like hot artist chicks and dudes with thin glasses drinkin' cognac or Metaxa. The whole patio didn't even have one seat and the music was electronica that went real cool with the lights hangin' inside aluminum bubbles. I found Raimis at a table in the corner...he was drinkin' some Carlsberg beer with Varna. And it was the first time I seen Varna's girlfriend, this girl named Terese, like a film director. Also there was another dude with them, this super thin guy named Gidas. When that whole crew seen me they all started laughin'. Raimis made sure I had a place to sit with them.

I didn't know it but Raimis was tellin' everybody my story, which I guess was a hit. Varna bought me a glass of Jameson, this super good booze I never tried, and I sat there havin' drinks with total strangers. They laughed pretty much anytime I said something, even normal questions like, "Who knows where's a laundry?" It's weird to ask questions to Lithuanian people cauze they don't really answer, just get real ironic about shit. Like Terese said, "So much a clean man need laundry?" and then they all laughed. But I was laughin' too, kinda. If you'll believe it, even though they spoke Lithuanian a lot and had a tough time explainin' some things, I felt like we all knew each other maybe back in high school. Compared with makin' barbecue at my mom's or hangin' in Gunther's basement, sittin' around ŠMC was way easier.

After a few drinks and some weed on the patio, Raimis let me use his computer. The inbox was filled up with bullshit messages from Jen where she was foamin' all over the place, *Oh my god, your place is empty. Are you evicted ? Are you evicted?* Then it was messages with guilt trips cauze they figured out I'm in Vilnius...probably cops did it for them. In lots of them messages Jen was just raggin', *Mom's givin' me shit right now and you don't even care, don't even answer your e-mail on purpose.* Hittin' delete on all that, I almost erased the most important message...

Andy, omg, where are you? WHAT THE HELL ARE YOU DOING IN VILNIUS?!?! You're spending time at SMC? That's a weirdo bar, druggies hang out there, so I'm not surprised :)

I've called the hostels and some hotels where I thought you might stay. But I can't track you down. You're broke? Andy, I have to find you...it's very important. If you're here, I need you to do something for me. When you get this message, this is my mobile: +370 687 258 41. Also, virtually daily between one and five o'clock (sometimes longer), I'm at the hospital with my father (but it's better for you to avoid that place). Please call my phone. In the meantime, I'll try to find some way to track you down. Love, Audra.

Dude, *Love*. <u>*Love*</u>, Audra. Not "Your friend," or "Best," or "Sincerely," or any of them five million slogans she could of used. Audra put *love*, a real important word where you can't throw it around like wet pants, especially if your an English teacher and they make you study all the most hardcore words they got. I knew

I was seein' too much in it cauze I was kinda high and buzzed. But it didn't stop me from feelin' all warm inside and jacked up.

I frickin' wrote her number down so fast on three pieces of paper, put one in the safe place, another in my notebook and the last one in my pocket. When I came back to the table Varna let me use his cell. And Audra answered in like one ring...she had this mellow business voice kinda like a secretary. I told her, "Hey...Audra? It's me. Andy from Berwyn." She didn't get excited or show any feelings, just said, "Andy? So, you really are here." Then it was this pause and I could hear car horns. "Can we meet someplace later tonight to discuss things?"

"Yeah. Just where?"

"I need you to hang up. I'll send a text message to the phone you're using right now."

That message took maybe an hour to come. Waitin' for it, I started gettin' all nervous, the same like when you go on a first date. I frickin' bought Varna, Raimis, Terese and Gidas a round to explain what the hell I'm waitin' for...not all the nitty gritty about the thousand bucks or Audra's family problems, but just how Audra was real beautiful and smart, and she bought me dinners and had a messed up husband. Terese said, "You come to find her? Yes?"

I guess I nodded. The gang had a million questions...what does she do and where does she work, what hospital is her dad in? The thing is, I didn't even know, so maybe they thought I was talkin' bullshit. But another round later, all of us nice and lubed, the text finally came in.

Varna read it. His beady eyes kinda looked us over real smooth and he flipped his phone shut, finished his drink so his big ass hair went shakin'. The only thing he said was "Absento Fejos," then he kinda nodded, a cool smirk like only me and him understood somethin' important together. Like he agreed with it and gave his stamp of approval cauze it was gonna be good.

Absinthe Fairies

Dude, right around the corner from ŠMC is this bar called *Absento Fejos*, which means Absinthe Fairies. The whole gang got real excited about it and now we were all gonna go down there together. For the whole time we were sittin' at ŠMC, that dude Gidas was real quiet at the table almost like he didn't like me. But now he got the most jacked up and smiled like somebody shoved a piano in his face. He grabbed my arm and went, "Trust in me, trust in me. For this bar we need for it to be very high."

Gidas had this plastic thing around his neck where he kept some real strong hash, said it came from Copenhagen. That dude rolled a killer jay, just one hit and I started feelin' like the ground was rubber and I could hear the most tiny whispers. Five hits later my hands got dipped in mint sauce and I had vibrations in the air, real mellow tracers. Like I thought maybe that shit had mescaline in it, but he said it was normal for Copenhagen.

We walked to this Fairies place kinda goofed out, Tepti stayin' real close by me the whole time. Comin' up to the bar, I knew gettin' in was gonna be a secret mission. Outside they had three bouncers dressed in tight black with slick smooth gel hair. And their frickin' leader had one of them bluetooth ear pieces. I seen the look on his face, like he wasn't gonna let no stoned Twinkies in his swanko bar. But Audra put info in the text

message, a secret password...*Say you're Dana's*[*] *people.* So
Terese went to do it *ketekeki cuss cuss cuss* and *klausykit Dana
shmeeshmaishmeel.* The bouncer just whispered some shit in his
bluetooth and looked at his assistant dudes. They checked us out a
little, shaked their heads kinda disgusted, but then we all got to go
in for free, even Tepti too.

Dude, let me just ask you to sit your ass down so I can tell
you about this Absinthe Fairies place. Cauze if there's a bar like
this in Chicago, for sure it's illegal, probably down a secret tunnel
for rich assholes to smoke opium with hookers. *Absento Fejos* was
totally shroom heaven, only more advanced. The ceiling lights
were kinda hangin' like grapes, some bunches of purple or yellow
or blue crystals. All the windows had red and dark blue curtains,
frickin' polished tree stumps for tables. Lots of the decorations
looked like melted wood, maybe drippin' dark red or green tree
roots. All them different colors went together real perfect and the
electronica tunes totally spaced my ass out.

Raimis told me, "We must to make some absinthe first." If
you never had it, it's this green syrup, only the stuff's maybe 500
proof so it lights on fire. You melt some sugar in the orange and
blue fire, then you blow it out and pound so it hits you more fast.
Absinthe goes real nice with hash cauze the flavor's like licorice,
plus you get a real mellow feeling.

After two of them absinthes, I was rocked through the wall.
The bar had this smoking yard over by the side...it was small and
without no ceiling so you could look up and see the Vilnius night
glowin' up there. I smoked a Dunhill with Varna and we seen
Gidas rollin' ONE MORE JAY at a small table. This was way too
much even for me...like I toked quick one time just to keep the
faith, but Varna told him *eyk pist, blet.*[**] Gidas smoked the rest by
himself so the piano was totally gone from his face. He turned like
a scarecrow just hangin' in the middle of the yard where

---

[*] Your supposed to say it more like "Donna". Not "Dayna".
[**] Go fuck, blet.

somebody shoved a stick up his back. And his face got green, totally Wizard of Oz so he would melt if it rained.

Finishin' my smoke, I went to look around the bar for Audra. Like I went in the last room, then down to the can and back upstairs, but I couldn't see her noplace. Raimis made me get one Absinthe "French style" where you mix it with water so it turns real cloudy, then just sip real slow and high class. I grabbed Tepti to keep him on my lap and sat at this stump table to chat with Terese.

That extra puff of hash was makin' effects. Mixed with the absinthe, I was totally flyin', but in this mellow, moody kinda way. Like I felt the good electronica all through my skin, and I seen all them real beautiful girls in the bar dressed with the most swank dresses and skirts. Terese was lookin' at me kinda intense...she was also a real pretty girl, but right there she got lookin' like one of them elves from the woods where Liv Tyler lived. I totally tripped out for a while, my body real light and my head kinda clear and free.

And right there I had a total hash moment. I was starin' in one direction where it was a big group of people. But pretty soon they started spreadin' out one by one totally connected with the music rhythm like invisible power was pullin' everybody apart. A path got made for me to see Audra in the corner...she was also drinkin' absinthe "French style." Her three wiggly fingers went wavin' at me and she was smilin' like she can't believe I'm finally makin' eye contact. Cauze she seen me a couple times already though she didn't say nothing.

Dude, Audra totally cut her hair super short and colored it the most dark black. She was this new person with green contact lenses and shiny silver earrings, frickin' jeans, a simple blouse and a black leather jacket. I went by her table with Tepti in my hands and for a while I couldn't talk. She didn't talk neither, but her smile got bigger and bigger till she started laughin'. She went, "Your dog? Your clothes?" and laughed so frickin' hard at me that her eyes got watered. "What the living hell are you *doing* here? Andy, what's this shirt?"

I shrugged. "All my real clothes got dirty. I was in some deep shit for a while."

"Deep shit," she said. "Yes, deep shit," and I could finally see she was absinthe wasted. We clinked glasses real smooth like a high class lady and gentleman, not two tools fucked up in a drug bar.

That girl Dana came by our table...she was one of the bar managers with a blue tooth in her ear and a real fancy black skirt that sparkled. Audra introduced me, "This is my good friend Andrew from Chicago," but I barely even remember lookin' at the girl or tellin' her thanks. Varna came by and tried actin' real smooth to show off his English, talk how he's a lawyer. Terese kinda pulled him away to go smoke, but then Raimis came around so tanked he couldn't talk no language. He just rubbed his bald head and said crap like "Elm mleh" or "Shmuka" then "Yesss...yesss." He shaked Audra's hand probably five times, talkin' "Good schmuka, yesss." Later Varna gave him a bunch of shit, sayin' *taxi** *taxi* lots of times. Them dudes disappeared somewhere.

I told Audra everything, how I met these people at ŠMC, even about my one night stand with the butterfly. She listened real intense to every word like she was tryin' to memorize the whole thing. We stayed for maybe one more drink, though we didn't talk where we're gonna go or what we should do next. Audra needed to go ask Dana something, so she was gone for a while...I seen them talkin' like a serious conversation. Then me and Audra just went outside by a taxi stand, like a bunch of real nice cabs in the middle of a square, some of the Russian drivers smokin' by a classical music theater. By accident I seen Gidas with his arms raised in the air to worship the building. I told Audra, "That guy gave me hash today." She made this stone face. "Andy, that's Dana's ex-husband. The girl was pretty upset when he came in with you."

---

* It sounds like "tuxy".

Our cab was this little mini-van. We didn't talk all that much and sat kinda far from each other, Tepti down by my feet. But I knew we were goin' to her place, so it got me paranoid, like pressure to say things romantic. The cabbie was haulin' ass down a narrow street, then down a bigger one where you could see the old castle tower lit up real nice. We cruised by the river, seen the small skyscrapers and some museum buildings, went over the bridge where I met Tepti. Both of us were quiet till I came up with something to say. "That guy Raimis. In his back yard they got train transmissions."

Audra was just starin' out the window. And I seen how bad she was spaced out...she didn't know what I said, only that I talked. Then it was like she woke up, "Oh, Andy. I...yesterday at the hospital."

"Right. I forgot...probably your thinkin' about that."

"No, please. Please, I want to tell. Yesterday at the hospital, the things he said. Because he thinks he's seeing ghosts."

"Who you talkin' about?"

"My dad." She had her forehead on the window and her breath kinda made little ghosts on the glass. "He thinks my mother's coming back. At night. Thinks she comes and sits on his bed."

I was quiet for a while. "You think it's true?"

"My father's an atheist. He never believed in God."

"Really..." After a long time when it was quiet, I kinda started thinkin' out loud. "Yeah. Though I never thought too much about it. I guess God is like a ghost too. Like the main ghost, the first one. But who knows what's more freaked out, if I seen God or my wife. Probably I'd rather see God than my wife, if she's dead. Though maybe not...depends if I liked her. Does she talk and walk around?"

"Andy." She turned to look at me. "She doesn't *do* anything. She's not coming to him. My father's going insane."

Now the taxi was pulled up to the front of this old building made with gray cement. We were in a totally new part of Vilnius on the other side of the river, a neighborhood with lots of trees and stray cats and kinda blue street lights. I seen a couple kiosks, like these stores set up in little sheds by a weird grocery, frickin' sausages hangin' in a window totally covered with birdshit. Around them kiosks it was these drunks rubbin' up in the shadows and strikin' matches, coughin' quiet. Tepti almost jumped out from my grip when he seen a stray.

Audra took me to this two story wood house. It had bars on the windows and a huge door in front. The stairway smelled like old garbage, plus cat and dog pee. Audra said, "Mine's upstairs by the naked light bulb." Up there it was one light bulb hangin' off a real dusty and crooked cable. And Audra's apartment was just one small room, super simple...a wood table and little bed, some chairs, a couch and a lamp with a yellow shade. In the corner it was a little fridge with a hotplate on top. Audra pushed away the drapes and the bright sky kinda gave the room this haze. She opened the window and we could smell the river real strong, kinda grassy water.

Behind this weird rubber curtain she had a bathroom...just a toilet bowl, sink and cramped bathtub. Audra stayed back there runnin' hot water to wash up with fruit soap. I kicked back for a while, laid down on the couch just lookin' at clouds through branches, how the sky was already light blue behind buildings. That's when I seen the little Jesus she had on the windowsill, a statue of him wearin' a red robe.

I'm gonna tell you this right now so you'd know. I never got into no religions. For real, most of 'em wig me, especially them people who believe magic shit, like a dude who comes back to life. Or the story with a snake talkin' to a girl and the girl don't freak out, she just believes the snake. That shit never made no sense to me.

The thing is, my dad was kinda into it, though he didn't talk about it too much with us. When I was real little, like three, I found some pictures of a guy with all his ribs showin' and thorns in his skull, plus a hole where somebody shoved a spear. Nobody told me that was Jesus, so I didn't know. Over by one bathroom door dad hanged another picture where it said "The Sacred Heart."

That one was also Jesus, though he looks real different with open bleeding holes in his hands, and some lights shooting out from his heart, only it's wrapped up in thorns to drip some blood. I didn't know that picture was supposed to make you holy or bless you. For real, I thought dad put it so everybody would know that's what happens when your not a man. It used to scare the shit out of me so I didn't talk nothin' about it or even look at it. Like sometimes I'd go down to the other bathroom by our kitchen.

Now here I was in Audra's place wasted on absinthe and hash...she was clinkin' around in a bathtub and runnin' water. That Jesus made me real confused and suspicious, like probably it ain't hers. I wanted to ask about it, how come she has it, only I thought maybe it would remind about her dad when she don't want no memories.

Audra was sittin' on her bed with the lamp on and the sky was crazy dark blue behind her. She was washed up without no makeup and her hair was wet. I seen them green contact lenses got put in a plastic case. Kinda automatic, I said, "Your real color's more pretty."

"You think?"

I faked a yawn. "Why you wore them contacts? How come green?"

"To hide, Andy. You know me. I'm fake and I hide."

"That ain't true."

She laughed some puffs from her nose. "Your sweet." And she looked me dead through, a warm and sad feeling straight through me.

I started feelin' super shy. "But, I like your haircut." She could hear I was gettin' nervous in my voice. "Also, when you wash off your makeup. Cauze you look younger." The room started shrinkin' a little. "I mean...not *that* way, I don't mean *that*. Not like your old. You don't look old anyway...anyway, cauze *all* chicks have to wear make up. But, you could wear even trashed stuff, and it would be totally fine."

I kept on babblin'. The room shrinked even more and the sky got more bright, like more and more blue. Audra came to kneel down by the couch. First she rubbed my head like I was too excited and needed to calm down. Maybe it worked a little, but I kept talkin' till she went *Shhh* so quiet and warm right by my ear and deep in my hair. Audra started kissin' my temples and cheeks real slow with wet lips and her mouth kinda open. I felt all my joints in my whole body, like my knees and elbows and shoulders go jello, then a buzz all over all my skin. She kept kissin' me, my forehead, my ears, my neck real soft, then my chin, the hard part of my nose, my lips... little warm and wet patches anyplace she put her lips. Audra was only wearin' a robe and moved my hands to let me feel her anyplace I liked, and when I wasn't sure I could do it, she put my hand to make sure.

I shivered real bad when she took my clothes off. It was weird...I felt like twelve years old but also more manly than ever before. I guess I was a little dirty so she took me to wash my whole body with a small cloth and that fruit soap. Then she dried me down with a real soft towel and brought me to her bed where we did it with the morning comin' on so it was like she planned it. Like the sun's gonna come up and she's gonna lay there under me without no makeup and no clothes so I could see her true blue...so she could sit on top of me and I can understand how she's totally real, not no fantasy or fairy. We kept doin' it even though we were tired, hung over and thirsty. But then we finally passed out together and she pulled me real damn close. We slept that way deep and hard with the fresh river smell outside and a warm breeze blowin' in real gentle.

A Surprise Visitor

Then a bunch of noise woke me up. First the phone went ringin' this violin song all the way on the other side of the room. That violin kept on and on and then somebody was knockin' on the door real loud. That made Tepti bark and he started runnin' a circle right by the door, sometimes sniffin' under the crack. The old boy would come by me and poke with his nose, bark bad breath in my face, then run back by the door. The dude on the other side wasn't too happy and kept bangin' real hard, sayin' *Audra!* and *Kelkis!* (wake up!). I finally went over there with my eyes all fogged.

Dude, I was *frickin'* hung over, totally thirsty and a headache. Audra was still wrapped up half way in a sheet...and for a second it was like *yeah, we did that, didn't we?* The cell phone kept goin' and the guy kept bangin' so Tepti wouldn't mellow out. I went just to check if the bolt could handle shit and seen the door was a Lithuanian special with scientific locks and hardcore latches...no way could that pissed off dude knock it down. So I just found my pants and tried to wake up Audra. Had to poke and use cold water, but then she kinda leaned up and blocked the light with her hand. I said, "The phone and the door. It sounds important."

She answered the phone first. *Nu, ko?* I don't think Audra was totally waked when she stood buck nude in the middle of the room. The guy stopped bangin', but she just kept askin' stuff like, *Ka?* (What?) *Kaip?* (How?) *Kada?* (When?) Then she finally

59

figured out the guy by the door was the same guy on the phone. Audra put on just a shirt and a robe to let him in.

I thought it was gonna be some weight lifter or a tough guy, but the dude came in real scrawny, like smaller than me. He looked like a lollipop, a white stick with yellow hair. And now he got real quiet, just sat on the couch, didn't care about me at all. I said "Good Morning," *Labas Rytas* and shaked his hand. But he showed me the time on his watch cauze it was frickin' past 15:00. Audra went to wash her face real quick so they could have a hardcore talk in Lithuanian.

The guy's real name was *Kuolas* (Kwo-las), like the most wigged out name I ever even heard. It means "fence post" or just regular "post," the kind where you tie a horse or hang the telephone lines, so from now on I'm just gonna call him Post. He didn't talk almost no English at all and I never figured him out too good, just from stuff Audra told me. The main thing...he was the guy drivin' the wagon when Audra's twin brother fell off. From that time he felt like he owed Audra to help her anytime she needed. The thing is, also he gave orders and could be mean, especially if he thought she's drunk or on drugs.

Sittin' in her small room, he was talkin' with real strict sounds, explainin' shit like a traffic judge. And when Audra heard what he came to say, she couldn't talk or do nothin'. For a while she just sat real hopeless, her face kinda hangin'. Post let her sit like that, but then he went *Dabar, Audra. Dabar*! (Now, Audra. Now!) She didn't look at me, just said, "Andy, we have to go to the hospital."

I didn't think the "we" had me included. I was super hungry and Tepti needed to go for a walk. But Audra already had a gray T-shirt for me and everybody understood I'm comin' along. She changed behind the curtain while I walked the dog real quick and then we left him in the apartment. Post drove us to this hospital near the river where we were gonna visit Audra's dad.

Dude, the old man was in real bad shape. The stomach operation made him better for a short while, but then other stuff went bad with him when Audra was livin' in Oak Park. Her dad got a small stroke that gave him shakes, plus he had a lung removed and parts from his intestines. He got throat cancer and needed to get most of his throat cut out. On the day I called Audra from Varna's phone, doctors were puttin' a feeding tube. The reason Post was bangin' on the door so hard was cauze Audra's dad woke up from the operation and ripped that tube out. He told everybody in the family he didn't want no life support or nothing artificial to feed him, so he ripped it out when he found it.

I ain't gonna lie. I wasn't lookin' forward to no hospital. For real, I felt like I didn't even belong there. I expected a guy with stuff connected everywhere and one of them machines with a heartbeat dot, probably bloody sheets. But it was real different. A Lithuanian hospital ain't like MacNeal where it's machines and stuff in the walls. It's more like a youth hostel with bigger rooms and a bunch of beds. That's all we found in there, lots of beds and this old man sleepin' in blue sheets, the kind for a little boy. He was real thin and white like tissue paper. Also he didn't have no teeth, so his lips sinked inside his whole mouth. Two nurses were watchin' him, though all they did was give morphine drops. They didn't have no cures left...without no feeding tube, they were just waitin' for him to die. Just to starve.

Me, Audra and Post were standin' around the guy's bed. And that's what I was thinkin'...*dude, your lookin' at him and he's starvin'*. And it wasn't even polite cauze I was hungry too and my stomach kinda growled a couple times. But Audra didn't hear it...she was lookin' at him totally shocked and hurt. Her eyes shaked a little so Post put his hand on her shoulder. Dude, I felt a mean jealous rush inside me that was weird, kind of a surprise where I didn't expect it.

This nurse brought a couple chairs. Then Post's phone went off so he went in another room for a long time. With a chair between me and Audra, she kinda changed into one of them manikins, totally froze like I couldn't see if she's breathin'. The old man started twitchin', then his head shaked and some wrinkles went in his face. Audra kinda grabbed his hand real soft but he didn't even move or know she's there.

It was a real weird moment for me. Last night I got the thing I came to get in Vilnius, the only thing I wanted. I'm gonna tell the truth about it, cauze now I wanted to go away someplace, wait for all this sickness and stuff to be over. I never seen nobody dyin' like this...the old man had maybe two days, definitely not no more than a week. My stomach kept growlin' and my mouth got super dry. Audra was whisperin' some mumble words, and down one hall behind us a nurse messed around with some metal, like a drawer filled with knives. That startled Audra up, maybe got her from a daydream. She grabbed my wrist and took me so I had to follow her.

Outside we just sat on this bench were you could see the river. Post was gone...like his car wasn't there no more. Audra picked a bunch of grasses and field flowers growin' by a tree. And she just ripped them blossoms apart or squeezed 'em, her fingers covered with pollen dust. Sometimes it was like she was gonna say somethin', but then she would squeeze more flowers. I probably sat with her like that for 20 minutes, some logs and plastic bags floatin' in the river.

Finally a taxi showed up to drop off some old ladies. Audra asked me, "Would you come with me, please? Please come with me."

"Where?"

"To a place. I don't want to go by myself."

Dude, I didn't want to go noplace with her. For real, I wanted to go hang with Tepti, maybe take some walks. But I told her, "Sure, Audra. I'll go with you."

The cab drove us right back to that taxi stand by the classical music theater, the one right by Absinthe Fairies. She paid the cabbie and we went down this other direction, a road that got real narrow. Down there it was a couple churches with Russian letters. That street had some weird amber[*] shops on one side, then this gate with a huge back yard. In there I seen old women and

---

[*] It's this orange or yellow or brown jewelry. They make lots of amber in Lithuania.

homeless dudes with their bandaged legs and pictures of Jesus and Mary, some junkies hangin' around. It wigged me cauze some of them people were in real bad shape. Audra just said, "Don't look at them, Andy. They're all alcoholics."

At the end of the street was something like a bridge, a building goin' over the road. It was totally bright white with this dark red trim...in castle times, that place used to be the gate of the city, an old one called *The Gates of Dawn*. Lots of tourists with cameras and sandals were hangin' around there to take pictures and buy some post cards. Audra said, "We have to go in this door." It was on the side and real small, like I thought it's gonna be a store or a restaurant in there.

But then I got shocked. Inside by some stairs was a huge Jesus, like three feet tall and hangin' on the cross. It was real uncomfortable and tweaked how some old women were lined up by him so it got real crowded in a tight space where you could smell everybody. That statue got its legs and feet rubbed for maybe two hundred years, so them feet didn't even have no toes, all of them totally worn off. Some of the paint got chipped so Jesus looked like he had scabs on one leg. No way could I touch it, but Audra kissed his feet.

Then we went up them stairs where it smelled like a Berwyn school after a flood. One old woman went climbin' on her knees and she held some prayer beads real tight in her hand. So weird...it was *frickin'* quiet in there, like you could only hear shoes on the ground and echo whispers. We were goin' *up* stairs, but it felt like we were headin' *down* in a dungeon.

Up on top was one more real old and creakin' heavy door. Behind that was this small room with a little stage for Mary. I didn't know too much about Mary, only from Christmas movies how she was kinda poor and had her kid in a barn. But this Mary got made out of gold, like a huge silver moon underneath her and a golden sun behind her head. The weirdest part was her face, like a ghost floatin' in a piece of real rough glass.

All them people were prayin' *hard* in that small room, kneelin' down to pinch beads or they would push knuckles in their eyes. An old man stood up and then it happened automatic...I ended up kneelin' down on this marble thing cauze it was right in front of me. Audra kneeled down right by me and for a while she was holdin' my elbow and lookin' at Mary. Then she lowered her head and folded her hands so her knuckles turned white...for a while I thought she's holdin' her breath till she mumbled some stuff.

Lots of Lithuanians believe that *Gates of Dawn* chapel can make miracles for sick people. You look around and all the walls get covered up with little pieces of silver. Like your supposed to make a silver eye or a heart or a leg, whatever part is sick, then you hang it up in the chapel and pray. Audra didn't have no silver pieces, but she was askin' Mary for a miracle. She frickin' fell apart, cracked up right in front of me, started tappin' her forehead with them tight hands and totally cryin' out her whole damn insides. And nobody reacted weird or nothing like that. It was like this is what the chapel's for.

I just stayed by her, but got real confused and unsure. Cauze even though she was cryin' and felt real terrible, I thought she was so beautiful and like the most smart and special person I ever even met. With golden Mary and all them old ladies, I was totally rememberin' that sunlight on Audra's body when we were together. But all them other people in there were thinkin' only how somebody's gonna die or some horrible thing happened. So I really wanted to go back someplace else.

Right there Audra told me I should go down by ŠMC cauze it was only three blocks away. Kinda secret, she put some money in my pocket, told me to go eat and she'd meet me. So I went back down that street past Absinthe Fairies again, totally blown away how a drug bar can be so close by this crazy religious place.

The day was kinda cloudy and cold so ŠMC was pretty empty. Raimis wasn't there and they only had one waitress. I ordered a piece of fried fish and a cup of the strong coffee, then wrote all this shit down in my notebook. This artist chick let me bum a smoke and I ordered a glass of Jameson to sip with some water.

Feelin' more mellow, I kept lookin' out the window to see if Audra was comin'. It was really a lot of traffic in the street, lots of tourists and people goin' home from work. Just by accident, I seen this guy kinda wanderin' toward the cafe and he went right up to read the food menu hangin' by the window. There was something about the way he walked and the way he moved his hands. He was wearin' a Grateful Dead shirt from 1978, plus pink and purple Tevas. At first I didn't know how come I can't take my eyes off from him, but then it hit me hard like lightning bolts! The dude was checkin' all the prices and rubbin' his chin. When he scratched his face and put his hand in his pocket, I frickin' knew exactly who I'm lookin' at! Shit a brick, Andrew, cauze you're lookin' at Big Beard. It was Big Beard standin' there with his whole face shaved clean, the same like in that wedding picture at his house.

Itchin'

For a second I thought he was gonna come in ŠMC. But then he looked up and down the street, shoved his hands in his back pockets and wandered down by this old city hall building maybe 60 feet away. Me and Big Beard didn't have no eye contact, but he saw me good, saw my body for sure, just I couldn't know if he recognized me.

He was gone and my brain went light speed on crack. *Get off your ass, dude! Get up! Go follow his ass. See where he's livin'. No! Cauze if he sees you, your dead. Gotta call the hostel, make sure they don't say my name to nobody. Get Raimis to call cops on Big Beard's ass, bust him for drugs...get him deported. He knows I'm here for sure and now he's lookin' for me.*

"Crazy motherfucker." I kinda got buzzed up right there, but it was only Raimis with Varna sittin' down by me. The waitress brung them coffee with brandy cauze both them dudes were still hung over pretty bad, kinda grumpy like they swallowed rocks. We drank some coffee, but I didn't say nothin' about no Big Beard...like I pretended nothing happened, just said I'm waitin' for Audra to pick my ass up. They seen I was gettin' impatient, wonderin' what's takin' her so long.

Finally she showed up kinda winded with her face a little red. She ordered vodka with a lemon squeezed, plus a small mineral water. The guys got more quiet, maybe tryin' to remember what hammered bullshit they talked at Fairies. Audra asked lots of

66

Lithuanian questions, but them dudes only shrugged and looked real unsure, starin' at me sometimes. It was like ten minutes or more when Varna finally told her *Gerai* (Good). He looked at me, "Come, Endee. I take you in my car."

Without me really havin' a say or anybody askin' what I thought, Varna was drivin' me to Raimis' place so I could get all my stuff. Like I didn't even know what was goin' on till we were walkin' to his Subaru. He asked me, "*Nu**...now you to live with this woman?"

"Dude, I don't even know." I got in the car. "It's a life of its own right now. I guess I'm just stayin' there for a while."

He started drivin', a real weird smirk on his face and his big pile of hair kinda bouncin' around from the bumpy road. "Endee. What you think about this Audra?"

"She's real nice. Sometimes."

"Sometimes nice?"

"Cauze her dad's real sick. So she ain't feelin' too good."

"Endee...her father. I hear about this family. Do you know, her father very big Communist?"

I just shrugged. "He ain't got too much time left."

Varna kinda nodded. For a while he was thinkin' some shit, tryin' to get his smokes while drivin' the stick shift. "You know, Endee, woman like this Audra..." We were stopped at a red light so he could light up. "You are young, Endee. Young, but you should believe. This kind of woman is good for penis. Yes, true, good for penis. But for brain is very very bad. Also, bad for pocket."

I didn't say nothin'. The light changed green and Varna kept talkin'. "Yes, I know one man, one rich *advokat*. He have big house...good house with *balkon* and garden...but then his complete big house go poof! Just poof!" Varna blew smoke out his nose and rubbed his hair. "You know, one minute you king! With blonde

---

* This means "well." Kinda the same like "Well, I dunno."

woman, every person see you...they thinking, 'Aha, *pizdiets*[*], this man is *pizdiets*!' Maybe trip to Spain and Italia. Money, cognac, car, suit, champagne, chocolate, caviar. Sex in car, kitchen, swimming pool, garden. Yes, sex in Spain and Italia." He made this fist. "But another minute, *blet*!" he waved his hand. "*Blet*, what they do to you. You wake up. Everything empty. Cognac bottle empty, stuck up in your ass. She put cognac bottle up in your ass, and that's all."

"But I got nothin'. What's she gonna take from me?"

"Ha, aha! Endee, the young young rooster." Varna took a drag from his smoke and raised a finger. "Woman like this, she needs only destroy. And what destroy? Who cares...destroy everything, especially man. For her is it sickness or maybe only game? This nobody can know. But you make sure, Endee...make sure, sure sure sure. With her you must do only only only with preservative."

"What preservative?"

"Strong preservative."

"What kind?"

"Like...gums. With gums."

"What frickin' gums?"

"Gums on penis! *Blet*, you put gums on penis!"

I was laughin' pretty hard when we pulled by them massive train axles and transmissions. "No, Varna. It ain't preservatives, dude...it's frickin' life preservers."

When we came up to Raimis' door there was all this noise goin' on in there. I thought maybe he forgot to turn off the radio, but it was two totally smoked up chicks blastin' *Dancing Queen*. For real, them two were like high school girls and the munchies had 'em eatin' salami with bread rolls, their shoulders kinda goin' to the beat. I just took my stuff without thinkin' too much about it and Varna had a beer in the kitchen. Walkin' out, he said, "You see? It may be better stay with Raimis."

---

[*] They say this a lot. It means like "right on" or "fuck yeah!" Though also it can mean how something sucks.

Varna left me at Audra's place since he had errands. I had to wait a long time for her to let me in cauze she was crashed pretty hard. Tepti was real quiet like he was ashamed, kinda hidin' near a drape. Dude...me and Audra left him too long and he totally took a crap in the bathtub. Even though it was kinda smart for him to go in there, still it was totally nasty, but I cleaned it up real fast. Audra stayed crashed and didn't even know about it.

Post came over later and woke her up real rude. They were havin' another hardcore talk...this time Audra was only sayin' *nezhee know, nezhee know* (I don't know, I don't know). She was real annoyed and kinda whinin'...Post got her to dress up to go someplace. She had all this stuff ready for me, a map of the city where she made circles on important stuff like ŠMC and her place, plus the bridge where I met Tepti. She gave an extra key and a calling card, writin' down her number just in case. Then Post drove her back down by the hospital.

Dude...right there I started feelin' pretty weird. Like I totally knew this situation ain't normal, and probably there's something real uncool about it. It was kinda like "Okay...*now what*?" cauze I needed to make a move. Only what the hell could I do? For a while I just looked out the window at cars goin' by, thought maybe I should ask Raimis or Varna if they knew about a job. Cauze I counted my cash and seen how absinthe night cost me about 100 Litas. So I felt real dumb from it.

My dirty clothes were stinkin' like a dead skunk. And that apartment started feelin' real cramped, especially since Jesus was starin' at me kinda sneaky. I had to get the hell outta that place, so I made triple sure I got the keys and me and Tepti went for a walk around Audra's neighborhood.

The whole time I was thinkin' *what kind of jobs they got for illegals over here*? Cauze I could totally take one, save up for a plane ticket home, which would be a good move. But walkin' around, you don't see no dudes mowin' lawns or cleanin' up the street. For real, it was a pretty depressed neighborhood over there, them shadow drunks rubbin' up in the daytime the same way like at night. Down a little ways past that birdshit grocery, I seen some more kiosks, only these in a little bit better shape. Workin' them kiosks is probably a minimum wage job in Lithuania, though for some reason only old ladies work there. Each kiosk is like a little jail with bars and a small window, and them ladies sell so much different crap...smoked fish in a plastic bag, tooth brushes, box juice, junk hair dryers and digital watches from like 1990. In one window I seen some false teeth.

But then I couldn't believe it cauze one of them windows had one little pouch of Ariel detergent. Totally frickin' the exact same Ariel you can get in Cicero corner stores or in the Berwyn Fruit Market. Holy shit, dude, that little bag of Ariel kinda wrecked me. Cauze I started rememberin' all this Cicero and Berwyn stuff, like Mexican candles in the stores. Frickin' Sterling College. Miska's Liquors on Cermak road, Freddy's Italian Ice on 16th. Scatchell's super good hot dogs. Diesel smoke from the Burlington Northern freight. Your gonna think I'm a serious idiot, but I totally bought that little bag of Ariel.

At first I was thinkin' I'll show it to Varna and Raimis. "You guys, this shit's from Berwyn." But then I realized Ariel was a total score cauze I could do my laundry. So I walked kinda fast back to Audra's place, real excited how I'm gonna clean all my shit. I made the bathtub water super hot, washed my clothes like Mama Bluegrass till my hands got red and wrinkled.

Audra came home when I was hangin' all my wet shit on windows and the chair. She barely even paid no attention to me, just pounded one huge shot of vodka, set up her cell phone alarm and crashed real hard in her bed. I was tired too after workin' like that, so I finished up and passed out on the couch.

Maybe we slept for two hours. But then it came super sudden...Audra got up straight in the bed, this total shock that woke me up. She seen Tepti layin' by the window and looked around the room to see all them hangin' clothes. Then she started scratchin' all over her whole body. First she talked in Lithuanian, but then she started sayin', "Fleas. I got fleas." She took off her shirt and sat on the couch to scratch only in her bra. "Your dirty clothes..." Dude, it was a serious wigout with her scratchin' super hard...you could see red marks on her skin from them long nails. She was scratchin' in her hair and her neck and then pulled her bra straps to scratch her back and shoulders like she can't control it, her whole face real tight.

Now she was bendin' over to scratch her ankles. I came up closer but she yelled at me, "No! Don't spread them!" I got scared she was gonna start fightin' or kickin' if I touched her, but finally I kinda grabbed her hands and her whole body went limp. She snapped out and looked around...it was like she's wonderin' *What's going on here?* Dude...the whole thing was totally sleepwalking. She was scratchin' like that in her sleep.

Audra fell on the couch for a while and covered her face with one hand. Her chest was half-naked, only not sexy at all...it was actually real uncomfortable, like she don't know she's nude. I put the blanket on her cauze she got the shakes. Audra sighed out real hard and said, "Wait, Andy. Wait. Wait." She grabbed my shirt tail with two fingers. "Look...go down to a store for me. Get me coffee. One cup, but really really strong."

I went down to birdshit grocery to get stuff that had a picture of a coffee cup on it. When I came back, Audra was passed out with the bathtub goin'...it was gonna flow over any moment. The water was so damn hot like she wanted to boil, so I put some cold and mixed it up usin' a vodka bottle. Then I figured out how to make coffee with that hotplate and a small pan. (Lithuanians just mix coffee with hot water sometimes and drink it straight without no filter.)

She asked me to wash her back and neck. I was pourin' water on her shoulders and over her head. That was the first time I could tell she was real thankful to me and thought the bath was real nice. Her phone rang and she took my arm. "Let it go, Andy. I don't want to talk to him."

I just sat down on the closed toilet bowl. She was movin' her hands under the water to make little waves and the phone finally stopped. After a while, she whispered kinda nervous, "Andy. Listen. I'd like you...if you could. I want you to tell me the truth."

I just nodded.

"I'm all scratched up." She touched her arm and her neck where it was real red, almost to blood. "This hurts. But I don't remember."

I smushed the sponge in the sink.

"Did I make you do it? Did I tell you to hurt me?"

"No way."

"Then what? Tell me the truth."

I told her the whole thing just how I seen it. From her face, I knew she didn't pretend it...for real, Audra couldn't remember wiggin' out like that. The bath water was already gray and gettin' cold, so she stood up and took a towel. Audra just told me, "Please boil more water, Andy."

We sat drinkin' tea by the window...Audra had these chipped up and real old tea cups with gold paint. The evening was turnin' real pretty, this crazy pink and orange between longass clouds. And she was starin' in the sky and talkin' with whispers. "It happens to me a lot. Especially out here."

I nodded.

"I forget whole hours. Forget where I'm going. I get a trolley to go to the hospital, but I get off at the market. And I forget how I got there. Then I don't want to do anything. I'd rather just sleep. I could sleep all day, and I don't even need liquor."

I put down my cup.

"Sometimes I feel like nothing's real. What's real...what's permanent? I know it's stupid to think that way. I hate myself for it. But then I feel like there's no purpose. When I feel like that, I hate myself even more. I get scared. I guess it scares me." Audra took a real small sip from her tea.

I said, "It's cauze your dad, right?"

Audra was quiet for a real long time. She said, "Yes. But no. No, Andy." After a while, she said, "I don't know. I could have gone anywhere in the world. I don't know why I came back here. What's wrong with me?" She grabbed her tea cup real hard, like maybe it could crack. "I swear to God. I don't know what I'm doing here."

Then she just looked out the window at them clouds. It was like she was hopin' I could tell her some stuff to help out. I totally knew right there I should say about Big Beard, how he was lookin' for us in Vilnius. But she seemed like a real little girl, more calm now and feelin' better. Though also I thought she's a candle burned all the way down to the bottom and the most small wind would kill it. So I just moved my chair kinda closer by hers. And I didn't say nothin' no more that night, just sat with her quiet till we went to bed.

My Room

Okay, right now I'm gonna admit somethin' real private and weird about me that I never told nobody. It's like a secret fantasy I used to imagine all the time (probably from like high school) where I'm sleepin' by an open window. Outside it would be late, like almost morning and you can see a tree or maybe bushes, plus it's a nice breeze. I'm totally passed out and dreamin' some good shit, like a cruise in a beemer with buffass sound around Lake Shore Drive. But then out of nowhere this girl comes and she sees me passed out by that window. So she thinks, "Alright, I have to do it to Andy right now." And when I wake up she's givin' me head.

I knew I'd never get it, but still I used to want this so bad. While sittin' around in class, I'd imagine some girls doin' it. A couple of times when I got trashed at some house parties, I went up to look for an open window in the attic rooms where I could pass out and hope for it. If it happened to me one time, I'd totally get my ass down by a White Hen Pantry for a Lotto ticket. Or bet all my cash on a crazyass longshot at the OTB.

Well...guess what? I was passed out right next to Audra and she was rolled up by the wall. Even though we were by a window, I didn't think nothin' about my secret dream...like I totally forgot about it. I slept real good with the fresh air and didn't even know how tired I was. But then shit started to feel real surprised. I wasn't even half woke up yet but it was happenin' to me almost exactly like I always wanted. When I finally knew for sure how it was real, I felt like, "Holy shit! Don't do *that*. Stop!"

But I didn't say stop. I didn't even move. I just got braced for the bust like I was gettin' ready for a doctor to give me a shot. It kept on happenin' and happenin', slow and long like when you hear Lake Michigan waves. And the whole time I was thinkin' *Is this good?* Yes but how and why? Dude...what's *wrong* with her? Who the hell does this, especially with Post comin' real early to pick us up?

For the last two or three minutes of it, he was knockin' on the door real light. Sometimes he'd go, "Audra. Audra," and then it would be tap tap, tap tap, tap tap. At the end she squeezed me so tight I almost went yellin', but soon it was finished and my whole body went jello. She just checked her face in the mirror, gave me some time to put on pants. Then she let Post in like everything's regular.

He sat down kinda yawnin', dressed up in a brown suit like he's goin' to court. They had a mellow talk with him shruggin' the whole time, sometimes flappin' his tie on his belly. Audra looked upset and sighed a lot...she was tryin' on different earrings from a little box. When she found good ones, these little gold dots, she just looked at me and said, "Andy. Don't sit around. Get washed up and change. Take your stuff because we're not coming back to this apartment ever again."

I helped her carry a super heavy suitcase and some leather bags she had stashed under the bed. Me and Tepti got in the back of Post's car and nobody talked with us...so for that whole ride I was thinkin' just one thing. *What the fuck just happened?* Did I tell Audra about my secret fantasy when we were in the Audi? No way. There's no way. I had to admit it...this was the second time from my life when I got what I always wanted. And it felt wrong and dumb, my neck totally stiff and lots of things confused. I totally fucked up cauze I could of had a secret fantasy where I wake up and I'm the mayor of Hawaii or something more important like that. But if all you want is a blow job then that's all your gonna get.

Post parked the car kinda close by this small hotel made with rocks and bricks. And you could see the castle from there, plus a park underneath and the big church tower. I said, "Where we goin'?" and Audra mumbled to me, "This is where I grew up. They both live here."

She meant her dad and Kovas cauze they were still in Audra's grandfather's old apartment. The house was maybe four hundred years old, a little ways down from the main post office on *Gedimino Prospektas*. It was marble steps up three floors to a fat doorway that went creakin' when a little lady opened it up. For real, it was like Twilight Zone reruns gram really liked cauze that apartment was huge, maybe seven or eight rooms and one long hall. The whole place got decorated super fine with metal candle holders, then red table cloths and a longass red rug. The biggest room had a shiny black piano, plus huge ass windows opened up wide with a breeze. I seen paintings of a hardcore army guy with lots of medals, then a wigged out crow flyin' in the dark with crazy yellow eyes. They put Audra's dad on a wheel bed all the way by one wall and he was covered up with them light blue blankets. A nurse was watchin' him real good, sometimes puttin' drops in his mouth. And around him they set up some chairs, like a concert where we're gonna watch a guy till he's dead.

Dude, I was totally unprepared for all this. And Tepti was confused too cauze he stayed rubbin' on my leg like a cat. I could hear some voices way in back, like three or four old women, and I smelled somebody was fryin' pancakes. In a corner by this small table they left one old timer with a hardcore cane made from a branch. He had vodka and was hittin' it from a gold shot glass, already buzzed at maybe 10:00.

Audra took me to a small room. She said, "This is yours, Andy. You can stay here." It was real nice with a TV and little shelves full of books, then a window where I seen a brick yard. The desk had a laptop with internet, then there was a sofabed...I guess the place looked like an office or a library. I kinda sat down by that desk and Audra said she'll be back with some sheets.

Maybe she was gone only ten minutes, though for me it seemed like an hour. The feeling was real weird to try explainin' right now...this was the best room I ever even seen, but I felt trapped when I seen it. The worst part, I couldn't admit to nobody how I'm trapped cauze I got what I always wanted and Audra's tryin' to be nice to me. But now I wanted something else...like maybe Raimis or Varna could borrow me enough for a plane and then I'd pay them back later. At the same time, I was thinkin' *You can't ditch her. You can't take off like a dick.*

Audra came back without no sheets. She kinda looked white faced and buzzed up. There was this plant where she sat down to light a smoke and ash out the window. I was lookin' at her and she said, "Okay, Andy. I can tell your confused and upset. I *can*, so don't say it, don't tell me about it. Okay? Please." She went rubbin' her collar bone. "I didn't want to bring you here. Hell, I didn't even want to come *back* here, but right now there's nowhere else to go. The apartment we left...that's actually Dana's apartment. She needs it now, so we'll have to stay here.

"Those cows just told me my dad's only got a little time. How much...they won't tell me. Please don't blame me for anything right now. I'll make you comfortable here. I told them your my friend from America. Maybe they think we're fucking. Maybe they think your my husband's relative. Or you work for me. It doesn't matter. They won't talk to you, they don't speak English. Kovas speaks a little, but I doubt you'll even see him, he stays locked away. If you don't want to, you don't have to come out of this room until it's all over. And then I swear to God, I swear to God...all these people will leave and we can rest, just rest. We'll go somewhere, Andy, by the sea or a lake...we'll do whatever you want. Just please promise me you'll stay here while this is happening. That you won't go with Raimis or Varna or anyone." She grabbed my wrists real tight so it kinda hurt. "Promise. Okay, Andy? Will you promise?"

"Audra?"

"You have to promise. Because when this is done, after it's over with, we'll have this whole apartment. It'll be easier then."

"But what you mean? Cauze...what are we doin' together? You got stuff planned?"

"Andy, until it's over just stay here, will you? Will you stay with me?"

I guess I nodded. Or maybe I whispered *sure* even though I can't remember. Next thing I know she was huggin' me super tight and stickin' my head in her neck where it smelled like soap water with sweat. She said, "They're making breakfast. We should eat."

I guess Lithuanians make this tradition when your waitin' for someone to die. Audra called it *atsy sveykint*, which means to say good-bye. You eat for a long time and talk about stuff, drink vodka or cognac from golden shot glasses and look at pictures. Sometimes you go up to the dying guy and sit with him or look at him...some of them old ladies went touchin' his forehead. The booze gives everybody hardcore moodswings, like one moment all them jolly fat women were puttin' sour cream and cherry jam on pancakes. But then they were all boozed up, cryin' and holdin' hands, their frickin' makeup real sloppy and all over the place. Like a half hour after that, they would get cleaned up with new makeup and start laughin' real hard in the kitchen. They sang kinda pretty songs, but then they turned sad so they got sloppy again.

This was the first time in my life where I got plowed off cognac and it was just after breakfast. One old lady knew only five things in English. *Come to me, please. Live and let live. Where in the world is Carmen San Diego? I did it my way. Fuck police.* Like she would say one of them things to me and I would repeat it. Then we'd have a shot and laugh together kinda confused, but also like we were a team since she always winked at me. I tried teachin' her new stuff like *good morning* and *pleased to meet you*, but she would giggle and say "Ver inssa vorld is Kermin Sendiego," then pour another shot.

Dude, it took Audra's dad four days to die. People were always comin' and goin' from the apartment and the phone went ringin' every half hour. With so many old people boozed up all the time, I kind of turned like a decoration and disappeared. All them people were the dad's friends from work, so I guess most were professors or secretaries. Audra only told about one lady named Marta since she was the dad's girlfriend from a long time ago. One time late at night I seen her wasted and holdin' the old man's hand like she was totally in love with him. She had a little suitcase with clothes and stuff so she stayed in the apartment the whole time.

I guess lots of shit was botherin' me, so I hit the sauce hard just like all them old timers. Even though I was wasted, still at night I didn't sleep too good, kinda paranoid and thinkin' only *when's he gonna die?* Audra always laid down by me after the last people were gone. She would look at the shadows on the ceiling and I could hear how her heart would go thumpin'. The last night before her dad died, we were layin' like that and I knew she wasn't crashed. So I said, "Audra. What's your plan?"

She licked her lips and shoved her head back deep in the pillow. "I want to go swimming," she said. "I really would love to go to the sea."

"Swimming..."

"A sauna by the Baltic. Or I'd like to buy an expensive car, an Aston. Or a Lotus. And I'd drive the motherfucker full speed right into the side of a castle." Then she was quiet. "But to destroy a car like that? No, it would have to be my husband's car. Into some tree. Because a tree can grow back, but a castle has meaning."

"How come your talkin' weird?"

"I want to rest," she said. And then she turned real soft. "I want to know what it's like to be calm. But, dammit, I hate calm people. You don't know how much I hate them." Audra rolled on her side and shoved her forehead hard in my ear. Then she crashed right there.

This time I was the one lookin' at them shadows. I didn't understand none of the crap she was talkin' cauze it just sounded like cop outs...*it don't matter if I bullshit Andy*. On my shoulder I could feel the air comin' out her nose and it smelled like booze. For real, that was the first time I got real pissed at her.

I thought maybe I should return the favor. Put my face between her legs so when she wakes up she finds a surprise, like real awkward. I should of, though I only had the guts to imagine. She would wake up confused and uncomfortable, and she would wish I stopped though also she would want me to finish. And then somebody would tap on the door, one of them old ladies. Or her dad would do it...he would get from bed the last time before he turned to a ghost. But I would keep on goin' and Audra would wait till it's finished, coverin' her mouth tight to make sure no sound comes out even though she wants real bad to scream.

Dude, I got freaked out cauze somebody *did* knock. First I thought it's in the brickyard, but then I heard one more knock and Tepti gave a bark. That door had one of them beady glass windows and I could see somebody's shadow outline. It was a dude, "Audra, Audra," but not Post, somebody else. So I shaked Audra, but she wouldn't wake up. The knock got pretty loud and Tepti was barkin' and runnin' his doggy circle right by the door. I knew why that guy was knockin' so I put on a shirt and opened up.

Black Out

The first thing I seen was a dude's thin arms with roadmap veins. Then his bony body, them collar bones like a big coat hanger shoved in his neck. His face was like a mask, just skin and stubble pulled real tight on his head with a buzz cut. Seein' him got me stone cold froze, and I did a shitty job tryin' to act regular. It didn't matter cauze he didn't care about me, just kept on sayin', "Audra, Audra," with his head stuck in the room.

That tweaked out dude was Audra's brother, Kovas. And behind him was a nurse. She turned on more lights so I could see better how he was like a zombie. After a while he got panic, yellin' at Audra cauze their dad was gonna go now, right now. Kovas frickin' pinched her stomach and slapped her cheeks pretty good. But she wasn't gonna get up...everybody knew she just pretended to be hammered so stubborn, how she could take the pinchings and not even move. The nurse babbled real fast and Kovas went with her in the piano room.

It ain't true if I say I followed. For real, it was like a tractor beam sucked me over there. I remember how I got the shakes, though also I felt buzzed up cauze I knew I'm gonna see something real important. It all happened fast...I didn't even have no time to feel ashamed of bein' a stranger with Kovas. I still hoped Audra would come from the room, but she never even made no sounds.

The old man was like an alien with sharp ears and nose and long fingers, real thin and totally starved. His eyes bulged out and turned the same gray like dirty ice, the exact same color how you see in the alley after slush gets froze. The nurse gave him a shave to make him look better just for this, but she cut a couple spots under his nose and the chin where it was blood dots.

She was talkin' stuff to Kovas. Maybe the dude didn't hear cauze he just sat blinkin' and twitchin'. It was real weird to see how the old man looked almost frickin' exactly the same like his kid. One was old and dyin' and his boy was younger, but both had skin and collar bones with fat veins in real thin arms. I never seen no ex-junkie up close...all them twitches in his face were a real surprise for me. His eyes got crazy pink like bloodwater, like when you brush teeth and spit blood in the sink.

The old man had maybe ten seconds left...now eight and seven and six, I could feel it. He just stared up and I remembered all them pictures the old ladies were lookin' at...the old man's wedding, Audra when she was a baby, then Kovas playin' with some little toy cars. At the last moment the old man's face got shiny, but then some blood poured from his mouth and the nurse wiped it with a little cloth.

I didn't know it was gonna be blood. And I started thinkin' *Oh man, help him out!* But all the pain was already finished and he didn't need no help...he was disappeared, just a body without no more life inside. With the old man gone the place turned quiet almost like earplugs. Kovas rubbed his face and his eyes totally watered, but then he went by Audra and said some real nasty shit to her, just pissed off and dirty.

Dude, I know people who seen somebody die will know what I mean, cauze it was one of the most beautiful and peaceful things I ever seen in my whole damn life. For real, I was glad for him. Goin' out was way better compared with lyin' around on morphine, and all you got is hammered ladies fryin' pancakes you can't even eat. So it felt like a weird freedom for him. Inside me I got this private feeling real deep where I could admit something clear, like "Yeah, *that's* true, I totally feel like *that*," though nobody can say what *that* is, since there ain't no word for it. I washed up with good hot water and went back to my room with my face and hands still drippin' wet. Sat in the chair where Audra left her prayer beads.

The reading lamp was on and I watched Audra still fakin' sleep, probably hurtin' where her brother pinched her. I hope I never feel more sorry for nobody like I felt sorry for her right there. The bullshit got old for her so she opened her eyes and stared at my knees. She whispered, "Who's out here? Who's left?" but I didn't say nothing. "Andy, did he talk? Did he say final words?"

I said, "No. Cauze it happened real quiet. Not a sound."

Her eyes got a little wet and she nodded a bit, but Audra didn't show no feelings. Totally like a mule, like a frickin' brick box.

The funeral went down three days later, and for all that time it was high stress preparations, like settin' up special prayers in a church, then a wake before they could bury him. The church was this big pink one down from ŠMC and it was the first time I ever seen how they do stuff. They had lots of paintings with holy people, plus a huge dead Jesus on a cross, some blood on his head, and his body the same thin and starved like Audra's dad. The priest stood in front of that Jesus by an expensive table and burned holy smoke, mumblin' stuff the whole time. Later on he lifted this golden cup and ate some white crackers, then shared them with everybody, though Audra said I can't have one. I just listened to this girl sing a real sad song with an organ on a balcony. Without that song it would of been the worst vibe since only ten people showed up in that bigass church, so the music made it feel more filled up.

Audra said I didn't have to go to no wake or the cemetery. But she asked if I could help Carmen San Diego make lunch and set up the dining room, also to make sure she don't steal no expensive shit from the kitchen, like China and silverware. It's another Lithuanian tradition for funerals...you give everybody a big lunch with salads and fish and mashed potatoes, plus big

meatballs called *cutlaytis*. More people come to your funeral if
they know it's gonna be a good lunch, cake and some tea made
with flowers. Carmen also had vodka and beer ready for it.

She showed me how to do everything with sign language
when she needed help. My main job was to peel like fifty potatoes,
then boil and mash them up. Also I had to set up the table, copy
the example she put for me by one chair. I totally didn't fuck it
up...for real, it looked nice with glasses and knives and the little
folded napkins. I got real surprised when Carmen busted out a
shirt and tie for me with pants. Like the pants were kinda big but
the shirt fit pretty good. Who knows where she got it, but she told
me "Good boy, good boy," when I was dressed and ready.

All the people came together at the same time after the
burial, kinda early in the afternoon. They were stone quiet and real
tired, some long faces and sad vibes. But after they got some
vodka and buttermilk soup (it's cold and mixed with beets and
potatoes), that perked everybody up. People started conversations
and did more vodka, ate some pickled fish, cucumber salad and
these beans mixed with beets and vinegar. For real, that food made
everybody feel a lot better so you could feel the whole room get
kinda relaxed and more regular. Like people tossed Tepti stuff
under the table so he could eat.

Dude, pretty soon Carmen brung the meatballs and mashed
potatoes, so right there people started givin' toasts, like ten minute
speeches. The thing about a Lithuanian toast, you don't just sip
some beer or brandy when it's done. Every frickin' Lithuanian
toast gets one hundred grams of vodka, almost like a double shot.
The old man gave a toast and then Carmen San Diego gave a toast.
Then another lady said some words and pretty soon Marta gave a
long speech. Finally Audra said some stuff real warm cauze
people liked it and clinked their glasses and looked in the eyes. So
right there I was finished with six hundred grams of vodka, like
more than half a bottle in maybe forty-five minutes.

It got so everybody was talkin' at the same time and passin'
around food, some big meatballs and mashed potatoes and
mushrooms with cream and bacon. Tepti stuck his nose right in

my crotch and his whole body shaked cauze he was jacked from all the smells. A lady gave me a bottle of dark beer that foamed all over the glass and tasted so good and cold, kinda sweet. Right there the old man stood up cauze he wanted to tell a funny story about Audra's dad and everybody had to listen.

He totally started talkin' like poetry. Frickin' the dude said some stuff, looked at everybody and then everybody was laughin' real hard from a real small whisper he made. I laughed just cauze that's what happens when everybody's laughin'. But also I was so shithead wasted, probably a banana peel or a snot rag would of been funny. The laughs kinda mellowed out pretty soon and the old man tried tellin' more story cauze he wasn't finished. But guess who was makin' a fool?

I was holdin' the table cloth. The tip from my tie got stuck in mashed potatoes, real messy and rude. Audra told me later it was maybe two minutes before I figured out I'm the only laughin' idiot and everyone else was shut up. I remember Carmen was starin' at me with her lips kinda tight. I guess I finally stopped and it was quiet for a while till the old man started talkin' again.

But now I got super paranoid. The whole room went spinnin'. Audra took my tie out from the potatoes and I looked at her, seen four eyeballs. Some stupidass beer goggle shit went through my brain, stuff like *That Carmen San Diego lady's actually kinda decent lookin'*. Marta poured me another 100 grams and I knew there's no way I can handle it. The walls were closin' on me and Audra was cleanin' the potatoes off my tie with a napkin. So with the old man still talkin'...he was almost ready to bust out a punchline...I just screamed it out, "Fuck police! Fuck 'em all!" And I started howlin'ʹ and blowin' raspberries and pullin' on my tie.

Dude, shit hit the fan. Audra grabbed my arm. The ladies didn't know how to handle this, though the old man figured *screw it* and just drank by himself. But Kovas got super pissed at me. During the whole lunch he was just sittin' there quiet and grumpy, not no reaction in his thin face. But now he slammed a salt shaker on the table five times. Lookin' at me, he went, "You! You say me *now*, who you?" When I only laughed at him a little, he slammed the salt shaker one more time. "You say me now! Say me now! Who you? What want you here?"

I guess I babbled some stuff, but Audra told me to shut up. She went over by Kovas and they started arguin' loud and hard. Marta and Carmen tried to mellow them out, but Kovas and Audra just kept on screamin' hardcore at each other with crazy power, like Audra pinched him and slapped his face once, but he stood ground and didn't care. The old man just sat at the end of the table with his hundred grams and a meatball. But for me the room was spinnin' even worse like before, so I knew I had to get the hell outta there. The last thing I remember is lookin' for the bathroom before I blacked out.

Secret Things

You know that feeling you get when you wake up and your still wasted? Like the white hot sun's blastin' on your face and a dog's lickin' your mouth cauze he thinks your probably dead? The light hurts your brain real bad and the dog's breath is gonna make you puke. But you can't even lift your head or open your eyes cauze you forgot how your body works.

I woke up in the same bed where Audra's dad died. The only reason I didn't freak out right there was cause I was still ripped and didn't barely know nothing. It was like, *Where am I? Who's this dog? Fuck, that's right...I went to Vilnius. God damn funeral.* Under my ass it was a phone book...sleepin' on it numbed my leg so I thought it's dead forever. My mouth was like chalk and somebody put a chainsaw in my head. I needed water real bad.

Dude, the whole apartment was totally trashed. They left old food plates on shelves and the rugs were pushed around crooked. Somebody opened two closets and all the clothes got dumped on the floor with some shoes kicked down the hall. All them old people were gone, just the radio in Kovas' room was playin' rap and I could smell him smokin' in there. On one couch I seen Post sleepin' real disgusting in his ballhanger underwear. Audra was crashed in my room on the sofabed with her friend Dana, the exact same one from Absinthe Fairies.

The girl was wearin' pink peejays and she was already kinda up. Her one arm was hanged over her forehead and she was lookin' at the ceiling. But when she seen me in the door she started laughin' hard so her whole body jiggled around. Audra got pissed and yelled *Nutilk* (Shut up), then hugged a pillow real tight. Dana covered her mouth though she didn't have no way to stop laughin'. In her real strong accent, she told me, "*Endee*, do you find moon in sugar?"

I didn't know what the hell she was talkin' about. For real, I figured she's probably still hammered just like me, or maybe baked from Copenhagen hash. But she wouldn't leave me alone about it. After I drank some water, she kept askin' "But where you throw moon? Now moon broken. Poor poor moon." And she laughed with that body jiggle.

I sat down by the desk. "Dude, your smokin' the bowl."

"No, no. No smoke in bowl, only sugar. And moon. Don't make lie. I know you remember. Because you remember *all*." The girl started makin' a mimic of me, *My gramma, her sugar, important bowl, only who needs moon? Who needs fucking moon?*

Dude, I didn't remember nothing she was talkin' about. Dana wasn't gonna believe me, though I swear I *still* don't remember nothing about finding no moon in sugar after I made a mess at the lunch. I guess I went back to the party after I puked, and I was makin' an ass for a while. Audra had to cut me off, made me drink tea and gave me a sugar bowl. So I stuck my whole hand in that bowl sayin' I'm gonna find the treasure. "I'm gonna take it, sell it for plane tickets."

I got reasons to explain all this. It's cauze gram used to keep important stuff in her sugar bowl, like her secret hiding place for a locket and a gold ring. Audra's bowl didn't have no rings or treasures, just clumped up sugar shaped like a banana. So I told everyone, *Dude, it's a moon. I found a moon.* Went liftin' it up the way the priest showed them crackers in church. *This is a moon, this is a moon. Who gives a crap?* Then I threw it out the window and yelled some stuff about treasures, money, plane tickets and Jameson.

Hearin' Dana tell that story got me real embarrassed. She was still laughin' at me so I said I needed to take a shower. And when I came out she was already gone with Audra to eat someplace. Me and Tepti took a walk in the brickyard and then I passed out in my room, woke up when it was already night.

It took me two days to shake that hangover. But for Audra it took maybe three or four. She just watched Mexican soap operas and drunk tea or seltzer, plus this medicine called *margan sophie*, some water that smells like metal. Me and Post pretty much cleaned up the place, put that dead man's bed in a back room, made the rugs straight and washed all the dishes. I did it just to have something to do cauze Audra was spaced out all the time and slept way too much.

Dude, I was frickin' bored out of my brain. And I was gettin' frustrated hangin' around that apartment. Audra didn't tell me nothin' like *don't go anywhere, stay here*, but the way she would look at me made me feel so damn guilty, though I didn't even know why. When she got better from the hangover, she didn't do nothing at all. For real, Audra didn't have no reason to be anyplace and didn't make no plan for nothing, cauze she didn't have one thing she wanted to do.

Like every day she would think where we could eat lunch or what kind of stuff was happenin' in town. But then she would get hardcore moodswings. Sometimes she would be quiet like a rock and just sit on the balcony or look at the street. And she would talk weird stuff. "Andrew, now it's quiet. Finally it's quiet." No it ain't, Audra. Cauze we can hear Kovas blast his Wu-Tang Clan. "The air's so nice. We can go for a walk somewhere. I wish Vilnius had a zoo. But it's a shame how they trap those animals."

She talked like this. And she started askin' me to do stuff totally useless, though I had to pretend it's damn serious. One day I had to pull all the sofas from every wall cauze she thought important things fell behind a long time ago. She acted like we're lookin' for key shit when it was just her imagination.

It was maybe eight days after the funeral when Kovas had to go to the clinic for the first time. It meant he was gonna spend the night...Audra never said why, only it was normal and happened a lot. She felt real free and maybe proud, like the house is all hers now. When Marta came to clean Kovas' room, that made Audra feel real good, like somebody's doin' service for her. But then she had a moodswing. "Andy, I want you to watch Marta because she's stealing spoons." No she ain't, dude, but I had to go look in Marta's purse anyway just to settle Audra down.

The only TV we had in English was CNN and BBC, so I started watchin' news, like war and killing and government lies. I watched tennis on Eurosport, frickin' swimming and motorbike races. Then I tried readin' Audra's books, like this tool George Orwell who killed an elephant just cauze peer pressure made him do it. And almost every day I wrote some stuff in my notebook. Here's one example...

Man shes crazy. I hate when she sits on that balcony crakin them hazelnuts. With stuff like this goin on, probably its better to go homeless. Cauze your homeless Drew, maybe it looks like you aint since you got this nice room with TV and internet. But thats smoke. Just get on with it...like I wanna escape at night when its dark. Though she would go find me, call me a traitor. Tepti totally hates comin back here. Fuckin free food but the stray dog hates comin here. The thing is your full of shit right now. If you leave you will hate it and your gonna think about her the whole time cauze its like a curse. So you better stay here. Frickin when Big Beard finds my ass then whats gonna happen to me? I should say <u>Audra I got no way home</u>. But shes gonna say why you wanna go home? Where you gonna live and what you gonna do?

I guess I was hopin' she would get more normal with some time after her dad died. Like finally she would talk friendly with me or ask how I feel or what I think. But she just kept getttin' more and more weird. For real, she was sleepwalkin' a lot...a couple times she came in my room real late and took off all her clothes to sit in the reading chair. Wakin' up, she pretended it's normal like she planned it. The whole time she seemed tired and would get spaced out in daydreams. I would be askin' her questions about some stuff I seen on BBC and she'd just loop out, ask *Kaip, kaip*? (How, how?) totally like she was talkin' to herself. One time I knew for sure she was sleepwalkin' when she went outside only in sweatpants and a robe. I ran down to get her by the brickyard and whispered "Wake up, wake up." But she just said, "No, Andy. I'm okay. I only needed some air."

Even though all this was happenin', pretty much the whole time we were still makin' sex. Sometimes it was simple and easy, but other times it could get complicated. She liked to spring it on me, especially when I was unprepared or takin' a bath or just tryin' to watch tennis. A couple times I said I don't want to do it cauze I was almost passed out, so she got super pissed and called me "Egomaniac!" Some of the stuff she wanted is only supposed to be on the internet, like with a blindfold or straps. And I had to make up English names for her, only some of them made her pissed. One time she asked if I'll wear a ski mask but I said that ain't my thing. She moped around and threw the ski mask in the garbage, went to crack hazelnuts on the balcony.

It was three weeks after her dad's funeral when she went back to the cemetery the first time. Like she left me sleepin' and didn't tell me, but then came back and said she was plantin' flowers over there. It kinda made her feel better cauze she was more mellow. And she put on happy music, like some guys playin' horns. She started goin' by the cemetery a lot in the mornings and I would be in the apartment way till the afternoon, just Tepti with me and Kovas in his room. And that's when I found Audra's notebooks.

That one real heavy suitcase I helped carry from Dana's place was full of notebooks. They were leather ones called *Moleskine* that fit real neat together in stacks. Them things were totally crazy inside and real surprising cauze Audra wrote in English a lot. She also drew real good, like professional, though lots of them drawings were perverted stuff or painful things...somebody cuttin' a girl's eye with a razor. She drew car crashes and some wrinkled hands with long nails holdin' a rope. One weird thing...she would color a whole page with crayon wax and then scratch words with a needle so her handwriting was like kids. Wigged words that didn't make no sense like *Choose a name* and *Son in armor*.

The thing is, I couldn't stop readin'. For me it was like riddles. If I found a part where I needed to figure out the meaning, I would copy that part down in my notebook. So right here I can show some of them things she wrote. The numbers don't mean nothing, just to organize it better.

1

When I told him what I wanted my voice cracked. He heard me. He heard me. Men find it impossible to ignore a woman when she sincerely tells what she wants. Don't you know what I want? All of me? No? I told him, Couturier, something new and something old. Sew it to virgin fabric. Afterwards, give me something that will come alive. A little one who'll learn to harbor secrets before it dies. Amazing how men listen when you tell them what you want. Cowards, their faces pale with fear. Ironically, they are all children.

2

On the other side of a hill is a little shack already gray and tired. Sunlight and rain have warped the roof of wooden planks. At dawn a cock crows to remind me of my lies. I know very well whom I've betrayed. At the horizon of the shallow valley, the sun is only a dome of red gold, but it grows and the day quickly turns yellow, then silver and gleaming white. A flood of birch trees, their dark green leaves. An iron bell sounds from beyond the hill as horse hoofs clomp clomp against packed dirt. Children laugh in the wagon, unaware that adults have lied to them about the future.

I first held a scythe in my hand when I was four. That scythe is my earliest memory...I had been curious about it for a long time, the most interesting object on grandfather's land. He had forbidden me from ever touching it. I knew how violently it could cut because I had seen the men using scythes in the fields, keeping time for their masculine songs, leaving stumps of grain that used to cut my legs when I'd run with the dog. I was interested in the scythe, but not because it was sharp and dangerous, or even because of its elegant curve. Perhaps I believed one became strong by holding it. I expected it to be heavy, but what did I know of heavy things? The heaviest thing I had ever held was a vase filled with water. When the scythe fell, breaking a window and frightening a cat, the metal clanged against the floor so that grandfather came from across the yard.

He shouted at me and cracked me with a switch. Then he told me something I didn't believe. "Audra, you will always be a girl. You will never be a boy!"

3

Our neighbor has hung wind chimes. I can hear them from every room in this house, very faint in the basement, but there is no place to escape them completely. Expensive little sounds, little jewels, little shattering crystals. With a better gust, the crystals explode...so beautiful to see sunlight fall through a storm of crystal shards and slivers, a beautiful death for a woman made of glass.

My punishment for hatred and jealousy: cut snowflakes for an entire storm. Bend over the table. Name each flake before you drop it in the cold. They are only little sounds, little jewels, little crystals. Now you've cast them down to melt against headlights, to fall into the wiry strands of a wool hat. Other flakes drown in the black saltwater of potholes. But my favorite flake (I refuse to remember her name) falls on the sidewalk where an Oak Park mother is about to crush it under her boot. She has returned from the store where she bought the wind chimes hung outside the window of her newborn's room.

I wanted to quiet the wind, to press the button that halts all air. There is a woman in the world who knows how to find the button. She has written the secret in a private notebook that her daughter will discover on her nineteenth birthday. (A daughter, certainly a daughter.) When the girl reads the book, the chimes will stop, the crystal won't shatter anymore. And all glass women will finally remember their names.

Dude, there was a whole suitcase full of this! And the stuff I'm showin' right now actually makes a little bit of sense, cauze sometimes Audra only wrote some lists of words, like a mixed up dictionary about eyelashes and a missing girl or a baby's laugh. Even though I didn't understand it real good, I couldn't stop

readin' that stuff and copyin' parts I liked. This next one gave me
the most hardcore vibe.

4

I lost the pliers. He'll need them.

Do you believe in finding what you lose?

*Where does the clock tick that way that it won't quiet down,
that I can hear it when I walk in rooms with peeling wallpaper?
My husband said "Only you notice it peeling. No one else notices
a small peeling corner." Well, what would he notice? There was a
moth sleeping on the wall, just one shade darker than the paper. I
caught him easily with a plastic cup and he was still fluttering
when I took pliers to put him in the candle flame.*

*Look in your mirror and tell the face you see, now's the time
that face should form another. Whose fresh repair if you do not
renew, you do beguile the world, unbless some mother. You are my
mother's mirror, and she in you calls back the lovely April of her
prime; so you through windows of your age shall see, it's time for
you, it's time it's time it's time. Pillow, flame, suffocation. Ends
gray moths along with brothers twin. Nothing against time's
scythe can make defense against such kin. So long's they suffocate
or nothing see, so long dies this and this gives death to thee.*

Dude, even though it sounds like bullshit, for real it ain't. I
felt real close to her by copyin' it down, definitely more close than
puttin' a blindfold and callin' her Samantha. Just to make a test
when I got curious, one time I caught a mosquito and used
tweezers to put him in the gas flame on the stove. It was real
intense...the little guy cracked and disappeared without no ashes.
Like dyin' without no funeral and mess to clean up.

It was maybe four weeks after the old man died when I took
Tepti for a walk one day...we went all the way down by ŠMC.
Varna was on vacation in Rome and Raimis wasn't gonna come in
the bar till night time. I was dyin' so bad to tell somebody all the
stuff happenin' to me, though also it was cool just to sit outside in
the shade with Tepti and drink coffee. I brung my notebook and
took it out from my backpack. And in there I seen a big surprise.

Audra drew a picture. It was a girl peekin' around a corner...only one eye and cheek and half a mouth was showin'. That girl looked kinda sneaky, like she was runnin' away from somebody chasin' her, though also she looked real curious. Underneath the picture Audra wrote, *If you want to leave just tell me. I'll get by on my own.*

I got this crazy buzz all over my body, totally like I got haunted. She let me know she read the whole notebook cauze she underlined stuff I wrote on each page, things like *She's nuts* or *But you have to leave sometime anyway.* Holy crap, it made me feel real ashamed. But also I got paranoid like somebody's watchin' me...someone's spyin' on me with binoculars. I just had to pay my waitress and find Audra to say I didn't mean it, none of it at all.

Noplace Else

Me and Tepti went wanderin' down this street *Didžioji Gatvė*, which just means "Big Street." Right by there it was this huge dig where dudes were fixin' sewer pipes. It was maybe one block down from ŠMC and all of a sudden I just stopped walkin'. Like I stood watchin' them guys workin' in a sandy hole and totally takin' it easy, totally smokin' on the job. Maybe right there I got inspiration to find a seat someplace and think this thing through real calm and good. Cauze I didn't know what to say to Audra. Like I didn't even know how to bring it up.

That *Didžioji Gatvė* is more like a parking lot than a street, just a triangle by that old city hall building that looks kinda like the White House. Around there they got a couple jewelry stores and cafes, like one of them just sells sweet milk and cake for old ladies. But then there's a bar with a statue of a dude poundin' a beer and some umbrellas in front, a couple regular people sittin' around. I thought a drink would be good cauze that strong coffee had me too jacked up to think clean. So I ordered *alos didlee prasho* and a real pretty girl brung me a foamin' beer.

Dude, I thought real hard while starin' at Audra's handwriting... *I'll get by on my own.* On the next page from my notebook I only put one thing...*It aint fair since now Im scared to write stuff in my own notebook.* Then I remember thinkin' if I should write one more thing. *It was real stupid to come out here in Vilnius and get involved in her crazy ass life.*

96

Just by accident right there I looked at the other side of the bar. It was a real long room made from wood with farm tools hangin' all over the place. Way down by this window I seen Dana sittin' with some dude. First I just thought *Oh, cool, it's Dana.* But then I noticed the guy she was with and it was like a trapdoor opened up for my whole table. Cauze Dana was sittin' with frickin' Big Beard.

He totally seen me right away. Like he *knew* it was me, so he started rubbin' his beard all serious...it was already growed back a little bit so his cheeks looked black. There wasn't no way I could pretend some crap cauze it was hardcore eye contact, plus a little nod. Dude, all my bones went metal inside. Maybe I could pretend I'm wasted or insane and just scream *Fuck Police* or *Moon in Sugar* and run away. And maybe I would of done it if Dana wasn't sittin' right next to him. Cauze she was wavin' at me with her small hand, kinda invitin' me to come sit with them.

Sometimes you just gotta face stuff. So I took my beer and backpack and kinda moped over. Dana whispered some stuff to Big Beard and then she smirked a little...I seen he was surprised since I came over so easy. I turned real sad and put some disgrace in my voice, probably overdoin' it. Words just started goin' automatic, crap like "Yeah, I'm here in Vilnius too. I already seen your ass one time. Probably you were gonna see me soon enough again. Guess I'll say my real name...it's Andrew Nowak, not Nate. I mean...yeah. Yeah." I probably drank some beer right there or played with the napkin. "It's gotta suck for you. So you wanna kick my ass. She probably took off with lots of money. For real, I'd say how much, like man to man, though I don't even know. A bunch of this shit is my fault. Though not all. She came to the laundry just before you did, like she had that planned to piss you off. So it's kinda by accident how all this shit happened. Dude, I never thought Audra wanted...you know, like a houseboy. I mean, I *hoped* she wanted, like....I mean, I *wanted* it...not like your wife ain't hot or nothing like that. That ain't what I mean."

"*'Scuse* me?"

"No. No, cauze I'll fess. Since probably I know how you feel. The first time she paid me a thousand bones. But then we met in Absinthe Fairies and she took me home for free. So right now I kinda don't even believe it myself. We buried her dad...for sure, the church cost cash, plus hospital and twenty-four hours nurse. She cut her hair, probably expensive...so maybe you don't recognize her easy. But she's around. And she's okay. Depressed, but okay."

The guy was looking at me dumb fuck confused with his mouth kinda open and his eyebrows raised high. Dana was holdin' back laughin', but then it all sprayed out her mouth like a shaked up beer. I said maybe one more thing but then Big Beard started laughin' too. And the next second he was talkin' *ketekeki va va va* to Dana, so right there I figured out it. This wasn't no fuckin' Big Beard.

Before you think I'm a moron, I wish I had a picture of that guy. Like if I could post his picture on Myspace with Big Beard right next to him, there's no way anybody could figure out which one's fake. You'd get it after a while, like if you look more close, cauze Fake Big Beard was a little younger. But they looked damn identical, like a young twin with an older one.

I guess I sat there real awkward. Dana and him started shakin' their heads all sarcastic and the guy opened up his metal box of smokes for me. "Sorry," I said. "I thought you were some other guy." We went outside for a smoke and they bought me 50 grams of the most super cold vodka so I would sit with them.

I can't tell you Fake Big Beard's real name, since there's risk. The thing about that dude, he buys and sells lots of drugs in Vilnius and has E parties, acid nights and secret whisky tastings where married rich women (like wives of political bastards) come to mess around. From now on I'll just call him Big Head cauze his head was shaped almost like a watermelon. He was Dana's cousin from Los Angeles and lived in California during the winter and fall. But he could speak Lithuanian good enough and real fast when he got drunk.

It was kinda fun to sit with them. Especially Dana had a bunch of questions, so I told how I got to Vilnius, like a PG version. Right there I could feel how hardcore I was *dyin'* to talk to someone about it. Dana was real interested, especially since I didn't have no plane ticket or no apartment in Berwyn. She asked me a real good question, "But you Audra's boyfriend?"

"I guess," I said. "I mean, I act like one. But also I don't know, cauze I'm a houseboy. It's hard to tell."

She waved one hand at me. "Ah, you boyfriend."

They asked what I was gonna do that day. I said, "Nothin'. Probably Audra's wonderin' if I'm comin' home soon." So right there Big Head looked at me kinda sly and said, "You want to come to a shroom party?"

"A party?"

"Good shrooms."

"Where?"

"Start at my summer house. But then we're going to a club."

Dana said, "Yes, Endee. You will like."

"Who's goin'?"

"People I know," he said. "People you like to meet." He was trying to talk like Bill from *Kill Bill*.

"Well...yeah, sure," I said. "But maybe I should call Audra. Maybe I should leave the dog."

"The dog's cool," said Big Head. "Keep the dog."

"Here, I have phone," said Dana. "You call."

Audra didn't answer. I left a message and said I found Dana and her friend and we were gonna hang out for a while. I'll tell you straight, cauze I was kinda scared to hit shrooms, especially after seein' a guy die in front of my face and all the weird sex. But I totally needed to chill out someplace.

Big Head had this real cool Saab. First we stopped at a Maxima to pick up some stuff, but then we drove out to the woods, like way past the Vilnius projects and some trashed factories. Out there it's little suburbs and small concrete houses with fields and white trees. We had to go down this gravel road that was not even a half hour from downtown. Big Head's summer house was like a little farm with a small shed and a house with siding. I seen some gooses by a pond.

The house was kinda medium sized. Maybe twelve people were hangin' out stoned all over the back yard and jammin' on harmonicas and guitars. One girl had this wooden flute from India and her little baby daughter was runnin' around the pond without no pants. Another long haired dude was roastin' pieces of meat, this special Lithuanian barbecue called *shush likai*. It smelled real good and I ate maybe five or six pieces with ketchup and bread. A guy I didn't even know gave me beer from a keg buried in the ground. And he smoked me up with some kind buds.

Right there I was feelin' really a lot better and more calm with way less worries. Like I was lookin' at clouds and watched some kids playin' with Tepti. But pretty soon Big Head busted out the shrooms, like a huge jar he had in the shed. Dana was gonna hit them for the first time ever in her whole life. So I figured what the hell and grabbed a couple caps to go in for the ride with her.

She started gigglin' like a little girl even though nothing was happenin' yet. I watched her hop down the gravel road like a small bird. Further by this gate she collected a bunch of round pebbles. I went for a walk in the woods with her and this fat guy who kept sayin' *va va va* real fast. The whole time Tepti stayed by me real close.

Pretty soon the shrooms started kickin' in. I knew I wasn't gonna wig or get a bad trip cauze the whole place was real fresh. Plus Dana was so happy and sweet that it spread to me. Also, the nature in Lithuania is real gentle and the air smells nice...it's kinda special like a fantasy. You think some friendly giants or fairies live in the woods, like there's elves drinkin' absinthe on tree stumps.

I had birds whizzin' past me and bugs makin' tracers in my face, Tepti stayin' by with his fur turnin' shiny. Then the trees started goin' and breathin' with rhythm pumped through...it all came on real fast. I had echoes and the whole woods got wide open, super deep and goin' on forever with layers that kept on movin'. Beams of light went through the leaves and the wind was movin' them around under the leaf ceiling. I kinda felt like I'm underwater, the way the light looks when you watch divers on Channel 11. I told Dana, "We're swimmin'," but she said Lithuanian stuff. I watched how she wandered out in the pond up to her knees and dropped some pebbles in the water. Each time she dropped one, she smiled kinda shy from the ripples. And she made so many small ripples crashin' into each other that the whole pond turned like a big music dance.

Shit started gettin' real intense. I walked further in the woods, like off the path a little. All over the place it was motion and surges like waves. Tepti would bark and it sounded like he was 1000 miles away even though he stood right by me, right by my leg. Havin' him around gave me weird courage like I could go anywhere in them woods. I kept on goin' deeper, like miles and miles, and the deeper I got the more intense all the shit around me started movin'. It was tree bark and birds chirpin' and all the little grasses growin' and the sticks on the ground. Spider webs. The most small white flowers. Pine cones just breathin' like they're totally alive.

Dude, I'll try my best to say what happened to me out there. For a while it seemed like hours and hours and I was out in the woods all by myself. In the beginning stuff looked beautiful and funny, like a tree turned into Big Beard's sculpture with a big nose, so I talked out loud, "Your an inventor. You make inventions." Sunbeams started pourin' all over the place like the light went liquid.

But then my feelings changed real hard, kinda heavyweight inside my chest so I had to sit down. I found this pile of soft moss that was real comfortable like a cushion. And way inside me, like in the most deep part, the place where I know there ain't no mom or Jen or Gunther or Audra, where it's just me and nobody else...inside there I had this totally intense question. It didn't have no words but you could understand it anyway. It was like *What Do You Want?*

The question wasn't pissed off. It didn't think I'm a tool or I can't answer it. For real, it was real gentle and made a strong ass

promise...*You'll learn how to find it if you figure out what it is.*
Tepti was lookin' at me hardcore and I believed so bad he could
feel the question too and wanted me to answer it. Like he even
licked my face to say *just try, just try.*

Did you ever ask that question *What do you want* without no
bullshit? Fuck, I got so scared. Cauze when you ask it clean like
that, then you can see all the lies you say all the time to yourself.
So I had to be real with it...I had to go with the thing that was most
true.

I frickin' want money. Though not too much, not like Audra
has...for me it would be good just with normal money, something
more regular. Though how come? Cauze I don't want to worry all
the time how I'm gonna make it. I wanna know I'm okay, just
know I'm okay.

But you know your gonna die, don't you?

Fuck!

Yes...

I know I know I know. I know. I know it's gonna happen,
dude. But I never thought about it that way so hardcore...like *it's
true*, dude, it's so *frickin' real*, like the most real thing...nothin's
more real compared. Cauze when it comes then there ain't no
comin' back...not like a movie where the actor dies, but then they
give him cash and a prize. It ain't like them Jesus stories when
they beat his ass and kill him, only then he wakes up. It's cauze
people want to pretend death is fake. Since that makes it easy to
avoid them thoughts about it.

A real thing is blood in your mouth. Like you die and
everything goes away with some blood down your face. You can
taste that blood in your mouth, Drew. It's cause your alive. You
can pinch skin on your face with nails, pull it real hard off your
bones and it hurts like that with pain cauze your still alive. Your
totally like the trees and Tepti and that little girl without no pants.

What do you want? Dude, I want a place to be. I wanna see
it and know...this is the place I need to be. Cauze all the time I'm
wonderin' *where am I goin' now*? How come I'm goin' there?
Always it's like *turn here, turn there. Sit here, look at that.* Look

at that. All these ants in the leaves. Like the frickin' ants know *this* is totally the right place, a pile of leaves. And all the other bugs, the spiders know it too, the web is the right place till some asshole fucks it up. Tepti, dude, "You know where you need to be!" Cauze you don't need me to give you no piece of bread...frickin' you can find food all by yourself, even better without me. It's just, before you die, it's more fun to eat together with somebody else, that's all.

Holy crap, my mind kept goin' like this so fast I couldn't even catch up with it...then it went around and around and around till I started wishin' I could be a bug. The wind went blowin' the trees, and that made light shimmer all over. Through a hole in the branches I seen clouds changin' shapes real fast like smoke. Then out of nowhere...I didn't even hear no footsteps or noise...frickin' Dana came and sat down by me with her smile that went through my whole body.

She was all wet cauze she went swimmin' in her clothes. And she was breathin' hard like she got off the playground. "Endee, Endee." She caught her breath and told me, "I show you. Have to show you emayzing. It emayzing."

I just sat there.

She said, "No, don't be alone. A whole thing. More like anything you see here."

"No, cauze I need *to be*, dude. I need *to be*."

"Yes, I show." She stood and grabbed my hand and started pullin' me, draggin' me real hard. I got up and she ran off like we're gonna miss a train. But then I seen what it was, something so damn beautiful.

We were standin' by the pond. I thought I was wandered miles away, but really it was maybe twenty or twenty five feet from the pathway. The sun was already a bit lower in the sky and makin' this clean yellow light. Everything vibrated with color layers in the air, and blue and yellow vibrations comin' at me from the sky, and this feeling like all the air was inside me, pushin' through me and goin' in and out. I seen shiny minnows by the shore, how they swum perfect in a group. And all the ripples on the water went perfect with the wind. Way up high it was a hawk or some black bird makin' a circle, and the clouds lined up perfect with a plane's pathway. Then a frog hopped around in the mud footprints. And birds went crisscrossed with bugs, and all them water insects totally skated on the water like they didn't even have to try. Dana couldn't talk...she just clapped and shrieked out. Then she ran in the water all the way to the middle of the pond. She splashed and went screamin', kickin' water all over the place, tellin' me, "Come in! Come in!" Her hair was flyin' all over and her smile turned so bright, dude, like brighter than a lamp in your face. So I frickin' did it. I ran in there with all my clothes till I was up to my waste and me and Dana just splashed and screamed in the cool water that smelled like a bucket of rain. We dove under and jumped sideways the same way how whales do it. Our feet made breathin' mushroom clouds from mud. We kept kickin' with yells and let our feelings just rush and rush till finally we got tired and had to chill out.

We kneeled down with water up to our necks...she had some mud on her cheek. That was the first time I seen the scar by her eye. We kneeled like this just lookin' at each other and breathin' together. And we didn't move till the whole water calmed down with us and got so flat like glass, like a black sky mirror. And we were right there with it, right in the middle of it, totally connected to the whole thing like perfect parts. Didn't talk nothing cauze we both knew it...we're right here with it and we both understand. Right now, we don't want to be noplace else. We don't want to go noplace else but here.

A Circle

The next moment Tepti was barkin' and every other tool at that party wanted to go swimmin' with us. A bunch of them came from a sauna to jump in the water. The fat *va va va* guy was skinny dippin', so pretty soon the pond got real noisy and dumb, kinda weird with that little girl watchin' it from shore still without no pants. Me and Dana totally got out.

First we went explorin' Big Head's house cauze maybe he had some dry clothes. His place was pretty intense. He had old guns from pirate times and he shot some wild roosters. Also one closet in the back had three different silk robes...two were regular, but this red one had a fuzzy collar. Dana told me, "Endee, we can wear."

We both tried on them robes (she changed in the bathroom). I got the red one and hers was black with some golden Chinese designs on the back and arms. In the kitchen we found a dryer to stuff all our wet clothes...shoes and underwear and everything. When the machine started goin' round and round, Dana took some beers for us and just watched the clothes go in a circle. And then I totally remembered it, "Dude, the laundry!"

"Londree. What it means?"

"No. Dana, no." I was real excited. "The *laundry*. Cauze it's like totally happenin' right now. Me and you right now...we're in the laundry." I felt like I understood some damn huge shit and was gonna start talkin' all this shroom stuff like, "It's a big circle. It all

105

started in the laundry." But Dana didn't even know that the hell laundry means. So I told her, "The first time, by the dryers, I didn't even know how it happened, though I turned into a hooker."

Dude, the girl *busted out* laughin'. I got totally surprised cauze she was holdin' her stomach with her eyes closed and no way to control it. Her arms swinged around and she knocked over an empty bottle. Then she tried real hard to concentrate. "Wait. Wait, Endee. Because stuff. Stuff stuff."

"What?"

She grabbed her face. "Stuff stuff." Dana said it a couple times and lost her marbles again, slumpin' down on the floor. That got me laughin'. She kept saying "Stuff stuff" and I went, "Shoe shoe." She said "Cup cup" and I went "Beer beer" and she said "Water water" and we kept on with it, sayin' stupid words, "Cow cow," "Lip lip," "Me me," "You you." Each time she raised her finger like, "Aha, we so smart!" Pretty soon we got so tired, all we could do was fall on the kitchen floor and look up. Big Head came in there to get some stuff for the grill...he just mumbled some crap and took our picture.

We got dressed when our clothes dried. Outside it was turnin' real beautiful, one of them longass Vilnius evenings when it takes the sun forever to go down. But pretty soon the sky got this clean dark blue with big stars real low above trees. For a second I thought the top of this tree was burnin', but it was just a dark red moon comin' up over them woods like a barbecue coal. And soon all the frogs came out to burp their rhythm songs. Me and Dana sat on one picnic table and watched the whole thing, sometimes throwin' Tepti a stick or talkin' real quiet.

I totally forgot Big Head wanted to go to a club. Like he came around and said a taxi's comin'. I thought that's a lame idea, but Dana got real jacked about it and started talkin' real fast. Big Head totally had some VIP tickets...who knows how he got 'em. He just handed all them out and a taxi came and drove us to the middle of Vilnius.

Now let me just explain a couple things to you about dance clubs. If your one of them people where you think some of them discotecas on Ogden or any of them dumps on Cicero Avenue is a cool dance club, just a DJ, a couple of green light bulbs, some Miller Lite and a bunch of people suckin' face on the dance floor...if you think that's cool then you need education. Cauze the cab took us to *Pramogų Bankas*. This was a place like a Godfather mansion with pillars and lots of orange and red lights outside, and you never seen how many weird people come dressed up in shiny outfits with purple glasses. The girls wear skimp tops and tight rubber skirts with funk shoes. Dudes put on leather pants and suit jackets. Most of 'em were waitin' in line to pay, but I just told Tepti to stay by a tree and all of us trippin' idiots went to the VIP door with pond mud in our ears.

Dude, the *Bankas* is like red rugs and golden hand rails. I went past a casino and then this advanced dance floor with techno and house and green laser beams and smoke and a white plastic bar that had flashing lights in it. One more floor higher was the VIP room. Over there they had free wine and small beers...you could go behind some see-through curtains and sit on dark red sofas next to golden tables. Somebody busted out a joint and Andrew Berwyn Nowak got to drink red wine and smoke kind bud by a golden table.

Over by the bar area, I seen a dude I recognized. First I thought my eyes played tricks, but then I seen it was that dude Gidas...he was wearin' this bad ass suit. I was in a real good mood so I figured I'll say hi...like I didn't remember he was Dana's ex-husband. She was talkin' to Big Head about some shit and I went over by the bar to tell Gidas I'm on shrooms.

Dude, that guy was ripped so bad he could barely stand, like his elbows kept bumpin' people's drinks. He forgot I don't speak no Lithuanian and kept mumbling *shmeeshmaishmeel* to me, kinda havin' trouble controllin' his mouth. I just told him *gerai gerai* and kept on noddin', tryin' to figure out how to walk away from his wasted ass.

Dana came right up and grabbed my wrist. "Endee, now we dancing." I kinda shrugged to the dude and put my wine on the bar. She dragged me in the middle of the dance floor and just let me go, started movin' her little body all over the place real smooth and good. And she was lookin' at me real sly with her eyes and big smile.

Man, I can't dance. I only learned how to walk like ten minutes before kindergarten. But it don't really matter at them techno clubs. The whole place gets wigged on E and the girls get dressed in spacesuits, put on golden make up. One dude had this ace dance move where he was scratchin' his head and hoppin' up and down. I was still trippin' good enough to fly out, and them lights, music and smoke helped me get real tranced. I wanted to pick up Dana and throw her in the air cauze she seemed so light and small. Sometimes she grabbed my hands and we just pulled and pushed each other to the beat. And sometimes she would fall towards me totally trustin' how I'll catch her.

We were havin' a blast. But I didn't know Gidas was watchin' from a balcony. I seen him up there totally by accident cauze he was in this spot where a white strobe flashed on him sometimes, like how lightning flashes on Dracula in them old movies. And he tried to look all proud up there since he was also VIP.

Dana wanted to get some mineral water and have a smoke by the sofas. Big Head was surrounded by people and tellin' some story in his *Kill Bill* voice. Me and Dana didn't find no place to sit so we stood by the bar. And that's when I remembered it...even now it seems crazy...*Dana was married one time.* We were talkin' about music, like the DJ and how that club was almost brand new. I didn't know the whole time she was only thinkin' *when will Gidas come by?* He did come by and I remembered how Audra told me outside Absinthe Fairies, "Andy, that's Dana's ex-husband."

It was a weird moment. Dana and Gidas talked Lithuanian and I stepped to the side a little. I was rememberin' Audra for the first time all day and got a little paranoid, like I could see that drawing with the girl starin' around a corner. Dana kept tryin' to walk away from Gidas, but he would grab her sleeve and mumble one more thing, then one more, then another one. She was rollin' her eyes or starin' at the floor with her face like a real tough statue. I could tell how he talked down to her, how he was blamin' her for some shit, probably for everything, and talked real harsh. It was totally low class cauze he needed to hold the bar just to stand. Dana finally got sick of it. But grabbin' my hand all dramatic and draggin' me to a golden table was probably a bad move. I seen it pissed him off. So I said, "Dana, maybe we should get outta here. Let's go to ŠMC." But she got all worked up, "No! No! *He* go away. Not me. *He* go. Right now we have cigarette and dance more later with good time. Okay?"

She lit a smoke and gave me one, but I just held it. Gidas was lookin' at us from the bar with this smirk like *You pigs, you dirtbags.* Dana gave him a look back with hardcore poison, frickin' her look could of killed Saddam. And she blew this line of smoke, like a rope for Gidas to hang himself. They kept on havin' this staredown, a totally evil moment where they hated each other. I seen him take a huge drink from his whiskey, though he didn't swallow it. Gidas came over and stood right by us, swayin' a little with booze drippin' down his chin. Then he spit whiskey all over Dana.

Dude, it was auto pilot...I just jumped up and took a swing at his head. I missed and was gonna try again, but the club's bluetooth dudes got us...three of them came from nowhere and just grabbed Gidas, dragged him through the crowd. One guy grabbed me and shoved my face in the floor. There was all this noise and glass fallin' and people yellin' shit in the background. Then I was gettin' dragged and they trashed me out a back door.

I sat up to see what was goin' on...in a couple minutes Dana was kneelin' down by me. My eyes were totally full of water so everything went blurred. My whole face hurt bad cauze my nose was busted and runnin' down my face. Dana put a kleenex and held it there till it got soaked. Then she tore a piece of her sleeve real intense, real strong...I could see how she felt stupid, but also a little proud. Some of my blood was drippin' down her hand and all over her forearm, only she didn't even care.

Walkin' through that crowd with them ripped up clothes and blood all over her, I got scared people would think I tried to beat her ass. I said "Dana, we gotta take you home." Tepti came runnin' up to us when I went toward that tree. We just walked some way toward this little square, then down a road where she said, "This way is bridge."

The more we walked, the more she started to feel real sorry and upset. My blood didn't really stop total, though it wasn't so bad. The shrooms were already almost weared off and she started gettin' real tired...at the bridge I had to keep sayin', "Just a little further. Just two hundred yards," holdin' her up cauze she was crashin' fast. Walkin' across the *Neris* river, it didn't connect clean with me right away...we were goin' back to the same apartment where me and Audra stayed together. I only realized when I seen them kiosks with the drunks and the stray dogs.

It was insane to see the bed and window. The apartment wasn't changed, still real simple and kinda run down, but this time it felt totally different, more like somebody's real home. The Vilnius night sky was bright and made the whole room look soft. With that big window open, some wind blew in the river smell. Dana just laid down on the couch and kept whisperin', "Five minute only. I rest five minute," but the girl was crashin' fast. All I did was sit with her till she was sleepin' good. She had a folded blanket with a massive yellow smiley face and I covered her up, made sure she had a pillow. Maybe in a different apartment I would of kissed her forehead or touched her cheeks or something like that, but it felt weird. So I just left a note, *Dana, it's morning when you get this. Maybe afternoon. Sorry about what happened. Hope you slept good. I'll call you later on. If that's okay. Andy.*

Under the Table

Here's the thing...I wish girls knew how complicated it gets when us guys go thinkin' about them. Cauze we walk over rust bridges when the sun's comin' up and then we wander down some trashed streets full of fast food bags where drunks burned a plastic garbage can. After that our dogs take us by a sausage stand where sawed off dudes sell blackass coffee in small cups and you stand by this railing to drink it real hot. For one whole cup you just think about that one girl, how she looked soft and real pretty in that blanket. But then you put some sugar in your coffee and remember how she was laughin' at your ass. And in the window you see your busted face, so you start talkin' to yourself. Andy...she thinks your a tool. Probably she's pissed cauze you left her alone. So call her tomorrow if you want...she ain't callin' your ass back. Forget all this crap that happened and just finish your coffee and go home.

I don't really remember goin' home. But I remember real good how I woke up in my room at Audra's place. Dude, my ass was *kicked*...like my whole head and shoulders hurt. Blood got dried on my neck and hands, and my shirt was stuck to my chest so I had to peel it off. Both my eyes were shiners, blue spots under my lids and my whole skull and neck and upper back felt like hell for a week.

The pain sucked. But gettin' rolled was like a score since Audra got all sensitive about it. I told her the whole story...the thing is, when you get rolled in the VIP room at *Bankas*, everybody in all of Vilnius finds out in a couple hours. So Audra heard from somebody (maybe Post?) how I danced all night with Dana. And suddenly she changed real different, wanted me to feel real good with TLC and I didn't have to do no more chores. We never talked about them notebooks...there wasn't no whisper about it even one time. I got homecooked Lithuanian meatballs, plus tea with cognac and she didn't have no moodswings.

But shit was still weird. Cauze it ain't normal when somebody *makes sure* they make sex with you almost every day, like a plan with a schedule. *Andy, this evening we have to be together, so plan on being together.* It was just to make sure I don't go out noplace. Like there were a couple times when we were doin' it and I knew it clean...*Right now, she don't wanna do it with me and I don't wanna do it with her.* Cauze even though it felt good, also it felt boring and fake. You both know somewhere down the pipe something got messed up.

Dude, I was messin' up all over the place. I didn't have Dana's phone number or even her last name. It was real dirtbag when I frickin' stole the number from Audra's cell phone. So I felt weird for a couple days and didn't call Dana...but then I thought it's just cauze I'm too shy to do it. I called two times from a pay phone, though I left only one message, a real bad one, something like *Hi, this is Andy...like from that one night...we hit shrooms. But then I wrote you that one note. Um...yeah. Okay. Bye.* I hung up and knew right there she won't get the guts to call Audra's place. I should of went by her house or where she worked, but I wasn't gonna find the balls.

Like I would tell myself every ten minutes how I had to forget her. But then stupid crap kept remindin' me...my hurt nose or anytime Audra made tea. Also, I had to tell the whole story to people. Cauze after my shiners mellowed out a little, I went by ŠMC where Varna and Raimis wanted to hear all about it. "Endee, it is true Gidas spits? He spits!" It was a big surprise for me how they made fun of Gidas. Like Raimis got happy to find out some bouncers rolled him. Varna totally hated the guy, and his big hair was bouncin' around when he said, "To all places he always following us. *Blet*, he try to fuck Terese all the days." Raimis showed a real nasty ashtray and went, "This, Endee, this is brain from Gidas."

Raimis had to get back to work in the ŠMC kitchen after a while. So me and Varna just sat around smokin' his advanced Dunhill smokes. For a while he bitched some more about Gidas, but then I seen he was gonna bust out one of his crazy speeches. He told me, "Gidas marry this Dana. You dance with her?"

I just smoked and nodded a little.

Varna shaked one finger. "Former married, *blet*. I tell you, I know about this kind of girl...I already understand. She no good, Endee. No, *hooyova**."* He ashed. "Yes, because for this kind of woman, I tell you, for her is big sport to make fight. *Blet*, what they do to you? She make you think, O! O, I am man! Large, strong. Somebody kick my face and woman clean my blood. Yes, I am Hercules or Samson. But what happen to Samson, Endee? You say me, what?"

I didn't know who the hell Samson was.

"Damn shit, Endee! Don't be McDonald. Samson, Samson! Hollywood make old movie, you don't watch? Samson have long hair, longer like you have hair...it is man hair. His woman, what she do? She give him love and yes, he is feeling good. But then he fall in sleep so quiet, happy like infant. And trusting. Like infant trusting mama. Then *blet*, she take this thing...what called this thing?" He showed with his fingers.

"Scissors?"

"Aha, scissor! And fuckin' *pizda blet*, she make short hair. And then what has Samson? *Blet*, nothing! They burn eyes with fire metal, make him *nahooy*** blinded. Then he make suicide and that's all."

I fucked with him. "You think Dana would cut my hair?"

---

* That means your like a dick. Really, if you get called hooyova, it means you suck. It's a real bad thing to call a girl.
** On the dick

"Cut, *blet*! Cut." He started wavin' his smoke around and pointin' down the street, rubbin' a hand in his hair. "This kind of one like Dana, she make you believe you *pizdiets*! *Blet*, you Samson! This is woman trick, very common. You are Samson, but no, you are only Endee. And when you blind, she make you marriage...*yob vashoo mat**, she take everything. Passport, money, kick out friends, no more vodka, no more beer. All family...*blet*, she make to America big export...whole family with grandmother, uncle from farm and also goat. Imagine, Endee, no more friends, no drinks, only damn shit goat in America. *Blet*, think one time!"

"Dude, how long you know Dana?"

"Ack, Endee! Don't be rooster. Don't be Pepsi Cola."

"What?"

"Don't ask this stupid..."

"No wait, Varna. Cauze I gotta question. Why's she gonna take my vodka when she's into shrooms?"

"Understand it simple. Simple! This trick, simple trick, *blet*. They *all* like vodka in front." He got all worked up. "In front, they like mushroom. *Nahooy*, they like Spain and Italia, cognac. But *blet*, then only marriage ring and you get goat. God dammit, Endee, don't be Budweiser."

"I ain't no Budweiser."

"I am *saying* you! Never tell her nothing. No secret, no informations. She finds out anything, you will regret. You don't know females of Lithuania."

Man, he was goin' off. For a while I just stared at the ashtray and pet Tepti, kinda hopin' Varna might gas out. And he did gas out totally fast when Terese sat down by us real unexpected. Frickin' Varna changed gears and gave her this nice kiss, rubbed her shoulder all romantic and ordered fifty grams Amaretto. That's this lady liquor they pour in a special glass that looks like crystal.

Even though I knew Varna was talkin' smack, later on I thought maybe he had some good points. I remembered stuff Dana asked me..."Are you boyfriend?" For real, she dragged me to

---

* That's fuck your mother, only like a polite version.

dance only to make Gidas pissed off. It got me sad even though I didn't have no good reason to be sad...I was just makin' up bullshit in my head cauze I was seein' too much in stuff, makin' it complicated when it was real simple. Dana just had one good night with me, that's all, and it was nothin' more.

I knew it was time to get my ass back to Berwyn. There wasn't nothing for me in Vilnius no more, a real bad idea to come. For a couple days the only thing I did was think who could give me money for a plane ticket so I could pay them back with Western Union. Probably the only person who had the money was Audra.

She started talkin' again about takin' a trip with me. One night she got some dinner for us from a deli, this meat and rice rolled up inside cabbage. She was all perked up and actin' kinda girly. "We need to go somewhere."

"Where?"

"By the water. Because I want to go swimming."

I kinda tried to act excited about it. "It's real warm out."

"I hate the heat like this...I used to hate it in Chicago. Would you go by the Baltic Sea? Or the lakes by Daugai?"

"I don't know them places."

"I have to call around, see who's available. I know people in Daugai. Free place to stay."

"Like, when would we do it?"

"Soon. I'll call people tomorrow. Tonight I'm too tired."

I never knew if she called nobody. She talked the next day how the Baltic Sea was real beautiful compared with Lake Michigan, but Daugai was also good without no stupid German tourists. I only said, "You pick one. Cauze you know them places." The thing is, Audra got real confused to make the decision. She would sit on the sofa all the time and look at phone numbers, then go crack some hazelnuts or smoke in the kitchen. Somethin' was still real wrong with her cauze a couple times I heard her cryin' in the bathroom, though I didn't say I heard.

Dude, it was so good to have Tepti in them situations. We went for walks or just sat around on some bench in a park or by a trolley stop. Most of the time I just followed him anyplace he went...he liked the big park where we scored money in the grass that time. He also liked sniffin' down this one alley sometimes cauze I guess lots of dogs peed messages over there. But one day he surprised me and went a different way down a totally new direction. It was by the big post office on *Gedimino Prospektas* where they had a fashion store and fancy stuff in the windows, like jewelry and makeup. I was totally talkin' to him, "I probably only got one choice, Tep. Probably should e-mail Jen, get her to wire cash. If she would even do it."

Dude, I wasn't thinkin' even one thing about Dana right there. But suddenly it was like a big fate, like someone was writin' a book or a movie about it and lubed it up with perfect timing. Cauze me and Tepti turned around one corner and I seen Dana walkin' right towards me. She was comin' around another corner just one block away.

I totally wasn't ready for it. Like I didn't even take a shower. And frickin' Tepti decided he should take a crap by a wire fence. She was comin' toward me so I stopped by a pile of bricks cauze it was a construction site over there. She slowed down and smiled, noddin' a little bit...I'll never forget that brightass smile. There wasn't nothing fake about it, though I seen it had something secret in it, like something I knew she was gonna tell me and I would be real happy to hear about it.

Dana looked like a real lady. A light brown leather jacket with black jeans. And her shirt was red, like you could tell she picked lipstick to match on purpose. The red made her eyes super green like them jewels in the store window. Dana was so small but also so awesome, like so smart and she seemed real strong, just the way she walked and held her head. When we stood by that pile of bricks and Tepti already finished his crap, stuff didn't turn awkward or dumb. She said, "Endee. You walking here."

"I'm walkin' the dog."

"Yes." She went down to pet him. "I never learn name. What dog name?"

"Tepti."

"What?"

I told her again how I named the dog *to apply ointment*. She had a little giggle about it, shakin' her head and shruggin' one shoulder. But Dana didn't ask no questions, just said, "Yes, Tepti. Why not?"

We went over to that *Pizza Jazz* place cauze it was close and Dana said they had good coffee. "Very good one from Italy." We sat in there and Dana didn't waste no time with small talk or bull crap. She said she was real sorry my face got trashed. And Gidas was a total pig. "But if I marry pig, what it make me?"

I kinda felt some courage. "Dana, I don't wanna talk about that guy. Who cares, cauze it was just a bad scene, that's all." Then I waited a little bit. "We should talk somethin' different."

"What should we talk?"

"I don't know," I said. "Maybe tell me where your from."

She told about her family and how she was born in this tourist town called Nida. Sittin' with Dana at *Pizza Jazz*, I wanted to know everything, so much like she could tell. "How did you get your scar?"

"Scar? What it is?"

"You got a scar. Right here by your eye."

"*Oi*. Is this scar? *Oi nu**. I fell. I fell on scene."

"What scene?"

"Yes...scene. You know, for singer. Also for actor sometimes. In theater where we stand." She had to draw me a picture on a napkin. I said, "That's a stage..."

"*Nu*, stage. Yes, I fall on stage. It was premier spectacle and many people come to watch...maybe I am too nervous. So stupid, I fall down from chair on stage and right on head."

"Your an actor?"

"*Pfuu*, no no." She said *pfuu* like an actor is some stunk up rotten crap in the back of the fridge. "No, I am voice student. Yes, for voice. For sing."

---

* This don't mean nothing, but Dana says it ALL the time. *Oi* means like "oh" and *nu* is like "well".

"That's in a school? They got somethin' like that, like a singin' school?"

"Conservatory. Here in Vilnius." She pointed. "Close by park."

"For real? But what they teach? Lithuanian songs or stuff like that?"

"No no. Opera."

Dude, this totally blew me away. The only opera I ever seen was from cartoons like Tom and Jerry and Bugs Bunny. "You know that one Bugs Bunny? The one where Elmer Fudd kills Bugs with a spear and magic helmet?"

"Elmer? No no."

"Yeah, he does it. It goes like this." I started singin' *magic helmet, magic helmet, magic helmet.*

"*Oi*, yes yes...that Vagner. Of course, I know. Very famous."

"So that's real? Dude, Bugs gets dressed in girl clothes with makeup, like a Viking hat and boobs. Frickin' Elmer falls in love with him...or...I guess with *her*. But when Elmer's gonna kiss Bugs, right there the hat falls off. He totally almost kissed a dude, like he would of been gay. So that gets him pissed and he kills Bugs with a spear and magic helmet."

"*Nu*...Vagner not really like that."

"What's the real one like?"

She got a little annoyed. "*En*dee! Vagner, this maybe six hours long."

"The cartoon's real short."

"My God...six or more hours. I don't remember."

"Maybe you can sing like a short part."

"No, Endee. Vagner I don't like, not really."

"Who you like?"

She gave me this list that sounded like a Starbuck's menu, frickin' crappachini and Al Pacini. But the way she said all them opera names was real hot since she did it smooth with her accent. I said, "You can sing your favorite one."

"No, Endee. Not in restaurant."

"Why not?"

"*Oi*, you don't do like this, not in *piceria*."

"Pizza's Italian."

This made her laugh. "*Oi*, no no."

"How about outside? Or in the park. Or...at your place. I mean, or anywhere..."

She stared me down kinda sly. "If you want, you can come to festival. I am singing small part."

"When?"

"Yes, in one week. In Nida, by Baltic Sea."

It took me a couple seconds to remember that name of the sea. "Dude, Audra totally said *Baltic Sea*. She asked if I wanna go by there."

Dana's one eyebrow shot up. "*She* also coming?"

"No. I mean...she wanted to go by some lake or the sea. But she can't decide. She wants me to decide."

"Endee, yes, sea." Dana kinda leaned toward me. "Nida best place. Because my great uncle has home. And Nida such good place with fishing men and a big mountains, some sand mountains. And forest and food...you can eat, pick up mushrooms. Only *normal* mushrooms. Also can swim. Or have fire."

"I never went by no sea." I kinda got quiet, picked up the salt shaker and just twirled it around my hand. "The thing is...how big's that sea? Probably it's real huge? Cauze Audra only said Baltic Sea. Not no Nida."

Dana waited for a moment. "Listen." She took out cigarettes, them long and thin kind where they look like candy sticks. And right there I got this smooth surprise cauze Dana stepped on my foot under the table...it was kinda hard, but also mellow so I got a buzz all over me. That foot stayed right there with her smokin'. She said, "I know something."

"Oh."

She shrugged one shoulder. "I know, if you want. Yes...because you can come to festival by Nida. If you want to come. Especially when I sing some very beautiful song, Endee. So you can hear."

What do you want?

Dude, when Dana had to go home I totally went hobblin' around Vilnius all kooky. Somebody shot me with helium and I could of jumped over the castle hill all the way up between fat happy clouds. For a while I couldn't even know where the hell I should walk or what I'm supposed to do next. Me and Tepti got a little bit lost by this one building with weird bubble lamps where I found this sign *Operos Teatras*. I knew it means Opera Theater, like even more proof how everything's a big fate.

That day was August 26, 2006. And I didn't even know it right there, but it was gonna be one of the most weird weeks from my whole life. When I got walkin' back towards Audra's place, I understood everything so clean and perfect. I'm goin' out to Nida and I gotta make sure to bring a present...something real pretty like flowers or maybe candy in a box for a girl. And I had to tell Audra, "Hey, next weekend we gotta go by Nida where it's the Baltic Sea. Maybe leave early in case it's a long drive."

But then it kinda hit me. One second I was walkin' fast and jacked, but when I seen my face in them shop windows on *Gedimino Prospektas* I had to slow my ass down. Not even fifty feet from Audra's door, I totally understood what kinda frickin' dirtbag crap I'm tryin' to pull. Screwin' a dude's wife and livin' off her coin. But then makin' her drive to a damn festival by the sea to chase her girlfriend around? That's totally dirtbag.

Goin' up them stairs to Audra's apartment, my helium ass turned like a regular popped balloon. I got super unsure, like a real stuck feeling, so I just stood on them stairs without no idea how to talk to Audra about it. Probably I would of stood right there a long time, but then I heard some footsteps comin' up fast and it made me nervous. I started tryin' to find my key, though all my pockets were empty...the frickin' key was gone. I seen Post was comin' up them stairs and he was real edged and stressed with his greasy hair and a smoke in his teeth. He totally ignored my ass and opened with his own key. That asshole tried to close the door in my face, though I stuck my foot in there.

I knew right away that something real weird was goin' down in the apartment. We had a visitor cauze they put a huge grocery sack by the door, like cabbage and bread and smoked bacon. The whole place smelled super nasty from Russian smokes since Kovas' door got left wide open. And I could feel a real stressed vibe.

A person was splashin' water in the bathroom. Audra was smokin' by herself in the kitchen...from her sagged shoulders I could tell she was a little boozed, a couple empty beers on the table. The way she was spaced out, I don't think she knew I was right by the stove. I said it real careful, "Audra. Who left grocery by the door?"

Her eyes were kinda bloodshot. She looked real tired with strong wrinkles around her eyes. Audra talked in this big sigh so smoke came out her nose and mouth. "We took Kovas to the clinic."

I wanted to ask *What's that mean, really?* but she acted like I'm supposed to know. I could tell this time it was worse than normal. Before I could ask who's in the bathroom, a lady came out holdin' a purse with two hands.

I never seen her noplace. She looked like one of them Lithuanian ladies who ignore all the other people when they wait for the trolley. Her hair was colored maroon with a perm and she put lots of hair spray, plus lipstick on wrinkled lips. She said

Labas and smiled at me, then went *shmeeshmaishmeel po nay*. Audra said I don't speak no Lithuanian, so the lady's mouth turned real tight. She sat by the table and Audra gave me the eye like I should go away. Pretty soon Post came in the kitchen from some other room.

I couldn't tell what the hell they were talkin' but I could kinda see them from my room, just a crack around the corner. They smoked up a mean cloud and got kinda noisy. Dude, you should of seen Audra. I thought any second she's gonna spit snake blood at the lady or tie her up and shoot her. I put on the tube to pretend I ain't listenin', but I tried hard to catch some words.

They were sayin' *Sima* (a name) and *dabar* and *nelabai* (not really) and *šitas* (this). Then they smoked with real heavy quiet. The lady said some stuff that sounded like questions, but nobody gave no answer. She talked one more time and it made Audra laugh this *evil* laugh, like cold ass metal on your teeth. After that laugh nobody talked no more and the lady went home. Post sat with Audra in the quiet and the place felt a little more calm. But then he also went home without no more talk.

Audra was makin' a bath and I ate some bread with cheese. On the kitchen table it was this letter with real fancy writing (Lithuanian handwriting kinda looks like them letters from Robin Hood times). The envelope didn't have Audra's name on it or no address, but in there I found three pictures. It was one boy about six years old and one girl with super curly hair...she was maybe two. The next picture was a whole family by a Christmas tree...them two kids and a guy with his wife, a lady with a long neck, her hair kinda bleached with black roots. She totally looked like Audra's family and I had this gut feeling, probably all this crap got sent from Audra's older sister, the one who ran away to Berlin, like this city in Germany.

Audra's bath took a long time. But when she was done she came in my room and we sat to talk. Her face looked like a squeezed wet towel. Even though she was clean with her hair

---

 Hello

combed back, I could feel all this poison jealousy and hate, though she tried real hard to talk happy. "Andy, we should go to the sea. Not the lake. Further away from here, right on the coast. To one of the resort towns, Palanga or Nida or Shvento...who cares if it's expensive, I'll pay." She was lookin' through a bunch of drawers for smokes. "Because there's nothing left here...it's time for us to get out. Tomorrow. Before that bitch comes back to talk more."

"I don't mind."

"I was thinking. Believe me...please believe me. I know all the young people go to Palanga. But if we're going to the sea, I'd rather go to Nida. Palanga is perfectly fine...it's pretty. But Nida's extraordinary, so beautiful. Have you ever been to Muskegon? Or Warren Dunes?"

"No."

"Sand dunes. But imagine an old little town, wooden cabins and a long long beach. Pine forests...god dammit, I can smell the trees." She petted Tepti's head. "In Oak Park, I used to dream I could smell them. When you sleep in Nida, you can hear the wind and the sound of the waves." She stopped pettin' the old boy and he kinda hopped over by the other wall. I seen how Audra spaced out a little. She pushed a real hard fist under her chin. "Andy...not now...I mean, of course, of course, you'll *listen*. Don't do it *now*...although...can't you? No, Andy, you won't hear it, will you? You'll have to try...just don't *think* about it, don't worry. Because Tepti will like it there, he'll feel free. Natural, everything's natural."

She was wiggin'. Any second and she was gonna start scratchin'.

"I was little the first time we went to Nida. Do you remember how I burned myself on a log?"

"You never told that part."

"In the daytime...the log looked harmless, just black. But it was hot coal. On my hand here, right here...blisters for more than a week. But my grandfather took care of me. He carried me in his arms for a whole day.

"I remember the sounds of the kids. We used to have climbing races, who's the first to climb a pine. But with my hand, my grandfather wouldn't let me. My brother...your not going to understand. Andy, I wish you could understand *exactly*. Exactly exactly exactly." She was tappin' her knee. "My twin brother used one hand to climb all the way to the tip top. And I remember him calling from up there. That was only a few weeks before his accident."

She went quiet. One of my socks was on the desk and she wrapped it around her hand like a bandage.

"So many children in Nida back then. I knew all their names. Sometimes I believe the kids are still there. It's simple to find them, just go to Nida...because they're picking mushrooms and climbing trees. Those kids are all up in the trees and I'm the only adult. But if that's true, Andy, if I'm the only adult, well then *I can't stand it*. If I end up seeing them in those woods, I swear to you. Dammit, I swear to you. If I could get away with it. Sometimes, my greatest comfort...I knew one boy named Paul. He died in a fire. It's true...sometimes God takes his pliers. Before we can fall in love, he takes them and puts us right in the candle flame."

She was scratchin' Tepti's neck and pullin' his ears a little. I said, "Audra. I'm real sorry I went in your notebooks."

She only closed her eyes and flicked one wrist a couple times real gentle. Then she shaked her head and made that sock more tight around her hand. "I know the kids are gone," she said. "They're not there. But it gives me great comfort. Andy, sometimes I imagine I'm Paul. His father's car has caught fire and I'm trapped, I can't get out."

"How come?"

Audra shoved her wrapped hand under a leg and sat on it. Now it wasn't part of her body no more. "You saw the letter on the table? The pictures?"

"Yeah." I was quiet. "It's your sister?"

"Sima." She kinda shrugged. "Made a woman deliver the letter to be sure we read it, so I wouldn't throw it out. She wants to come visit here, come see us. *Come back*, she said."

"Like soon?"

"I said no way in hell." She turned quiet for a while. "Did you see those little shits? Did you see that boy with one mole on his nose?"

"Yeah."

"Not hers, Andy. They're not her kids. I know they're not. Did you see them? Did you look in their faces?"

"Kinda."

"Where do you think she found them?"

"Maybe it's her kids, Audra."

"No way," she shaked her head. "No way. Curly hair? Impossible, because I know it's not possible. Sima can't change biology. She can't change DNA."

I just nodded.

"When we go to the Baltic, do you promise to swim with me? At night, I mean at night. Do you promise? I've always wanted to swim at night, but I'm afraid. I'm afraid of the dark water. No one ever wanted to do it with me. But you'll swim, Andy. Right?"

"I never swum at night neither."

She nodded and I thought maybe she was turnin' more normal. But then I seen she was startin' to space out real bad. Audra started talkin' weird and tellin' wigged stuff from when she was a kid. One story she told was her favorite kids story...her grandfather used to tell it, only to me it sounded more like a horror movie. I don't remember all the parts, just some stuff about a snake who lived in the sea. But then the snake went by a village and stole a girl to be his wife. Frickin' that story was real long, like an hour, and in the end the girl's brothers cut the snake up with farm tools, and that made all the sea waves turn into blood. Audra told it real strong so I could totally imagine a foamin' blood wave crashin' hard on the sand. And this girl standin' there to see it so she knew her family killed her husband.

I didn't really know if that story had some meaning. Audra said she liked it, but talkin' about blood waves was messin' her up, like she was tryin' to get sad on purpose. The story was done but she couldn't look at me, just kept starin' in the lamp. And she asked complicated things, "Tell me what you've lied about." I stayed quiet and she got angry. "Fuck, do you promise? Tell me...you've lied? No, you haven't lied, have you? Stop it...do you promise?" There wasn't no way out. She stared me down horrible with them hard eyes like rocks. "With me in the water, Andy. Do you promise? You promise to swim?"

"Don't worry. We'll go swim." I tried real hard to mellow her out, make her go to bed. But Audra kept on talkin' weird and mixed up, that bandaged hand under her leg the whole time. "Many trees in the world are dead kids. The forest in Nida is full of trees." Then she told *one* *more* long ass story about Shakespeare's wife, how she got ink stains on her hand and couldn't wash it off. "Because she can't create," said Audra. "It's why my husband hates me...it's why he sent me away. Because I can't create life. That's why, Andy."

"Sorry. I'm real sorry, Audra."

"What are you when you can't create life? Tell me. When the only things you make are empty or ugly? What are you...what are you fit for?"

"Don't talk that. It ain't true...you don't make nothin' ugly. You make stuff pretty all the time."

"Where? Don't be a fool."

"I ain't no fool," I said. "Cauze you make stuff beautiful. Like you just told nice stories. The snake one, it's good, I think it's a real good story. Also your notebooks, in there lots of stuff is real cool. I totally wanted to read more, figure out what you believe about. Like...the story where you can't be a boy. And how you made snowflakes for a big storm. For me that was real beautiful."

Hearin' that talk made her get heavy like she was gonna cry. With that hand still under her, she sat crooked and her eyes got big. Audra whispered, "Naive. You're so naive." Then she went to the bathroom to put cream on her face, only she forgot to rub it finished and left spots on her cheek and eyebrows. She pounded one beer in the kitchen, just guzzled it. Audra wandered by the sofa and pinched her nose real hard. She crashed with that wrapped hand on her belly.

Seein' her passed out was like I could finally breathe. Like I got unlocked from a chain and could wash my face with real cold water. Smokin' on the balcony, I totally passed out with my head on the table and Tepti by my feet. Some screamin' drunks woke me up when it was already almost morning, so I went in my room.

It was maybe six hours later when I woke up. Real weird, I had to take one moment to figure out where I was, almost like a hangover. Walkin' around the apartment, the whole place was empty...like the floors creaked extra loud without nobody in that place. Somebody cleaned up Kovas' room cauze it smelled like Pine Sol and Ajax and the door was wide open. Dishes got stacked real neat in the kitchen, but some stuff from Audra's purse got left on the floor, lipstick with some kleenex and coins. Probably ten minutes went by before I figured out Tepti was gone.

Dude, it was total panic. The *hell's* Tepti!? They put him out...that lady who cleaned the room threw him out. I yelled *Tepti Tepti* off the balcony, out the back window...probably lots of neighbors heard it. I knew my panic was goin' overboard but I couldn't stop it, couldn't calm down. I couldn't find my key to go look for him...without no key I would be locked outside again, a bad move. So I ended up alone in that apartment for like a whole day.

Shit got weird for me real fast. I called Dana but she was probably already down by the festival. Raimis and Varna wouldn't answer. I had to sit in places by myself, like the front room and the balcony and the kitchen. So many feelings started comin' out in me, stuff I didn't have no time to think about before, or I was just ignorin' it. Fuck, I was *real* sad...like *real real real* sad. When I figured it out, it was almost a surprise, like *didn't you know*? Frickin' I was scared about so much shit. What the hell's gonna happen to me...what am I supposed to do now? I swear I wasn't on no drugs at all, but I got hardcore paranoid. Them paintings were starin' at me with eyeballs like peep holes...a crow and that dude with all his medals...he was lookin' at me. I went in another room and found this plant everybody forgot to water. And right there I kinda wigged out.

That plant was already dry brown with some dead leaves on the floor. I lit one smoke and just stared at it totally dead, and that plant got me daydreamin' real intense. Like it finally hit me...I'm in the same apartment where Audra's bro got suffocated. Maybe it was in this room with the dead plant, right here on this couch with lots of pillows. Or maybe it was in the front room where the old man died by the piano. I remembered it one more time, how the blood went pourin' from the old man's mouth. Like a small river that mixed up with dark sea water, so I seen blood waves comin' toward me on the sand where I couldn't move, just stood there waitin' for the blood foam to hit my bare feet.

Nobody can stop it, dude. It don't matter if they water you or if you bring your own water to drink it. Holy shit, dude, I got so sloppy right there lookin' at that plant, seein' all them pillows on the couch. Like even my smoke was dyin'...you could see it burnin' up and runnin' outta time. So I went and laid down in my room again, ended up trippin' out to a real dark place, like a basement without no flashlight and a flood comin'. I could feel that question one more time, *What do you want?* Only now it was my dad askin' me real strict, *Do you want to live under the bridge? What kind of a life do you want for yourself?* Also my mom was tellin' me, *You want me to work all my life? I could of got rid of you, Andrew. But I kept you. Brought you in, but what do I got in return?* Dude, I rolled up in a ball on the bed with my face shoved deep in a pillow, just got sloppy all over it and couldn't stop. Don't know how much time went by cauze I kinda blacked out.

The next thing I remember, I felt a hand on my face. And now my head was on Audra's lap, like I was laid down on my back and it wasn't no dream. Tepti was right there, right by the bed. Audra was holdin' my head, pettin' my hair with that sock on her hand. First she was hummin' this slowass lullaby, *umma umma*

umma...umma umma umma and she was rockin' me a little. Nothin' about it felt weird, just nice and gentle so it calmed me down. That lullabye lasted a good long time and she was brushin' my face with her knuckles. Then she whispered, "Andy, did you think about it? Should we go to Palanga or Nida?"

I was so mellowed out, I kinda had to remember what she was talkin' about. But then I said, "I wanna go by Nida," and Audra nodded real slow. I seen how her eyes were more bloodshot now. Real red...maybe she got soap or face cream in them. She brushed my lips with her thumb and then she started to unbutton her shirt. I thought no way, but then she did it. Just like it was totally normal, like we did it together every day, she totally pulled one out to pretend she's breastfeedin' me. She tried to pull my head up, only it was heavy so I had to help. I totally did it, pulled myself up a little and pushed my face in deep cauze it was soft and warm like protection.

Dude, that was the best moment I had with Audra. For real, right there nobody was confused and both of us knew why we were doin' it. I don't know how long we stayed like that. We stopped only cauze the doorbell rang, and right there me and Audra kinda looked in each other one last time.

Tepti was barkin' by the door and Audra let in the maroon hair lady. I was gettin' some water in the kitchen where them kiddie pics were still on the table. This time the maroon lady brung a little photo album with more pictures of Sima's family. Dude...there was pics in Vilnius, Sima's kids playin' and laughin' in the main square when they were small, the same square just down the street from Audra's apartment. I got to see a couple more, them kids goin' to school, takin' first steps, learnin' to ride bikes and the first day in kindergarten. Audra talked with the lady in the kitchen for a while and tried to be polite with her, sayin' *achoo achoo* (Thank you, thank you). The lady kept rattlin' fast with her high pitched voice. Audra said *achoo achoo* a couple more times, then smiled and nodded and put water in the tea pot. It was real tense how the lady babbled *bootin bootin* (you must, you must) and Audra was lookin' around for some tea cups. And then out of nowhere BOOM! she just went off.

Audra went volcano. Her face got red and she was screamin', swearin' nasty shit in Russian, *nahooy* and *yobana* and *pizda*. She slammed a plate on the ground, hit the table with the sock hand, but the lady stood real proud like *I can't understand this crazy*, shruggin' and tappin' a finger on her cheek.

I remembered one word in Lithuanian, *nay raykee*, which means like unnecessary. I said, *Gerai nay raykee nay raykee* but the lady ignored it. When Audra found an extension cord to whip the lady's ass and Tepti started growlin' pissed, that's when the lady took her purse. She pretended she's all calm and smooth, way better than us. She just left the album on the table and went home.

Audra sat by the piano for maybe and hour and cried snot tears, her whole body hot and pourin' sweat. Sometimes she only whispered "Sorry, Andy, sorry," but no more. I sat right near to feel her bounce hard every time she cried. A couple times I thought now she's done, but then it would come back hardcore and she hit her hands on the piano and wrapped that crazy sock more and more tight. I wanted to bring her a drink but she grabbed my shirt and said, "No! Don't! We'll swim. We'll swim."

Pretty soon she got real drained and burned out so she went by the sofa. Without no horny or perved stuff, I took all her clothes and put sweatpants and a cotton shirt on her. Then I brung a good blanket and pillow and she kinda grabbed it all in a pile to hug. I laid down right there to make sure she don't sleepwalk noplace. Each time I tried to get up (cauze I wanted to hide them pics) she would grab me and say "Not yet, not yet." We both passed out together.

I got woke up when Tepti licked my face. And I seen Audra sittin' on the floor by the piano with all them pictures scattered all around the floor. She was flippin' each one, playin' a game like solitaire where you line up all them cards. When I came over, she rubbed her nose and smiled abnormal, almost like a pumpkin. She kept on playin' that game .

Audra almost didn't talk for a whole day, just mumbled a couple times, "We'll be leaving pretty soon." She chain smoked a whole pack and then took Russian smokes from her bro's room. In the kitchen she boiled some eggs. When we were eatin' them with mayo I thought she'd snap out of it. But Audra went back to her solitaire game with them pics.

Dude, I was *so fuckin' tired*! It was in my shoulders and I got that stingin' in my eyes. Frickin' Tepti needed to go for a walk and I tried to let him go by himself, only he wouldn't. You should of seen him...he thought I'm tryin' to ditch his ass or kick him out. So I took Audra's keys and went with him real fast, just fifteen or twenty minutes. But when I came back to the apartment the place was a frickin' mess.

She was cuttin' her toe nails with some huge ass scissors. And in the kitchen she got a massive pot of water boilin' full blast so all the windows got steamed. Them pics were lined up perfect on the floor, like she did it according to size and color. But also she dumped her purse and threw butter knives and spoons and plastic bags all over the place. Audra showed this face like she's got somethin' important to say.

She gave me a fat envelope. I knew it was full of money, so I said, "What the fuck?" But she just went, "Please, please," and tried to make me go away, pushin' me. But I didn't go. She did it one more time, *Prasho, dabar prasho*, and pointed for me to go in the other room, then hit me a little on the shoulder. I stayed right there in the kitchen, so she waved her hand at me like it don't matter any more and she don't care.

I kinda got froze watchin' what she was doin' next. She shoved them scissors hard in a plant and went by the water pot to look at all them bubbles. Audra unwrapped that sock off her hand...it was already nasty gray. She dipped a huge knife in that boilin' water, looked to see how them bubbles were dancin', almost like she wanted to dive in there. When I took a step near and said *no*, she moved real fast, just one flick. Audra took that knife super hard across her palm. Cut her hand clean open, straight across and almost down to the bone.

A Hole

When you see somebody do somethin' like that in front of your face, it don't matter if you know their secrets. There ain't no secret she can say that's gonna explain clean how come she went nuts like that. Sittin' by the table, her blood was goin' all over the wood and I knew I'm supposed to freak out or maybe get pissed, but that ain't what happened. I just thought *damn, that's what she did.* It was almost like an answer, like the whole time I was wonderin' what would it be like when she finally freaked out.

I called everybody's phones, but the only guy who answered was Varna. He heard how serious I was talkin' and didn't make no stupid jokes, just got the address and totally called the ambulance for me. And when the medics showed up, Audra just sat by that table like she didn't feel no pain. Pretty soon Varna also showed up...he didn't talk no smack but helped me explain things to the medics, totally smooth and helpful. They knocked her out with a shot to strap her in a wheel bed and Varna took Audra's phone to call Post.

Post showed up at the E.R. Marta was with him and they had a bunch of papers with documents that looked real important. He talked to Varna, told him I gotta move out from Audra's place and should go do it now...he would get somebody to fuck me up and throw me out a window if I don't do it. I shouldn't try makin' no visits in the hospital cauze only family's allowed, not no outsiders.

Varna drove me to get my backpack and clothes and then we went down by ŠMC. For the first couple hours, all that stuff Post said had me a little freaked out. But Raimis got me a bottle of *Moskovskaya* vodka (like a cheap brand) and I pretty much drank that whole thing. I don't want to admit how it got me talkin' stupid, stuff like "Why you guys like me?" When it got real bad and people in the cafe were starin' at me, Varna shoved my ass in his car. I crashed on his couch with Tepti on the floor.

The next day was Friday September 1st. Varna had to wake up real early to go to his job, so he put some ice on my face and pinched my little toe with a clothespin. He left me at ŠMC and said he would come around later with Raimis, probably in a couple hours.

Outside it was a real nice morning with people already hangin' around the patio. But my hangover had me grumpy, so me and Tepti went inside the cafe. I got coffee and a pancake with cheese. Then I counted my cash...around eighty Litas left with change. After payin' for my breakfast, the whole money in my name would be 32.60 USD, so right there I could of dressed in a straight jacket and moved inside a cuckoo clock. But then I remembered Audra's envelope.

If I would of found enough for a plane ticket in there, probably I would of got the next one out. But it wasn't no money...Audra just gave one of them Moleskine notebooks, a real little one that was smaller than a wallet. She wrote all kinds of shit in there with drawings, though I didn't want to see none of it. For real, I almost got pissed and threw that notebook in the garbage. Though I knew I'd regret it, so I shoved it in my safe place.

It was still early, maybe 11:00 or 11:30 when Varna's Subaru pulled by the cafe with Raimis ridin' shotgun. They had the car packed up with a box of beer and vodka, plus a pile of beach shit. Raimis came in the cafe decked out in his orange soccer shirt and some huge sunglasses. He said, "Ei, crazy motherfucker. What you doing?"

I just shrugged and showed my empty coffee, how Tepti finished my pancake.

Varna said, "Endee, *blet*. You ready?"

"What for?"

"*Nu*, fuck. Today Friday. Yesterday, we have plan. Go Nida, big festival."

Raimis said, "*Blet*, now hurry. In street already is too much cars."

Dude, I didn't know what the hell they were talkin' about. They claimed it blue in the face, last night we planned a trip to Nida. But I can't remember and still don't believe we made no plan. I think the guys planned it alone when they heard my story cauze they were super jacked about goin' to Nida, frickin' wired on coffee and babblin' shit. I got in the car kinda half-ass, still hung over and grumpy. The trip wasn't gonna bring nothin' good, but where the hell was I gonna go?

We got on this highway called *Autostrada*. Over there Raimis went crankin' Beastie Boys and Ludacris and RZA, plus some Euro garbage. Drivin' down that *Autostrada* was crazy, cauze in Lithuania you pass people even though there's a log truck comin' right at you. It's like Nascar, only worse, weavin' in and out and ridin' asses and playin' chicken with a log truck. Like everyone's tryin' to die and get it over with.

Up and down the highway shoulder I kept seein' lots of farm girls sellin' food, like sour cream jars and bread and fruits. We bought some raspberries, like the best damn raspberries you ever even ate, real cute and small with this awesome flavor. I ate a whole little bag, the Subaru flyin' at 150 k.p.h. and Raimis blastin' tunes.

I want to tell you about them farms just so you get a better idea what I seen on the road. Lithuania kinda looks like Wisconsin, some small hills and little woods. But also it's real different cauze if you give any farmer 32.60 USD he's gonna have a heart attack. Them cows are real thin with shoulder bones. And scarf ladies come up with buckets and a stool to milk them just with hands. Way in the back, lots of the houses get made from gray wood or cement bricks and they sag and lean a little sideways like they got tired. But its real pretty and mellow. Some forests with white trees, then fields with horses, sheeps and goats. There's blue and yellow and red wildflowers through all them fields, and the farm girls sell little bunches. When I seen that I told Varna, "Hey, dude, we gotta stop and get some flowers."

Both them dudes went "Ooooo, ehhh," but they frickin' stopped. I paid one Litas for a whole pile of flowers, kinda nice how the girl tied real them real neat with a fat piece of grass. Them flowers smelled good and so fresh Tepti was gonna eat 'em. It was weird cauze buyin' them made me feel a little more normal, less grumpy. Even if I didn't find Dana to give no flowers, it would be cool for me to see somethin' new in a different place. And try to forget shit, make a plan how I'm gonna go home.

Gettin' to Nida is complicated. First you go through this town Klaipéda where the main thing that happens is huge ships. You drive to this one advanced pier where you wait in line to put your whole damn car on a boat. Over there you can get beers and sausages from the kiosk ladies, and I seen one lady sellin' Ariel laundry soap. Like Varna seen me standin' over there and starin' at it, so I told him the story, how Ariel comes from Berwyn. He just said, "Endee, let's go better look casino."

The boat to Nida has a sawed off bar where you can play slot machines. In there it smells like armpits and motor oil. Russian truck drivers fire up their nasty smokes to mess up the fresh air, though it's a real nice view where you can see both sides of the lagoon. On one side it's cement walls with cranes. But the other has trees, patches of light brown sand and red roofs. We were goin' that way, toward a place just like Audra said...sand dunes and pines. You drive off the boat and all you smell is pines and salt water. It's frickin' real small towns where maybe twenty people live there.

But when you get to Nida they have a big sign and lots more people, tourists all over the place. We parked across the street from a school. All over the place it was real small cabins, some of 'em dark red but also white or yellow. And we seen a bigger orange hotel and a bar with a disco outside. People were sellin' smoked fish and jewelry on the same table and you never smelled no air like this, like totally perfect pine smell. Sometimes you catch a whiff of somebody's potato pancakes or smokehouse or their *shush likai* in the back yard.

Varna went to get us a place to sleep. He just knocked on some old lady's house and pulled some lawyer negotiations, cauze that lady let us sleep on her sofas for fourteen Litas. We had to make our own beds, but the lady said breakfast was gonna be at 7:00. I never asked for no vase, though she gave me one for them flowers.

The old lady didn't hear about no opera festival. And when we went to get some potato pancakes down the street (the restaurant was just somebody's house and you eat in the front room), the waitress never heard about it neither. Raimis asked some people walkin' by but nobody knew about no opera. So I knew right there Dana was just tryin' to play around with me.

Varna went, "*Blet*, what they do to you?" He put sour cream all over his pancakes. "But who cares, because in Nida is full of womans. First we make some hash on beach. And then more investigation."

We went to the old lady's house to get changed for beach clothes, and I turned around to see them dudes totally wearin' real tight speedo ballhangers. I didn't have no shorts, only underwear, but Raimis said he had an extra slingshot I could use, like his nuts were in it one time. I said no way, so he went off on me. "*Debilas*[*], *blet*. I wash. *Nahooy*, I wash with Ariel." But I still said no way. If Dana was anywhere around, she wasn't gonna see me wearin' no ballhanger. I went to the beach dressed regular, just jeans and a T with my White Sox cap.

Varna rolled a quality hash joint and we smoked it walkin' through the pine woods. Dude, it was so good to get stoned. I was hearin' the twigs crack super crisp and it mellowed me out. From far away you could hear the sea goin' *hush shhh...hush shhh* and Tepti took off runnin' through them woods with hardcore power, jumpin' over logs and bumps. It was like freedom for him over

---

[*] Like a tool or a shithead.

there and he went diggin' around by some roots, his tail flyin' real fast.

Dude, the Baltic Sea is huge and shimmerin' blue, the sun white and lots of puffy clouds. The beach has ballhanger dudes all over the place, like old timers and fat guys walkin' pecker proud. But there's lots of room and sometimes you can get a spot behind some tall grass in the small dunes. We went there so we could smoke cauze the grass blocked the wind. Varna and Raimis wanted to go swim so I laid in the sand and just looked at the sky where clouds were makin' faces at me and I could hear the waves real nice.

Them dudes were gone for a long time. After a while Tepti came runnin' from someplace and I seen how he started tryin' to dig a hole. So I kinda kneeled in the sand by him and started diggin' to help. It got me relaxed so I had lots of thoughts...like what would happen if I asked Jen for cash? And what if I moved in with her for a while? Maybe Diego knew somebody who could loan some cash...or maybe Varna could do it.

Dude, I totally got carried away with the diggin'. When Varna and Raimis came back from their swim I was in the middle of a hole maybe four feet deep, a huge pile of sand next to me. By accident, I kinda buried Raimis' towel and he said, "Ei, monkey. Ei, *pridurak*[*]."

Varna said, "*Naftamenas*. American thinks everyplace it is oil."

"Hide dinosaur bone."

When I heard them talkin' shit, I was gonna tell 'em off with somethin' real good. But then I seen Dana just a little behind Raimis. She was dressed with a green bikini and starin' at me kinda confused about the hole. Dude, I totally felt the buzz all over me and a soft sinkin' way inside, like a piece of gold got dropped in a jar of syrup. Maybe I waved or tried to fix my cap. Just said, "Hey, Dana. We made it for the festival."

---

[*] That's Russian for moron.

Very Romantic

Before she even seen me, them dudes already told her I was "afraid" of wearin' a ballhanger, so for Dana this was totally a riot. Varna and Raimis whispered lots of stuff in Lithuanian, more jokes about me in a hole. And she looked at me kinda sly. But none of it felt bad. Everybody could tell she was real happy to see me cauze her face turned pink. Dana didn't even think I was gonna come to Nida. Since I never called her.

I said, "Where's it gonna be?"

"It be? What be?"

"The festival."

She got all perked up. "What this means? What *festival*?"

"For the opera."

"Endee, what you talking?"

"You said I should come. Cauze it's an opera festival in Nida."

Now she turned even more pink. "No...Endee. No no...because *you don't understand*. I just say party, opera *party*." She made little fists and crossed her arms. "I don't say *festival*. I say party."

Dude, your probably thinkin' she's right and I'm wrong, but you better believe Dana said festival. In my head I can still hear *festival* real good and clean, like I can see *Pizza Jazz* and remember everything better than a Mac could do it. But here's the best part...it didn't matter who said what or who remembered. She

138

could of said its a convention or a roach motel, it was just good to see her turn pink.

Hangin' out on the beach was real easy. Varna made one more joint and we hit that thing behind the grass to laugh and say nonsense about each other. Then we kicked a soccer ball and made Tepti chase sticks in the water. I met people from Dana's family, like other singers and a violin player. That *va va va* guy from Big Head's shroom party was workin' his gut on the beach, pickin' hair in his belly button like nobody seen him.

Dana invited us to eat by her place. Big Head was in town makin' *shush likai* and everybody was goin' over there. First we stopped by the Subaru to bring four bottles of vodka and some beers. Dana showed the back yard where Big Head was cookin' on a huge box grill...he got kinda happy to see me and slapped meat on plates for us with black bread and ketchup. This always blows me away in Lithuania, how you can just go over to somebody's back yard and they'll set your ass up with meat and bread, then pickles and cabbage. An old lady came out with a wet bowl of *ugrast*, some weird berries like green eyeballs. They tasted kinda sour but went damn good with vodka.

We started boozin' it and Varna talked funny with strangers by a picnic table. He was makin' toasts, talkin' *blet* and *nahooy*...pretty much anything he said had people rollin', maybe a little embarrassed. You should of seen it, cauze anytime we polished a bottle, somebody else had another one in a bag or by a tree.

In the middle of all this, Dana took my wrist kinda private and told me, "Endee, I must dress up for sun."

"What?"

"I come back soon. Then we go together."

She just went to change in a cabin, but I stayed drinkin' by a table and felt real normal, like the booze barely had no effect. After some time, Raimis got up and went stumblin' around the yard by this hammock in the back. He laid down in there and snored up a mean saw, like people in Vilnius could hear it.

Dana showed up wearin' jeans and a blouse with this blue and white thing around her shoulders...also, she made her hair in a small braid. All she said was, "We go, yes?" and put her hand on my shoulder. Tepti followed us down the main road to this little pathway with log stairs goin' up them dunes. And we ended up on top of this huge one.

Dude, up there it was five thousand times more amazing compared with the pond in Big Head's yard. The sun was goin' down right in the Baltic Sea and it took a longass time to disappear behind the water. It was like 22:00 at night, but the sun was still up and slow in the air, kinda floatin' there real heavy. All the best colors came out, dark purple and yellow clouds with the light pokin' through real sharp and pointy like glass razors. I shoved my fingers under the sand and me and Dana stayed real quiet. Only Tepti ran way down by the water to bark at us.

It was like I woke up on a new planet. Cauze now the sun was sinkin' intense and makin' a red pathway go toward us, this shiny sidewalk where the waves were pullin' back on the wet sand. Dana sat in front of me and leaned back so I could hold her. We watched it like this and I could smell her hair, feel how she was breathin'. Pretty soon the sun was just a little bump, like somebody dumped the barbecue over there. And seagulls were goin' real low in big curves, the waves stayin' foamy slow.

Dana whispered, "Endee, we must go back for *opera party*." I didn't really want to go to no party, like I would of walked all the way down the beach only with her. But she got up and brushed the sand off her ass and held her hands to me. We yelled for Tepti and went back to that yard.

Holy shit, you could hear from far away how they were partyin' and singin' with music. There was a good bonfire reflectin' bright off this old man's silver accordion, like a real expensive one. Another guy next to him had a fiddle and one dude was playin' a beat up guitar. At some smaller tables people were liftin' beer bottles and swayin' together to sing booze songs. Raimis was still passed out in the hammock, but Varna found a picnic table with three women, two of them sisters. He was lightin' smokes for the ladies with his zippo and actin' real smooth. Me and Dana just sat down on the grass by the fire.

Most people in the yard were Dana's family or good friends. The old man was her great uncle, Dėdė Liudas, and he was like the leader of the party. After a song got done he would shout a name, *O dabar Jurgita!* No matter who he said, everybody would cheer or go "Ehhhh!" and a person would come up to start some music. When this dude Povilas came out, everybody shut the hell up real quiet. Somebody gave him a fiddle and he totally busted it out, playin' super fast. Then he was done and everybody clapped loud or they hit the table with bottles.

Before the old guy could say who's next, Dana shouted *Gerai, o dabar Varna!* If you can believe it, Varna kinda looked around and got shy. He tried to say *ne ne* but the girls poked him. So he stumbled over by the fire with a smoke in his teeth. Dana said he talked some real embarrassing shit, how they don't teach no music in Law school. Then he tried to sing Stevie Wonder *I Just Called to Say I Love You*, holdin' a beer like a mike. It was like a real bad shithouse to hear him sing so the whole party whistled and threw bottle caps, some people yellin' "Uuuu!"

Dėdė Liudas kinda calmed everybody down with some little music and a nice talk. He had a real soft voice and started sayin' *something something shmeeshmaishmeel, O gal dabar Dana?* Right away the whole party went "Ooooo!" and people started clappin' and knockin' the tables. Dana looked at me and her one eyebrow shot up like she knew exactly how she's totally hot. Then she walked around the fire like a lady and everybody shut the fuck up.

Dude, her voice totally changed. Now she was the woman in the movie who makes all the guys kill each other. And she was older, like 35. Dana totally loved how everybody was lookin' at her...it was like food and she was like a magnet. She talked Lithuanian and asked Dėdė Liudas to give her some notes, like a starting place. When she was gettin' ready to sing, the whole frickin' forest shut up and the fire stopped crackin'.

I thought the song was opera, but she told me later it was jazz, this real famous song called *I'll Be Seeing You*. The first sound buzzed me up with goosebumps. There's no way you can believe how it sounded. She's only 110 pounds and so tiny, but the song came out from her whole body, especially her chest and guts. And it was slow, *so damn slow* and quiet...like the song was holdin' back and holdin' back and holdin' back even though it was gonna bust, just not right now...wait a little, just wait a little more. It was so damn sad but so damn real...nobody in the whole place was even movin' or breathin' too loud to fuck it up.

The song's words go about a girl by the wishing well...then she's by a small cafe and the merry-go-round where she used to have dates with some guy. But he dumped her and now she sees the moon to remember him...it's way up there. So Dana sang these words real high, the highest word pushed all the frickin' way up with her lungs. And right there Raimis started snorin'.

I was gonna go over there and deck his ass. But then the song was over and all the people were clappin', sayin' bravo and hittin' the tables. Dana didn't turn pink from it. With everybody clappin' she turned like an even bigger magnet.

Dude, the family made her sing again. This time she busted out a booze song from Italy where everybody in the back yard knew the words...the whole back yard went swayin' to sing with beers and mugs. Finally it was over and Dana came to sit down by me, but everybody *still* asked for one more song...*Dar viena, nu dar viena*. Frickin' you don't know how much Dana loved it. She jumped up like somebody got her a present.

This time she wasn't gonna fuck around. The third song was the first time I ever heard anybody do hardcore opera. I know probably lots of you never heard no opera before, or maybe you seen it on Channel 11 around Christmas when it's just a fat woman and a guy in a tux singin' real bored. But let me explain some shit right here, cauze most opera ain't like that. Most is totally insane and tripped out. There's always some girl who loses her marbles, like she finds out her husband made sex with a demon queen, so she cuts up her babies and poisons her husband and then falls in a fire pit. There's always a devil up to no good...he helps this nasty old guy turn into a stud so he could get the hottest girl in town for one more good time before he goes to hell. Another real old opera goes about a whorehouse in Turkey. In this one called *Mephistophe*, some ballet dancers come on stage for a serious orgy with devils. Opera writers make sure to put lots of sex in there, only it's not regular sex where your done and just sleep. In opera you can't handle it, so you stab a poison knife in your chest or jump in a fire. A beautiful girl singin' that shit will kick your ass all over the place.

Like the first sound Dana made scared the shit out of me. She spit fire right through my guts. The whole song was made from energy feelings, like "That's it. I'm gonna have one crazy music orgasm in front of 25 people." She had to breathe real fast and quick, but each time the air went deep in her lungs and her head flicked fast and her whole shoulders and arms made power. And fire kept comin' out, like inside she was burning. It makes you real horny cauze she's givin' you opium and sayin' evil promises. You know it's lies and you should never believe it, but maybe you should believe it...yes, you should, you should say *damn straight*, let's have one minute of crazy fire love and then get burned up in a forest fire!

Dude, I almost forgot there's other people around. And I barely remember how they yelled bravo and Dėdė Liudas kissed Dana's hand. The song was over but the feelings she made and the energy was still all around me. When Dana came back to sit, two young boys went by the fire to sing farmer songs that everybody knew, but I can't remember how they sounded. And I don't know how we left the party, if Dana took me away or what. We were walkin' down the main road and I still felt that crazy energy. I couldn't talk for like a half hour when we were already down by that hole I dug in the sand dunes.

Tepti left us alone. The wind was stone dead so my ears turned real alive and our footsteps made the sand crunch loud. The waves got real lazy and crashed slow, plus the air turned real warm with the smell of the salt and the pines. Rememberin' this right now, it's like I forget how the whole thing is real and not from a picture. Like a video where she's turnin' pink. And she's lookin' at me so I can tell what she means...it's totally invitation. And all I'm thinkin' is don't say nothin' stupid, don't fuck up...dude, for real, don't talk nothing at all. My heart's goin' lightspeed. Just kiss her...maybe on the forehead. Or maybe right on the lips, just classy, not no tongue. No, you tool, say something first. "Dana." Now your fucked...you gotta say something else. "Dana, hey. There's lots of stars."

She nodded, her face real pink.

"Your real pretty tonight. More than usual."

She nodded one more time and her one eyebrow went up. She was super sneaky, though also kinda unsure.

"I brung you some flowers. Though I forgot them for you in the old lady's cabin."

"Hmm...Endee?"

I didn't say shit.

"Endee...now, don't be engry." She was noddin' all pink. "Now...okay? Okay?"

"How come? No...I ain't angry."

Dude, she took my hand real soft and started gigglin'. "Okay?" She kept on gigglin' and shrugged one shoulder when she put some sharp corners in my hand. "Don't be engry."

I looked at it. She gave me a rubber and her face went super pink. "Just for safe. But very romantic. Because look, I pick red, you see? Yes, I pick. You should see. A red one. Very romantic."

That Fateful Tuesday

I never had that much fun with nobody before. We got laughin' like little shits playin' a game. With Dana it was totally easy, cauze makin' sex wasn't dirty, not like you broke rules or wanted to act wrong on purpose. I didn't think no nervous crap, only heard the waves shishin' quiet on the shore and had that salt breeze goin' over all our skin. When we were finished, she just fell on top of me kinda sweaty and we were breathin' together. The night stayed real warm so we laid on that mound and looked at the sky. Without no moon, it had all the stars and a milky way like somebody spilled jewelry all over soft black.

Dana said, "I have some sand. You know, in one *place*. Not comfortable."

"You wanna go skinny dip?"

"What it is?"

"Just swim naked."

"*Oi*. Yes, why not?"

It's real intense to go in the sea at night. The water's frickin' dark, like way darker than the sky so there could be a rock and you'd bust your head. But we went floatin' on our backs with the mellow waves bouncin' us up and down. Then Dana played a trick and went underwater.

Holy shit, the girl can hold her breath for like two minutes. I got paranoid cauze the sea was like dark oil. And then it started remindin' me about *dark water*. There wasn't no way to stop them

145

thoughts of swimmin' with Audra...for real, it was like I *remembered* swimmin' with her even though it never happened. The thing is, all girls in the whole world have ESP to find out when your thinkin' about another girl. And when your butt nude that ESP has like triple power. So I had to snap out of them thoughts before Dana popped out.

She did it real smooth and quiet behind me. All I felt was hands on my eyes and her body on my back. She whispered "I catch you like fish," and pinched my nose. Then it was a judo move to flip me back and we stayed down where it was pitchblack and cool and wavy with the soft sandy bottom.

But soon enough we got out. We forgot to bring towels and just stood goosebumped in the breeze to dry off. Dana bent over to squeeze some water from her hair. I thought maybe I'm hearin' things when she said, "Audra, I want to ask." She looked at me real soft. "You know, we must to talk about it."

"Dude..."

"Endee...wait, let me *say*."

"You said Audra?"

Her eyes got real big. "What?" Dana crossed her arms real tight. "*Nu* Endee, hear what you call me."

"Not me. You just called me Audra right now."

"No I don't."

"Totally. I heard it. You did it."

"You called *me*. Don't make bullshit."

"No way. Cauze you gotta admit it."

We had a pretty solid but also kinda embarrassed laugh. What the hell else were we gonna talk about? Dana already knew from some gossip friends how Audra was in the hospital...and the only guy who seen what happened was the "American friend". Dana asked, "She cuts hand? Is it true?" When your on the beach puttin' on your pants and it feels normal to tell that story, that's when you know your totally in Lithuania.

Me and Dana went down the dune to that little path. Them woods at night get almost the same dark like the bottom of the sea, but Tepti was right there waitin'. It was real cool to see Dana with him, how she said *Nu Tepchookas, Tepchookas* in a special way, almost like Tepti's her dog too. If you have a pet, then you know what I mean.

The old boy showed us down that dark path so easy. And we gave him three pieces of fat *shush likas* meat left cold on the barbecue. In the back yard some people were still boozin' by picnic tables, though all the music got put away. Me and Dana didn't feel tired at all. We sat by this plywood table where the stools were tree stumps, real ones with roots still in the ground. Dana found some mineral water and we totally started talkin'.

For real, it was the first time I tried puttin' the whole story together, all of it in order from *That Fateful Saturday* to the boilin' water and the knife. Lots of stuff took a while to remember. But all that shit from the beginning...the laundrymat and Big Beard and Audra's surprise visit...it was like all them things happened a million years ago to a totally different dude. Tellin' it out felt real good, to say *everything* about the breastfeeding and scratching, the weird sex and Audra's dad. Dana didn't get shocked by nothing, only nodded and listened real careful.

That's cauze she was gonna drop a bomb on my ass. I guess I never wondered how Dana met Audra. Maybe I figured they were old friends from someplace...like they grew up in Vilnius or hung out in school. But Dana's only one year older than me...during that summer she was 21. Dana met Audra in high school on her junior year cauze Audra was her damn high school English teacher.

"It is special school for music, so most student creative, not so stupid. Audra was good teacher. She say all the time *be your own way, be your own way. Don't listen what they say or you turn like them so stupid.* But then she was stripper, big scandal. Only for me, really, I think very little about it. Audra was gone from school and soon I forget her. Because I have my own problems. Have to start conservatory. And then I have big stupid wedding."

Dude, when Dana graduated high school, she got in a conservatory for opera. Then this theater group invited her to sing for a play. Over there she met Gidas since he was workin' like an actor. And they got drunk one time, frickin' engaged and then it was gonna be a wedding.

Dana was just 19. The party was on a farm, like three days long with moonshine and 125 fresh killed chickens, plus opera and vodka lubin' everybody up crazy. Dana had this one real jealous older cousin who was almost 30, but all her life she couldn't get no husband. To prove how Dana didn't score nothin' good with Gidas, during the wedding she banged him real low class behind some barn. And gettin' pregnant was an extra score cauze now the cousin could get Gidas by the nuts, plus show everybody how Dana's marriage was garbage. It was barely even four months after the wedding when Dana found out about all this crap. So she dumped Gidas' shit out a window.

For a while she never ran into him noplace. She didn't really go out too much, just to school and some crappy jobs or gigs. "Endee...later I get job at Absento Fejos. This is May, right now just before summer. For me this very good job because tourist give bigger tip in Fejos. But soon Gidas learn where I am working. Thanks God...for him Fejos is too expensive. So he was coming only one time in week, maybe two.

"But it was a stress. He want to talk all the time. I try to ignore, but few times I talk with him. He say lies, so typical I don't repeat to you. *Dana, later maybe meet someplace. Dana, my mother like you most.* Drunk and embarrassing like this. I just tell him very polite, 'Gidas, I can't go with you to any place. And please don't come when I working. Please please.'

"Then later, yes yes, the most crazy night I never forget. Endee, for me it is *That Fateful Tuesday.* It was July...yes, this summer. I see him come through door. And with him two friends from ŠMC, some stupid painters. I see Gidas smoke too much hash...you can see his eyes and how he move. He want to talk, so he grab my arm, but I say 'No, I am busy.' He start drinking, he drink five hundred grams vodka, more. Another people by us could hear how he talk...how he tell me *Dana, come home with me, why you leave me? Look, why you work here? You see who comes in bar. You only want find tourist man to fuck. To fuck one from London.*

"Oh my God, Endee, I get so engree. *Engree engree* like knife made for killing. He talk *How many them you fuck, how many? That one?* He point like this. *Or here, this one from Spain?* I was drinking Cola Light. So I take Cola Light and spill whole glass on his trouser...*nu*, here on dick. Oh my God, Endee, how he start screaming. And with shouting and yelling. Say to me such dirty things, *Tu pizda yobana*. But our security kick him out. And they say he can never to come back.

"*Oi*, I was shaking. The rest of night I feel it, terrible upset. I just go for one cigarette to stop thinking about him, because Gidas is idiot.

"Endee, you saw inside Fejos? The place where they make smoking yard? One lady follow me there, but I do not look who is she...I not even think or care. She sit by small table very near and look at me sometimes. I think maybe she is girlfriend from Gidas. I am almost done with cigarette and then she talk to me. *Excuse me, please. Tell me, is your name Dana?*"

Dude, Dana didn't recognize Audra. For real, she didn't feel like talkin' to no one and almost said, *No, that not my name.* But Audra was lookin' at her real intense. Dana just said, "I'm sorry, I don't know you."

Audra started talkin'. "But Dana, I remember you. You went to special music school. You sit behind *so and so*...in front with *so and so*. Part of your family live in Nida, correct? And your dad die when you were 11, yes? I think you write about it in class.

"*Endee*! So suddenly, I remember. And so strange when I remember. I see myself...I am in her class, and suddenly I get so calm. But why? In school I was never calm. And I stare at her...stare and stare her green plastic eyes and black short hair. Why I stare at her, why she remember about me? Audra ask *Who is boy they kick out? Why he talk like this to you?* We have conversation, but soon she go away. Then, Endee...for two days, I can't forget about her."

"Yeah," I said. "For me it was like that."

"Later on she come back to Fejos. It was Friday. Oh my God, Endee, I get so nervous. So so *nervous*. Suddenly, she is like magnet for eyes and my whole body. I only want to work, to ignore. Because who is she? I have thoughts...I want to sit with her and make all person go home, all music shut up. Very uncomfortable...this feeling I can't understand. I know she come to see me. But I can't believe. Why she do it?"

Audra stayed in Fairies till Dana got off work. They went by Double Coffee, this all night cafe. The girls hit some gin and talked about guys, how they mess stuff up all the time, how they're garbage. And the next minute they were in a taxi goin' to Dana's apartment. Dana told me, "For me, it is like experiment. Like I am curious, because why she is magnet? Suddenly, I *must* to know. Even if I regret. Maybe you are only person who understand, Endee, because she make you believe it...if you can be with Audra, you will learn some great big thing. You find something emayzing. But in truth she is only crazy. With her all feeling is big pain. You are scared, you don't say *Audra, you are big pain to me*. Because maybe she make bigger pain. You understand what I mean, Endee?"

"Dana..." I said, "Were you her girlfriend?"

She was tappin' this empty water bottle with her pinky. First her one eyebrow shot up. But then all Dana could do was shrug.

"Like...for how long?"

She said, "I don't know. For some time she is living with me. Bring suitcase. I give her key, then don't know how I can make her go away. With big pain, she say, *Thank you, thank you because I can't be home right now. No, I can't stay there.* I wish she leave, but feel so guilty. Don't know how, but somehow we make very much sex. Each time I regret. But later I want more."

"Totally," I said. "But she don't talk, so you don't know what it means. She don't tell you nothin', what's happenin' in her brain."

"You understand. Yes, Endee, yes." She was kinda quiet. "And then it is that night when *you* come to Fejos."

"To meet with Audra? With Varna and Raimis?"

"And *Gidas. Blet.* Audra say I should let friend in bar so you don't pay. *Nu,* but there is Gidas. I get so engree. How did he do it? And Audra has some boy, this small boy from America with terrible shirt...*you.* She says *this my friend.* But then she says she want to take you to apartment. Do you know how I get jealous? But also so stupid...why am I jealous? I say fine, take him my place. Who cares? For night I go stay with friend. And I tell Audra, have my place for weekend. Next day, I go Nida and visit uncle. Ask what is wrong with me."

For a while, all I did was whisper, "Damn...damn." But then I remembered something. "Wait. Cauze Dana...it was the *funeral*...on that night after the funeral?"

Half her mouth smiled.

"Did you? I mean, in the morning. Both of you together...when I woke up. That night?"

Dana didn't say nothing. She looked in me real soft for a while. Under the table she stepped on my foot again and kept it there. "Endee. Let's go in cabin to sleep."

Loaded

In her great uncle's cabin Dana took us up a step ladder that went to a real tight attic. That ladder got pulled up with a rope and turned like a trap door. Dana's stuff was real messy all around, like a purse and clothes, plus CD's, empty packs of smokes and some mags. On one wall was like this gumdrop shape window. Somebody made a mattress just from a pile of wool blankets covered with a sheet, though probably me and Dana could of crashed on the scratchy wood floor since we were so tired.

I woke up first cauze it was flies landin' on my face. And in the morning Big Head was makin' noise outside real loud, playin' garbage Euro pop *thump thump thump* and kickin' a soccer ball with kids. I had a smoke out the window and watched them kids scream when Big Head kicked a ball straight in the air.

Dude, I was so mellow. I guess I had a hangover, maybe some hash clouds in my brain, though for real I felt calmed down and loose. I seen Big Head's ball hit this flower pot, like a huge wood bucket, maybe one of them from a well. Starin' at that crap, I thought *ding* I should bring Dana's wildflowers while she's still sleepin'. That would be a real smooth thing to do. Also, I'll get some food. Cauze you can smell them fishermen makin' smoked fish all over town, and down the road there's a store with bread and sausage. If I got some coffee, that would be Lithuanian style breakfast in bed.

I knew I still had some money left...after payin' the old lady for the bed I never even used, then them potato pancakes we ate, I had maybe twenty Litas or more. But now I was lookin' through all my pockets, inside my socks and shoes. That money was gone, maybe lost in the sand or in the grass where some tool found it. The only thing in my pants was a two cent coin, this real light aluminum that ain't worth even half a penny.

You figure your supposed to go bananas when your finally broke for good. Like you need to cut your hand or tie a noose. Bein' *almost broke* is like there's a train comin' to smear your ass up and down the line, a real mean one with black smoke. But bein' totally broke...I just kinda sighed and went "Yup...yup yup," pressin' that dumbass coin in my forehead till it stuck. It was a small mirror on the wall so I stared at my dumb face, greasy hair and the stub on my chin till that stupid coin fell down lost in Dana's pile of girl socks.

So now what the hell could I do? I was tryin' to figure out how that trap door worked without me crashin' through the floor. And right there I got some wishful thinkin', cauze maybe my money got stashed in the safe place! I wrote Dana a note with her eye liner from her purse. *Went to get my stuff, will come back soon.* When I got down to the kitchen, Dana's great uncle and a lady with long gray hair were havin' tea. They stopped talkin' just to look at me, probably a little surprised, and I said good morning, *Labas rytas* even though it was way past afternoon.

Dude, I found Varna and Raimis passed out in the old lady's place. The room stunk some nastiness...farts and cigarettes and booze breath. Varna's one hand was real swelled up and his knees and feet super dirty. Raimis was in bed huggin' a bigass pineapple like a girlfriend. The old lady came in and started rattlin' off to me, showin' the clock, sayin' *dabar* and *kada* and *shmeesh-maishmeel.* I wanted to say "Sorry" *atsiprasho* but only came up with *atsisaysk,* which means "Sit down." Dude, that get her real pissed. I just took my flowers from the vase and she dumped the dirty water all over Varna, only he didn't even flinch. Before she could throw some shit at me, I just said *Achoo, labai nayko, viso gero* (Thank you, very nothing, good bye) and got the hell outta there.

Tepti ran up to me from the Subaru. Holy crap, I kinda forgot about him. With the old boy waggin' his tail all over the place and the bright sun and all them happy people wanderin' around Nida, I started believin' the money was stashed for sure. Me and Tepti rushed on back to that table with the tree stumps. But it wasn't no cash in the safe place. The only thing in there was Audra's real small Moleskine, another thing I totally forgot about.

That was a big letdown...I didn't even touch it, just got mopin'. Like I walked down by this cement boat dock, sat there watchin' some sailboats cruise around the lagoon. Some of them were real big and smooth, like white with silver poles and some color flags. And over there people parked cool cars, like BMW and Saab or Volvo. I seen a dude buyin' ice cream for his wife...he was dressed real swank with one of them blazers and his gold watch totally shiny in the sun. Them heels from the shoes sounded *click tap click tap* when he walked real proud so everybody could see his watch hand holdin' ice cream.

I knew I'm fucked. Like it was clean for me when I heard Dana sing...the girl's real talented and she's gonna be famous. For real, Dana could steal that ice cream dude from his wife if she wanted...fuckin' she could land any loaded guy with a sailboat. Or a diesel bodybuilder with a potato in his ballhanger. How come she went for messed up tools like me and Gidas? I had to think about that, cauze any girl who liked me, probably something was real wrong with her.

Dude, I moped all the way to that stump table, put my backpack over there, then got in the hammock to swing around. I had to admit stuff clean without no bullshit and no stupidass romantic stuff. Probably when Dana wakes up she's gonna say, *Thanks Endee. Maybe I see you in Vilnius later.* And she would go home in Big Head's Saab.

Dude, I had a pretty weird moment. Layin' in that hammock, I could see my whole future super clear, like the whole pathway right in front. Jen was gonna give me money to fly home, and she was gonna bitch about it all my life, hang that shit over my head how she borrowed me cash one time. I was gonna end up livin' close by the train tracks in Berwyn again. And I would get some crap job washin' windows or checkin' meters. No way would I ever get married. The only thing, I would get a dog, but he wouldn't even be half so cool like Tepti. With a half-crap dog, I would just turn like a geezer. My neighbor next door would have some nice daughters...all the time they would feel sorry for my geezer ass. Cauze I would have just a chair on the back porch and Old Style beer with the Sox game on the radio, the same like all them other Berwyn geezers. Sittin' there on that porch, sometimes I would remember Tepti and Dana. Like I would be 80...I wouldn't even know where the hell I left my teeth, but I would remember Dana and feel real soft inside, real missing. Then when I was in the hospital hooked up with machines, the only person in the room would be a nurse and she never heard of Lithuania. Finally they would have to pull the plug and I would totally see the pond and all them ripples in the water from Dana's pebbles. Remember how she used to say *Stuff stuff* and *Don't be engry.* That first time when she said, *I show you. Have to show you emayzing. It emayzing.* And the best night of my whole life when we went skinny dippin' in the dark water.

Dude, I kinda passed out in the hammock dreamin' this shit real hardcore so I could feel a machine hooked up. But then I woke up with them flowers on my gut. Dana was sittin' down on a stump by that table and she had a whole bowl of berries, plus a glass of water. I said, "Hey, I brung these for you." But she was readin' somethin' real intense and didn't even hear me.

Dude, when I was passed out in the hammock, Dana went lookin' through my bag for a lighter. That's how she found the frickin' Moleskine by accident. You should of seen her face readin' it, kinda wigged and confused. But also she couldn't stop and didn't hear when I said "Dana, Dana" a couple times. Finally I sat down by her and she looked up, didn't even see them flowers. "*Oi,* Endee. You engry I read in this?"

I didn't say nothin'.

"I can't believe. Here, look what she give you." Dana showed in the back of the Moleskine. I didn't even know about it, cauze them notebooks have some back flaps, like a folder on the last page. That's where Audra put her ATM card...it was from some bank in Oak Park and she totally taped the pin number for me. I barely believed it, like I checked the date to make sure the card ain't fake. I told Dana, "You think it works?"

"Why not? Because look what she write."

There was lots of stuff in that Moleskine totally similar to the other notebooks. Drawings of eyeballs, sunsets and body parts. She drew Big Beard's house in Oak Park totally memorized, like the exact perfect shutters and door design with the bushes in front. Them drawings were all real good, but Audra's handwriting was real pointy, kinda like barb wire. In all them writings she always mentioned my name...for real, the whole notebook was a weird letter to me. This part I'm gonna show here was on the last couple pages. It looks neat typed up, but her handwriting was real hard and bent, like her hand hurt when she wrote it.

Andy, you're sleeping by yourself in the apartment. I've taken Tepti for a walk. We've stopped here at Avilys, that's the bee hive, a brewery. Fitting, I think. Although I ordered tea, not beer, and some sweet brandy. Yes, Tepti wanted to go outside, but please keep sleeping. Don't listen to me or wake up, please rest. It's fitting. I'm sorry sorry sorry sorry sorry. Please, Andy. D, Drew, Andrew, I'm so sorry. I was watching you sleep–I realize how I'm tiring you. You know I lack courage. My cowardice wipes you out. But I want you to know–can you tell Dana and anyone who asks, my cowardice is only a single part of me that masks the rest and plans to kill what's left. But I'm trying to concentrate. You didn't come looking for a coward. I won't burden you to forgive me. Such short time keeps leaving. I'll find a way to let you know, answer all your questions, but don't you dare forgive me.

You flattered me. I did not in a million years ever expect you here. Andy, I am arrogant. In this sick and uncivilized world, I manage that much. After four years of it, 2002-2006, the headstone on my American life, I came out to Vilnius. Disguised myself, greened my eyes, cut my hair so they wouldn't recognize the woman buying milk or kneeling down to pray. Because when my grandfather died, over two thousand people came to his funeral. And most of them knew my face. Now nobody in this country remembers the narcissus or her family. Had I any courage or brains, I would have told you at Absinthe Fairies to stay away. I could dream up so many simple ways to make you hate me, run away from me on your own. Can you name one?

On one side was flattery. (Please believe it.) But on the other, shh shh shh, because someone's badly leading someone on. The coward loves her own hatred but fears those who might hate her. Or grow indifferent towards her–the coward is powerless against indifference. Equally, she cannot find herself attracted to a simple boy. It is impossible. So go ahead and lead him on. Convince yourself it's what you're doing, merely leading on. Leading like a leader, I don't need anyone, sincerely yours. Andy, it has always given me pleasure to see them wishing to know my wishes, to do anything to know them. What do I feel, what am I like? It is better to make the boy wonder if I care than to show him how I do. Ironically, you knew all this long before I did.

But you are wrong about me. My perversion isn't beauty. I thought you were speaking only to fill awkward silence, though now I realize you don't gild the looking glass, dress a whore in virgin white to be led down the aisle by the father who has ruined her. I mean this as a compliment, so please don't be insulted. The demons around you–Andy, you come to them with the trust of a child, naive as a cloud to the wind.

You look down on yourself in this evil world (call yourself a moron or a tool) because you can hope and accept. You have trouble loving because you are scared the ones you love will disappear, even when the ones you love are harming you. Because we are not like you. The rest of us can only lie, steal and destroy what we fail to abandon. I want to hope I haven't sunk my claws in deep enough to poison you for life. Maybe I shouldn't hope, sincerely yours. The least I can do is help you get away.

Look in the back of this book, in the pocket. I don't know how much, I'm not sure. It's enough for you to leave, to start something. (I wish I could buy away your memory.) The card is not a chunk of bread handed to a dying dog, or the time you gave a demon. I am legion, for there are many of us here. If you fuck something up, set it free. Don't you dare return to look for me. And don't you dare forgive.

All this seems like a bunch of heavy shit right now. It's pretty intense to write it down, to think how she wrote it...and right now I understand all of it cauze I got help to look it up, like the stuff from the Bible, and the narcissus is a flower. But readin' it the first time, me and Dana barely paid no attention to what it means. We got our butts down by the ATM to check for money.

Audra left me $2,124 bones. Dana looked at the little paper ticket with me, both of us holdin' it together. I seen them numbers and went *Dude!* This huge cash changes everything, so lemme just jump up and frickin' down. But then 15 seconds went by, and maybe 30 more went by, only I was still standin' on the ground and holdin' that ticket with Dana. She looked at me in a totally new way, like tryin' to be happy for me when she couldn't, kinda jealous though she was tryin' to hide it. Writin' this, I know for sure she had thoughts real similar to mine. Probably like...Andy, what are you gonna do now? Even more important...when are you gonna do it? Cauze when your loaded, you can do exactly the thing you want to do. And when it's right in front of your face, there probably ain't nothin' harder.

A Round

All I said right there was, "You wanna get some lunch?"

She was still holdin' on that little ticket like something's gonna happen if she lets go. She shrugged a couple times and put her hands behind her back. Then her one eyebrow shot up, "Food. *Oi, nu.* Maybe, sure." Dana brushed hair off her face, though she didn't have no hair there at all. And she started noddin'. "Yes, hungry."

But on the way to a cafe she said *she's* gonna buy the food. She knew a place where the pancakes were real good, these ones called *laytin bleenai su barveek*, which is like small burritos made with cream and huge mushrooms. Waitin' for the food, we sat there kinda awkward, just watchin' the people walk up and down that street. Then we got happy when the food came cauze eatin' was easier than talkin'. But Dana babbled a little during the lunch, talkin' how them mushrooms grow behind the cabin in the woods and you can pick 'em natural. They're like the most favorite food for all Lithuanians, more important than bacon or salt. She talked more but I don't remember none of it cauze I was only waitin' to say, "Dana, I'm gonna pay. You don't need to pay."

"No, I pay."

"But you should let me."

"No, because I pay. For both."

"But all this is real expensive. That fancy coffee and this mineral water."

"So what. I order, I pay."

"But I think the guy should do it."

Holy shit, you should of seen her eyes get huge and intense. And how she bit the fork with her front teeth. "The guy? You think the *guy?*"

"I mean, just cauze the way it usually goes..."

"Usually? Oh. *Nu*, yes usually." Dana said *usually* maybe 5 or 7 times. "Yes, is usually for guy to pay. But usually is also when guy have money. Because right now, very *unusually*, money come from crazy bitch. Crazy bitch fucked up in head."

"Don't talk that. It ain't fair."

"Endee! *Crazy* bitch. Because I know. And right now you crazy boy. Yes, I will say. Listen how you talk. You with such big money. *Nu*, who cares, because I don't need. Money for you, not me. Don't know for what you use, but not to pay my fancy coffee, my mineral water. You pay your *bleenai* and I pay mine. Everything...*fsyo**."

Dude, before I could come up with something to reply, she threw a hundred Litas on the table. Dana pounded her mineral water and stormed off...she was walkin' totally straight down the middle of the street with her sandals flippin' loud. Definitely she wanted me to chase after, but I was smokin' pissed. And damn shocked too cauze I never seen none of that comin' or even understood how the hell it happened so fast. You should of seen Tepti. He wanted to go with her and did about half way before he looked back to see if I'm okay with it.

The food cost way cheaper than 100 Litas, probably only 35 or 40. I paid for the whole tab with her cash and kept the rest to give back. Who knows why I did it like that...I didn't have no clean reason at the time. Just figured I'd see her in a while and we'd sort this stupid mess out. But then Varna and Raimis showed up. And before I could get back to Dana's cabin, she made Big Head drive them to Vilnius.

---

* That's Russian. A real hardcore way to say *I'm done.*

Raimis and Varna had that pineapple cut up and wrapped in a drugstore bag. Them dudes were a total mess. Varna got his whole hand and arm stung up by hornets, also some on his leg and back cauze he kicked a nest by accident in the woods...for real, he still had some pieces from leafs in his big hair. He couldn't remember too much, why the hell he was out in the woods. He just freaked out runnin' to the cabin and trippin' over shit. Raimis laughed hard at the story. But eatin' that pineapple in front of us, he was gettin' some infection on his face from the juice, like a big red clown smile on his bald head. "So what." He went, "*Ananasas pizdiets*. I find in street. Someone lose, but I take."

Dude, we were kinda in a nice family joint. But them dudes sat around the table talkin' hardcore swears with frickin' *blet* and *vashoo mat* and *zayabees*, plus *pizda* and *shoodas* and more words than that. Pretty soon the waiter came, though Varna and Raimis didn't feel like orderin' stuff from him, they just wanted to eat their *ananasas* (like my favorite word in Lithuanian). We totally got kicked out, plus dirty looks from people.

Goin' back to Vilnius in the Subaru, I told them what happened last night with Dana, how I got the Moleskine and the ATM card. For real, I started thinkin' real advanced, kinda turnin' the situation around, seein' it more Dana's way. Like let's say for example I was livin' in Berwyn and just mindin' my own business. Maybe I had a job in some bar like *Fitzgerald's*, or more swank like the *James Joyce*. And let's say Gidas would of been a regular over there sometimes. Now I'm only pretendin' about this...I'm only settin' it up to think about cauze no way would this happen for real. But just for example, let's say me and him got gay a couple times in secret[*]. And then after that Dana showed up outta nowhere, like a real big surprise. The only reason she came around Berwyn was to find Gidas, but next thing you know she's livin' in his place. After that, me and Dana do some drugs and have one romantic night by Lake Michigan. She's broke with no way home, but then Gidas gives her two grand so she can leave. So at our last

---

[*] That would **never** happen.

lunch together, like maybe the last time we're gonna see each other forever, Dana just looks at me and goes, "I'll buy you a burrito." Dude, that would fuckin' make me pissed and real depressed.

I started feelin' unsure about usin' that money. But Varna went, "*Blet*, spend it. Spend all. Yes, buy ticket. Go duty free, get best brendy. Only please, Endee. Please please don't fuck Gidas."

Raimis said, "*Pizdiets*, two thousand. Crazy motherfucker, you buy petrol for car. And for me one coffee, only good one." I paid at the BP and got him a nasty disgusting joe that smelled like sweatpants.

When we got back to Vilnius, Raimis wouldn't let me stay in no hostel. He said I should stay in his place...like it would almost be a favor for him. "Because always those crazy girls from my sister here come and listen their *nahooy* Abba. My sister, she have two daughters. I can say them, *no, you nephews don't stay here, because from America I have guest*. Endee, just help me clean room sometimes, wash kitchen." I thought that was cool and stayed with Raimis for the rest of my time in Vilnius, which was only gonna be a couple more weeks.

I tried to visit Audra on Sept. 5th, the Tuesday after we got back from Nida. I read the whole Moleskine and all her notes lots of times, and a bunch of stuff in there gave me questions. I decided I was gonna pay all the money back to her...for real, I believed I would do it. Then I could tell Dana the cash was only borrowed, cauze me and Audra made a fair deal. It was real important for me to tell her this, though now I don't really remember how come.

Dude, I found out Audra didn't go home after they fixed her hand. They moved her to a shrink hospital, like the same one where her mom went, only now it got spruced up. Anybody who wanted to talk on the phone with her had to give a number at the front desk where Audra could call back. I tried givin' all Raimis' numbers, though I knew she wasn't gonna call. I had a note to give, but a real young nurse over there was straight with me. "I cannot say for certain if patient will get note." Post and Marta made a deal to read any letters or anything Audra got first, but I left that note anyway, then went to write e-mail. Even though it's kinda short, it took me like two hours in this internet cafe to finish it.

Dear Audra, Hello. I read your Moleskine real careful. I'm real sorry too for everything and how it happened. I know you didn't want none of it but maybe right now you get a better chance to rest. Hope they let you and don't ask you questions too much. I just wanted to say I don't think I'm naive like you said. Cauze that ain't no compliment. For you it seems that way cauze you would listen to me, so I said things nobody heard before. Though if you go makin a guy confused on purpose then it ain't fair to call him naive or a cloud. Still I don't got no hard feelings right now. Sorry for all them things that got you upset and I hope in the hospital you get better.

The thing is, I can't take no money like this. Yeah, I'll use it for now, thanks a lot for the loan cauze I gotta go home finally. But then later I'm gonna pay it back, work some job and send Western Union. I won't know where, but maybe when you get out from that hospital then Varna or Raimis can find you and give it to you. For real, to pay it back is the most fair thing.

I wish we could of talked one more time. Get well soon, Audra. It's no reason to be no stranger just cauze you cut your hand. But whatever you do I won't be pissed. Your Friend, Andrew.

It was pretty easy not to worry about that message or what Audra was gonna think about it, cauze I knew she wasn't gonna see it for a while. The way I wrote it sounds like I thought I'm never gonna see her again, but that was bullcrap. I felt real strong I'm gonna see her again. Just didn't know when and where.

That was the first time I seen my e-mail box for like six weeks (I never really checked it at Audra's house). I was expectin' a whole load of crap from Jen, but only found a couple new messages in there. One said I'm a traitor and the worst asshole, like it ain't even worth it to write me no more messages. She wrote *your just like your dad where you skip town, totally the same like him and not no different.* Jen got married with Gunther, so now dad was only mine and not hers no more.

That message got sent in July. But in the middle of August she sent a couple more. One said she got a Glock and it was her new hobby to shoot since she was gettin' real good at it. Also she was gonna get her GED and take speed typing at Sterling College. That seemed weird cauze I never knew about no speed typing classes. But the most wigged thing was the picture attachments she put in. The message said, *I know you don't care, but here's some pics from my wedding.* Like she was wearin' a headband at the Justice of the Peace. The Wisconsin cabin party had people dancin' on tables and drinkin' Jim Beam, like a couple passed out on the floor. In one pic somebody wrote *I DO* with lipstick on Gunther's forehead.

Dude, that night I had this real important dream where I knew no way would I forget it. Half of it was nightmare and half comedy, though the whole thing had lots of meanings for me. It started in Berwyn. I knew Jen's wedding was gonna be in one hour, like the ceremony in a dry cleaners down East Avenue. That cleaners only washed wedding dresses, nothing else, and Jen needed fifty frickin' different ones with lots of colors. It was my job to pick them dresses up, but Berwyn was all mixed up with Vilnius...like I ended up around the corner from the Pavlak Funeral Home where it was the Neris River and the Gates of Dawn. Totally lost so I couldn't find no dresses.

The whole dream turned like a time bomb. I ended up goin' through back doors with rust chains and some *Exit* signs flickerin' red like a horror movie. Finally I found a warehouse and Jen was over there with all her dresses piled up. She started talkin' in Lithuanian and I could understand it. "They're in piles. Look at the boxes. Too small."

"But them boxes ain't heavy. I can carry."

Right there we had this dream argument. I seen a beach out some window and really wanted to go there. But Jen said forget it. "Dana's not invited to the wedding. I don't give a fuck."

"How come?"

"Cauze you don't invite nobody." She got super pissed at me. "You sit in the coffee bar, sit and sit and sit in the coffee bar. Hope she pops around by accident to say how your important. But you don't got no guts, Drew. You don't got no guts." Jen kept on raggin' and all I could do was pile up wedding dresses in boxes that were fallin' apart. I knew I'm never gonna finish in time and all of it would be my fault.

Maybe you had one morning like this where you just kinda pop up...it's like you just snap out from sleep. In Raimis' front room I seen some leafs from a tree branch movin' around by the window real mellow. Like I could hear the city, some car horns and a couple crows talkin' real far from each other. For a moment it was like Jen was right there...she was on the couch raggin' at me. But everything around me was totally calm, and real sudden I also *knew* something real calm. Like I knew exactly what I had to do next.

You don't know how mellowed out it made me, more calm than ever before in my life. For a whole day I didn't worry about nothing, just thought how to make a good plan. I didn't want no advice from nobody and I wasn't gonna spend a dime from Audra's money. So when I did it Dana couldn't get pissed at me.

In the evening I went out in Raimis' back yard by them huge train parts, one engine block almost bigger than a Volkswagen Golf. And I seen all this metal junk on the ground, like springs and bolts and little rings. All of a sudden I started laughin' cauze I knew I'm gonna make an ass of myself. But I had lots of practice for that and didn't have nothing to lose.

That night at ŠMC I came around when the crew was cleanin' up real late. I helped Raimis carry chairs and wipe down some tables. Then we sat around the cafe with the main lights off and smoked some LM cigs. He told me, "*Nu, bomchik*[*]. You don't read walls, ah?"

"What walls?"

"Already three days, four days on walls. You don't read?"

---

[*] That means like bum.

I looked around.

He said, "*Blet*...this paper." Raimis went over by a little bulletin board next to the shitter. People hanged flyers over there, like if a DJ was gonna spin or a rock band had a show. But I always ignored that shit cauze I couldn't read it. Raimis took a flyer and slapped it on the table. "Dana hang this, tell me 'Don't say him.' But *blet*, you don't read."

I saw the word *Operos* and looked a little closer at the rest. It was all this *shmeeshmaishmeel* with numbers, a picture of a piano and lots of names. In some bigger letters at the bottom it said *Dana Grybaitė*. Raimis said, "*Nu*, you understand?"

"When's this?"

He pointed to the date. "Two days, *blet*. Conservatory."

"She hung this up?"

"She say very important to me, *Don't say him, Raimis, don't say him nothing.*"

Dude, I'll admit I got kinda wigged and nervous. The extra day was key cauze I had to get an outfit and make something to bring to the concert. I totally knew how people get spiffed up for opera, so I borrowed a suit from Varna, kinda light blue with baggy pants. The jacket sleeves were too long, but I looked cool...just strapped them pants up with a serious belt and rolled them sleeves a little. Varna gave a black shirt and white tie so I could be total Euro.

On opera day I left Tepti at home with Raimis. The conservatory was right across the street from that *Gedimino Parkas* where I found money on the lawn. I came kinda early and felt a bit jumpy, so I bought this smoothass tobacco called *Samson Ultra Milde Shag*, sat down on a bench to roll a smoke. But frickin' some freestyle skaters or other shitheads put gum on the bench, exactly in the middle where I put my ass. And I got so nervous tryin' to pick that crap off, ended up wipin' my hand on the jacket to smear some gum over there. This totally messed up part one of my plan, which was *don't be dirtbag*. But I kept on goin' no matter what and stood positive.

That conservatory building is this real old one with shandeleers and scratchy wood floors. It took a while to find the recital room...in there some short guy with a yellow goatee was already doin' opera. The song was pissed off how he hates everything...for real, it sounded real bad, like a bunch of frogs in a blender.

I got kinda worried. I was late...the gum made me late. Dana was probably already finished with her songs and now only the tools were gonna sing. I sat down on this chair and it made the most loud creak. But that didn't matter too much...my eyes got better in the dark and I seen how frickin' nobody showed up, just some students and a couple moms and dads. Two bored old timers, that's all.

The show was some music marathon. After Yellow Goatee it was Jewelry Princess. Then Humpty Dumpty and a girl with hair like two ropes. They kept on comin' and comin' like cartoons and each one sang for way too long. All of 'em sucked...like the most boringass tunes, not even nothing insane or sexy. And I couldn't get the hell out of there cauze now it was more people and my chair was gonna make all that noise. But if shit didn't get better I was totally gonna light a smoke.

I guess the show did get better. In opera school they always end their gigs with the best students, so this girl came out with her hippy piano player, like Jerry Garcia in a tux. That girl could totally crank it, like a love song where she put her hand real light by her boob. So people totally clapped for that.

Then you frickin' knew Dana was comin' out, the last one since she was the school's best singer. It was a vibe in the air and more people showed up...they knew your supposed to wait in the hall for all the crappy people to finish. Some dudes coughed out their last noises and Dana came out with her piano player. She didn't need no fancy clothes, just a lady's black dress with some shiny earrings and a necklace.

Dude, she didn't waste no time...right there it was frickin' opium, like the first sound. The girl busted out this song where your whole eyeballs get melted and inside your chest a deep red ball goes super warm. The song was Italian and real sad and

lonely. It was a girl all by herself in a window on Taylor Street
waitin' for a dude to come home. But he was dead or messed up or
he loved somebody else. It didn't matter cauze she was waitin' and
waitin' and really believed he was comin' home someday, though
everybody told her she's nuts, totally crazy and dumb. And at the
end her heart was gonna break, like she was just gonna frickin' die
right there from how bad she wanted him home. I didn't even
really try to fight it....that music got me totally sloppy.

All the people stood to clap but I just sat tryin' to wipe.
When it was done, everybody wanted to talk to her and give
flowers and shit, so they all lined up. That gave me some time to
clean up with a napkin. With all them people lined up on stage I
sat down a little closer where she could see me. The last person
was done and her piano player gave her a hug, then she came up to
me not even a little bit shy. "*Nu.* Endee. Hi."

"Hi."

"You look..." She seen me good. And right there I could tell
she *knew* I got sloppy. "*Nu...oi.* You have suit."

"Varna borrowed it. Though I sat in gum."

"Hm," she shrugged with one shoulder. "Who tell you is
recital?"

"Raimis. No...I mean. Just...he showed some flyers. Like
hanged by the wall."

"Oh, he *show* you? Really?" She crossed her arms. "*Nu*...yes.
I not expect you, because it is surprise. For example, you don't
even *call* me." Now she got kinda sly and put her hands behind her
back, noddin' a little. "But you like song?"

"It's real good. Sounds way better with piano."

"*Nu*, yes piano. Of course, better with piano."

Right there we had one of them awkward breaks that was
way too long. And then we started talkin' at the same time, "I say
you," and "Sorry about Nida." Then "Go ahead," and "No, you
say." Dana said, "You not engree?" and I went, "It's a good song."
So we both started kinda gigglin' at each other and she hit my
shoulder. "*Nu!*"

"Dana. Like, do you wanna go for a walk down *Gedimino Prospektas?*"

"Endee... say correct, *Prospektas.*" She rolled them r's. "*Pro, pro.* Not Prawspacktis. Talk better. *Prospektas.*"

"Your right. So, just down the street? Just for a walk."

She stared me through. Then she smiled with half her mouth and that one eyebrow shot up. "But my feet so tired."

"Oh, yeah...we can sit someplace. Cauze they got cafes and stuff." I tried to think about some nicer bar. "Only you pay. Totally. You pay the whole thing."

She looked at me with her eyes half closed, kinda shakin' her head. "Sure...good. Very good. Let's go."

We were out on the street thinkin' where to go when suddenly she got an idea. "Yes! Endee, I show you very good bar. From all Vilnius one of my favorite. You never go, but you will like."

Dude, Dana totally took our asses to this wacked out maniac bar. It's real close to Audra's place, kinda behind the post office and that construction site in a little alley. The name is *Suokalbis*, a bar shoved real secret way in the back of this old building, like behind some black and gold stairs. At first it looked kinda swank with old fireplaces and black and white photos. But then Dana bought me a beer and said, "Okay, careful. Because you must to guard." I really didn't understand what she was talkin' and put my beer on a windowsill, turned to have a look around the place for twenty seconds. Then I looked back and seen this sawed off dude drinkin' my beer...like he was slobberin' all over it with his tongue and nasty mouth to make sure I don't want it back. This made Dana totally happy so she laughed. "I am saying you! You must to guard."

We got a table in the corner by a fire place (it don't work, just looks cool). Lookin' around the place, I seen it was a total freakshow. There was this dude dressed only in potato bags like some Holy Moses and he was playin' chess with an old guy, maybe 70 or 75, though he had a mean shiner. In another corner some guy was passed out on the ground with his feet on a chair.

This one woman with a purple wig was starin' at me funny like
she don't trust me. And every now and then she would stick her
tongue out. Dana said, "Yes, Endee. This is great bar, like a real
freedom."

Frickin' we got totally hammered in that place off the most
strong beer. I didn't pay for a thing. When Dana was buzzed she
started babblin' fast, tellin' me she was sorry about Nida. Like two
hours after stormin' off she was feelin' real guilty. For real, she
kept talkin' fast so I couldn't slide no words in there and had to
listen. Like she started talkin' stuff I didn't expect...asked me from
nowhere, "Endee, where is Indiana?"

"Indiana? That's next door. Right by Chicago."

"By Chicago? Not far. *Nu*...maybe you know Jacob Music
School? No, you don't know?"

"Never heard of it."

"Yes, because Jacob Music School in Indiana. I want there
to study for voice."

"How come you got to study? Already your real
good...should just start makin' gigs."

Here she laughed at me. "Endee, what you talk? I must to
fix...*oi*, so many problem to fix. Yes, Jacob Music School Indiana.
Where it is?"

"Not sure."

"My teacher say me about this school. She say very good
one. Because not many Russians. And Indiana small town, so easy
with bike."

"Dude, Indiana ain't no town."

"*Nu*...not town?" She shrugged around and finished her beer.

I waited for a while. "How come you start talkin' all this?"

"Start? Start what...not *start*, Endee. I want sing opera. Make
career. From time I am little girl I want sing. When I hear first
time Maria Callas* record." I nodded at her and finished my beer.

---

* This is a real famous opera singer from the olden days, almost the same
so good like Dana.

Then we stared at the empty glasses. Dana said, "I get for us more drink, yes?" and she just hopped by the bartenders.

The place was gettin' packed with the most happy and hardcore drunks you ever even seen. The bartenders were playin' stuff like John Denver, AC/DC, Eminem, then Ozzy...everything mixed up. Dana came back with two beers plus two shots of vodka. We hit the vodka right away, clinked the glasses and said, *Sveiks* (cheers). Then she asked me, "And you. What you will do?"

"Well. I gotta go back to Berwyn."

"Of course. Yes, of course. That's fine."

"It's fine?"

"Very fine...yes. Continue."

"I mean, Berwyn. I was in community college for a while. But I stopped. I wanna go back though."

"What you study?"

Right there the bartenders put *Money* by Pink Floyd. Holy crap, this was a huge hit and the place got jacked...them drunks just went "Ei!" and got dancin' on tables, on the fireplace and everyplace else. Moses was totally shakin' his ass on a windowsill (he was like 50 and real thin) and Dana made me get on our table. She put her hands over her head and just kicked the beer glasses all over the place even though they were pretty much full. Some guy grabbed one and finished off the little drop that was left.

We danced for the whole song so the table was wobblin' and all my shoes got wet. Stuff went real wild, like I got nudged by some guy and almost slipped. Dana took my tie off and threw it in the crowd. You never seen so many old timers kissin' and rubbin' each other, like holdin' their women real tight and sneakin' feels.

When we sat down again, our chairs were totally wet from beer. But we didn't care. Some people got on our table and we had to talk with their legs like trees in our face. A guy wiped out on the floor by us, but people just picked him up, rubbed him off and he went to get more booze.

The whole night went like this. We would talk...Dana would say, "What you want to do?" And I would say, "I don't really know." Then she'd say, "You would be good *sicko analog*." Later she changed her mind. "No. No, Endee. I believe it, you become good dog doctor." Ten minutes later she came up with another one, "No, Endee. *Yezus Mariya,* I know...you should build kindergarten." Then we would laugh and hit the sauce. Some song would come on, like *Bye Bye Miss American Pie* (that was even a bigger hit than *Money*) and we would go dancin' on the fireplace.

Even though that place was a total crazyhouse, we weren't allowed to smoke in the bar. Everybody went on them black and gold stairs by the front. So me and Dana were rollin' some *Samson Ultra Milde Shag,* our clothes a total mess of beer, sweat and gum, and we were *ripped.* I was tellin' her about it. "Like...I always thought about openin' a bar. Like one with hip hop and rock bands. Or I was thinkin' about a travel agent. But pretty soon computers are gonna get them fired from all their jobs."

She snuck in real close to me and rolled a smoke all lopsided so it looked like a fat minnow.

"Dude, I thought I could be a tour guide. Like in English." I made this microphone voice, "*This is Vilnius, land of Absinthe Fairies. Land where you can make some beers. Where it's opera singers.*"

"Where is matches?"

"*And down there is Suokalbis.*"

"Endee, *Suokalbis, blet.* Talk better. *Suo, Suo,* not Sock Ulbis. Where is matches?"

I gave them to her. She smoked her weird minnow, like a cig with a belly, and we just looked at each other all sweaty and messy. When half her cigarette was finished, she said, "Tell me true."

"What true?"

"True from today. At concert. Because your face, why was red?"

"*My* face?"

"Endee, you. Your face red with eyes, like this, with eyes. Why?"

I ashed over the railing. "Dana...I got sloppy."

"No...but tell why?"

"Dude...cauze. Cauze I get sloppy from shit. Like from the song."

Now she got pink. "From song? Really, from song?" And she snuck even closer by me and started talkin' real fast. "I thought you don't come. Because I wanted call. I'm sorry I don't call. Sometimes I too proud. But I told Raimis."

"Yeah?"

"So...from song. Really, from song? You know, Endee, I have some money. You can stay with me...I don't care. I pay for you, you so thin, don't eat good foods. Until I go Indiana. And then, if you want. Oh!" Suddenly she put her hand on her mouth real tight. Then she covered both her ears and closed her eyes, "Mm. Accident, accident. Drunk girl." She hopped down the stairs and ran out the bar.

Dude, I chased her down. She was so embarrassed, standin' by this totally crumbled up brick wall. I said, "Hey, don't run."

"Sorry. Sorry."

"Why you runnin'?"

Her mouth went like a motor, total babble trip. "I don't mean you chase me. No, I don't say *if* you want to...no, I mean if you *want*...yes, sure. Don't mean you go Indiana just because I go. No! Don't think, Endee, don't think *she so selfish, she so selfish. Want me wait for her.* American boy, he can have anybody, go every place. But, yes, why...because right now what you must to do? What you have, not children or job...you can be here. You can stay."

Now you have to picture it cauze it was perfect. We were standin' by this brick wall and Dana just kept on babblin'...she had to do it or she was gonna cry. Then behind me I heard this cough. I turned and it was frickin' Holy Moses comin' up to us with a smoke in his hand and lookin' for a light. He said some shit and went stumblin' around, though finally he came up by me and went "Kheh, kheh humf." Then that dude just sat down in the middle of the street with that smoke kinda movin' around in the air.

Dana said, "You see. Because here is everyone idiot."

"That guy's all right."

"No. You don't like here. You want go *Birvin*."

I took her one hand. And I was actually kinda laughin'. "Dana. Not *Birvin*. It's Berwyn. Talk better. Say Berwyn."

"*Birvin*."

"See. Also some stuff you can't say." Then I laughed real quiet, kinda imitatin' her voice. "Now don't be *engry*. Don't be *engry*."

"*Nu*...why you say this?"

"Shh. Don't be *engry*." I took one of her fingers and put it on, though it was too big.

She looked. "What it is? A round? Why you give me round?" It was the only ring I could find in the whole city for free, just one of them from the train parts. The thing was some dark metal, though I polished it up real good and clean. "What this rubbish? A round from rubbish? Endee, what kind round this is?"

"It's a ring, Dana."

She stared at it dumb fuck confused. "But what this means? No, because you say me. What it means?"

In-Laws

Dude, I hate weddings. I guess your gonna say I can't talk since I never got invited to no wedding before. But I seen lots of them Meg Ryan movies where you need a barf bucket just to watch it. And I went to prom night my frickin' junior year where the only reason they invented prom was for wedding practice. I know weddings get way more swank compared with prom, like real flowers instead of plastic and you don't have to hide your booze in the trunk, frickin' make sex in the limo. Weddings get more romantic than that, though lots of people still have them in a church right by one of them Jesus statues with all his ribs and blood. That ain't romantic in my book, just tweaked and fucked up.

I was still kinda ready to get converted to religion if Dana's family would of wanted. But gettin' married with a divorced girl is a total score. The family already made a serious deal one time with a huge wedding that backfired real bad, so nobody was gonna shell out again, especially since Dana needed cash for opera school. The family didn't need to waste no more from the savings (like they were savin' since she was little to pay for a good school). So our wedding was gonna be fast, simple and real cheap. The only thing we needed first was the stamp of approval from Dana's great uncle, Dėdė Liudas, and her mom, Ponia Grybienė.

I already seen Dėdė Liudas and Ponia Grybienė together one time. They were them people drinkin' tea in the kitchen when I came from the attic...the mom was the lady with long gray hair. Probably a different mom would of got pissed, said *who the hell is this guy*? But Dana's mom ain't that way. Before I even came to Nida, Dana already told her she met this "American boy" and she was tryin' to forget about him since he was gonna leave.

Here's the thing...Ponia Grybienė is totally one of them spiritualized people, like she thinks she can read minds and see the future. It started when Dana's dad drowned in the sea and Ponia Grybienė ended up good friends with a meditation teacher. That teacher gave books about Buddhism and Hindu, plus this old Lithuanian religion called Pagan. Maybe Ponia Grybienė took that stuff way too serious cauze she started believin' she's a magic healer and a witch...like she would get dream predictions from ghosts talkin' with her. Frickin' her dead husband and other people from the olden days like knights and dead farmers.

Dude, I totally had to get prepared for this shit. We were goin' back to Nida cauze Dana's mom was gonna check me out with Pagan. For real, a first grader could of looked at me and said I'm homeless without no job and I do way too much booze and drugs, so nobody should marry me, unless you hate yourself. But Ponia Grybienė totally needed better information than that, stuff only ghosts could tell. I kept askin' Dana what all this means, like what would happen, but she just rolled her eyes about it. "Endee, my mama crazy because she sad and alone. But she only crazy, not stupid."

When we came back to Nida, Ponia Grybienė was dressed with this orange and blue swirly shirt, plus she had her gray hair in a nice pony tail. In the daytime Dėdė Liudas looked super old (he was 91) and real wrinkled up. When he shaked my hand his fingers were hard and strong like iron grip, but also you could feel he was totally a gentle guy, especially when you seen the way he played with Tepti. He said Tepti was a real dumb name, so he called him Mikis, gave the boy a huge hambone to chew, then mushed some old bread for him with sour milk.

It was rainin' pretty hard so we hung in the kitchen, drank this real strong tea called Yerba. In the beginning Dana's mom was quiet, just watched me with her light blue eyes and real thin face. Dėdė Liudas only stayed like 3 or 4 hours with me...like he said that's all he needed. For real, all his hard questions went to Dana and she never gave me no translation. It was real intense to watch her explainin' stuff to him, since lots of deep feelings came out on her face.

Dėdė Liudas wanted to tell me stuff to see my reaction, so Dana had to translate a couple things. He told me, *Endee, our Dana do not need man for support. Because she smart, have strong family, very big one without hungry people.* This was real important for him to say lots of times, *Our family is many musicians, but not even one hungry person.* Later on Dana told how Dėdė Liudas was a prisoner in this place called Siberia, which is the cold lands where Russia put prisons. For five years out there he had some real rough times. Talkin' to Dana again for a while, Dėdė Liudas made sure she told me one thing. *Endee, you will never be hungry. Your all life you will be having food. For good home, one bread on table every day is enough. But give bread to fool, he will say "Where is butter?" Because fool cannot be happy.*

Pretty soon after that Dėdė Liudas left us alone with Ponia Grybienė. Probably he seen how she was gettin' impatient to do her Pagan...you could totally tell he thought that stuff was weird so he went to listen to the radio. And with him gone the mood changed...now nobody was talkin' nothin' at all, only Ponia Grybienė was starin' at me real soft and gettin' messages from the ghosts. Then she started tellin' me stuff, makin' sure Dana translated all the parts.

It was real mixed up without no order. First she said my dad's still alive and I'll see him again someday. Also (and this was real important for her) in another life I used to be Lithuanian, that's why I fell in love with Dana. But I had to be real careful cauze I got Polish blood and this can mess stuff up, though she didn't say how. To help deal with my Polish blood I should read more books, especially smart ones about young guys who learn truth (which was totally her favorite word). She said the main reason I can't get a job is cauze I don't sleep enough. Someday I would burn myself real bad and I would remember Ponia Grybienė. That day I had to make sure no strangers talked with me.

Ponia Grybienė was gonna say more, but Dana got real sick of translatin', almost pissed off about it. So her mom went quiet, just reached my hand to press. Then she looked at Dana and I had a crazyass moment right there, like a real intense one. Her smile went straight through my whole body, cauze it was the *exact* same smile like Dana gave by Big Head's pond...definitely 100% no bullshit the *exact* same face and look, only older with wrinkles, gray hair and them eyes light blue like a baby blanket. That was the first time I could feel the big difference between a girlfriend and a wife, like how a wife would get old if you don't fuck it up. It made me feel advanced and more grown up, like I could see one thing that used to be invisible.

I thought we were done. But now Ponia Grybienė busted out the real Pagan stuff. It was a little pan with wax and a water pot, plus a bag with some dry brown herbs and branches. Dana got annoyed, but Ponia Grybienė was lightin' candles real serious and warmin' the wax till it went liquid. She made me pick from a deck and I got the seven of spades. Then she shuffled it up one more time, squeezed the herbs, said some mumblings to Dana and picked four more cards. Them herbs got sprinkled on the wax and she poured it smokin' hot in the cool water. It made shapes in there, a bunch of goops and gobbs.

Dana had to look in them goops and tell what she seen, the same like one of them shrink tests. She said it was a butterfly and some real thin fingers. So now Ponia Grybienė picked four more cards and looked at them real careful. She poured more wax in the water and then it was my turn to look at them gobbs. But the first thing I thought was it looks like diarrhea. Then I seen a couple butt cracks and cleavage...no matter how bad I tried I couldn't see nothing different from that. The girls were waitin' for me, totally starin' at me with pressure. So I told Dana, "It's another moon in there. Like a banana shape."

Ponia Grybienė thought this was totally hardcore. Cauze the moon had lots of meanings and she talked all this stuff, pointin' at cards and gettin' real excited, touchin' my hand real soft. It took maybe ten minutes to explain the moon in the wax, how it went connected with a butterfly and thin fingers, but Dana didn't translate them details. She only told me, "Endee, very good. Because it means together we very good couple."

So that was it right there. The official stamp of approval. The next day we had a small lunch with some relatives and Dėdė Liudas got kinda emotional, maybe a little bit wasted. He busted out the shiny accordion and sang some songs. Later on he poured some homemade *samagonas*, which is like Lithuanian moonshine, maybe 8000 proof with pine sticks in the bottle for spice. Dude, fifty grams of that stuff blew me and Dana over the dune, then Dėdė Liudas kissed my forehead and squeezed my ears. For him this was totally a good marriage ceremony without no huge party, cousins or any frickin' Pagan.

He wasn't gonna go back to Vilnius with us cauze he said it's a dump, real loud and only liars. But Ponia Grybienė came on the bus. You should of seen how pretty she got dressed, like an amber necklace and earrings, plus a real flowing dress made from gray linen, which is this special Lithuanian cloth. When Dana wasn't lookin', Ponia Grybienė got kinda sneaky and gave me a small cloth sack. In there she put two amber rings, like the same ones when she married Dana's dad. I guess I looked shocked, maybe unsure, but she told me with her real rough accent, "Pliz pliz. Yiss yiss. Fir you." The ring I made out from train parts just got stashed someplace in a little box.

Me and Dana got married on Sept. 21, 2006 in this real small office. You could see the Neris river from the window and a hill with trees. Raimis was my witness since he lost the coin flip with Varna. When I busted out them amber rings, Dana got water eyes, though also she turned real proud. We signed all the papers, paid like a hondo and Varna took some pictures. Then we all went by this cafe called Ramovė since it was the main hangout in Vilnius for singers. A bunch of Dana's family and other musicians came by so people totally sang booze songs for maybe four hours straight. After that we did it Vilnius style, goin' by ŠMC and Suokalbis and Double Coffee till the sun came up a bright white heat ball.

Me and Dana totally had a plan. I was gonna go by myself to Bloomington to get a job and set up a place where we could live. I never been to Bloomington and didn't know nothing about it, but that didn't matter. Gettin' married with Dana, I felt real different, like I could totally pull stuff off without messin' up. She was gonna come after she got her visa, and then would do her audition for Jacob's School in March. If she didn't get in Jacob's, we would try another place and move wherever. Cauze I totally didn't care where it would be.

I left Vilnius almost right away on Sept. 28, 2006. It was just a couple more nights with Raimis and Varna at ŠMC...they said they would come to America and visit us for sure. Me and Dana and Tepti had this hardcore good-bye in the airport, though we didn't make no sloppy scene. Totally trustin' me, she gave a thousand bucks from her family savings. And then that was it...I wasn't gonna see her till she got a visa, which the embassy said would take a couple months.

But it took way longer than that. Homeland Security does that shit on purpose cauze they hope you give up tryin' to bring your wife. Dude, we totally gave up on Tepti cauze it would of cost too much money...Dana left him with Dėdė Liudas in Nida. It took four longass months with phone calls, letters, paperwork, cash and bullshit for them finally to give her the visa. They wouldn't even let her in for Christmas cauze George Bush knew about a secret Lithuanian plan where opera singers blow up New York. Dana frickin' missed my 21st birthday, though she came about a week later on January 30th, 2007. By then it was already hardcore winter in Bloomington, like wind and ice.

Dude, my eyes opened up to lots of stuff during them four months in Bloomington. For real, I thought maybe we made a big mistake comin' to Indiana cauze Dana was probably gonna hate it. Compared with Vilnius, most stuff seemed real ugly and felt totally weird. If you never been away from the USA for a while, then you don't know about it, how comin' back is a total trip, sometimes real fucked up. You get off the plane and it's a total shock right away too see the fat people...the cabbie *and* the waitress *and* the guy at the Motel 6 who's way too big for his chair. Then a whole family can't fit in no booth at Denny's, though they get extra large fries and ice cream. It just don't seem normal...how come it happened? How come it's so many people like that?

It was only five days for me in Bloomington when I took the first job somebody offered. It was a late shift waiter at a fast food joint, though I won't give that dump no free advertisements, just call them Beefin' Cream. At first it was fine since the pay was eight or ten bucks sometimes with tips, but pretty soon my boss started gettin' on my nerves. He had two stickers on his Ford Ranger...one was that fish that's supposed to be Jesus, but another one said *Immigration control courtesy of .357 Magnum*. He told me I'm a traitor for gettin' married with an immigrant wife, though not so bad since at least Dana was white. That guy was one of them dudes who thinks your gay just cauze your smarter than him. Like if you ride a bike to save money on gas and a car payment, then your gay. Though if you got a Ford Excursion with a gun and a Jesus sticker, plus your white and pay your child support on time and eat too much and never go noplace outside LaFayette County, then your perfect and God loves you. Maybe it would be normal if I met a homeless dude under a bridge who talked stupid crap like that. But this tool was my fuckin' boss. My frickin' MANAGER.

My landlord was this real old hippy, like white hair, pechooli in his armpits, some shirts from Woodstock and the Filmore, and he told bullshit stories how he partied with Pig Pen and Janis in Vegas. But also he rented me a decent studio down Kirkwood, maybe six blocks from Jacob's School and right by a BP. The apartment cost 390 and had real tall windows, plus a balcony, though the only thing you could see over there was the gas station.

Sometimes one thin tweaker dude who worked there would wave at me if he went for a smoke.

People think Bloomington is just hippy vegans who shop by organic stores. There's definitely lots of stuff like that, mostly in the neighborhood by Indiana University and Jacob's School. But other parts from town get ghetto, frickin' jacked up woofers in trunks to vibrate your whole apartment. And lots of them people who come by Beefin' Cream at 3:00 am totally think the same like my boss, cauze I would hear conversations at tables. The thing is, I could say anykind of stuff I want about them people...but they all had better jobs compared with me. Or they had parents bustin' out for them to be frat boys so they could stiff the waiter and act hardcore. Eatin' at Beefin' Cream is way better compared with workin' for a guy who talks smack about your wife. A guy where so much shit makes him unsecure so he just puts it down.

And it was workin'. The more time went by with Homeland Security makin' delays, the more I kept thinkin' Dana didn't really know who she got married with. It was gonna be a shock for her...how come I didn't explain better about the USA? If your livin' in Vilnius, you don't got no way to understand Bloomington or Berwyn, people like Gunther, my mom and my boss. Talkin' to Dana on the phone, I pretended I was feelin' normal, explained how I got furniture for the place, a rug and some drapes. But I didn't tell how I was feelin' wiped out workin' where I hated it and couldn't find nothing better. I knew I'm a trash kid from Berwyn with a fat mom and a tweaker sister, a dad who's run off. For real, I didn't even call Jen or mom to say I'm in Bloomington or send some e-mail. I knew they would say I'm frickin' the same like dad, a guy who takes off and never calls home, and I would know they were right.

The day I picked up Dana was totally freezing, so the Indy airport (it's 45 minutes from Bloomington) had lots of delays and I had to wait a couple hours. I kinda forgot how small Dana was...her hair grew totally different, more long, and she had new clothes with a coat and gloves. She seen me and turned real pink...no matter what we did, she wouldn't stop talkin' even though she was dead tired.

"*Nu* Endee, how far from here is Jacob's? We take bus? Not so long to wait, fifteen minute. *Oi*, look how nice this bus...feel chair, how comfortable. Look outside, now snowing. *Blet*, where you think this lady get so good coat? I need also so good like this. *Look*...over there big cars from movie...this one is Cadillac? Very pretty this road...why you don't say Indiana is hills...so big farms and so much land. Already this is Bloomington? But where is Jacob's? *Oi*...this our house? *This* one? Endee, how you find so big? So nice our flat with curtain. And smart, next door by petrol store...it work all night? Very good because when I run out of tampon or need ketchup. And they have toilet paper?"

Dude, Dana totally thought Beefin' Cream was good food, especially the beans and chili. Takin' a walk down Kirkwood one day, she thought the homeless dudes were frickin' high class. "So polite. And clean, not even drunk. Without bandage or broken foots." The only stuff she hated was toast bread, French's Yellow Mustard, Lipton tea and diner coffee. She also got real confused in the hippy store when she seen veggie dogs. "Because stupid. Someplace they make carrot from sausage?"

Like two weeks after she showed up, Dana got a job pourin' cokes and makin' popcorn at the movie theater. Every day she practiced her opera hardcore so people down the block knew a singer moved in. Dude, I didn't even know how March came so fast and it was audition time. Frickin' she was crazy nervous, but Dana didn't have no problem gettin' in Jacob's...they gave her half-off tuition and all them professors went e-mailin' her to join their class. You should of heard how happy she got tellin' her mom on the phone, totally proud and bright pink.

The whole time till March came, Dana was talkin' how we needed to see Berwyn, though I tried not to think about it. We kinda got in a big argument about it, a good one with screamin', and I said I don't want to talk about it no more. Dana didn't say nothin' more till the audition was finished. But when it was done, finally she didn't have no stress and just said it was time to take a trip. Frickin' in the library she found books about Chicago, like travel guides with bar lists, stories about gangsters and butcher shops. For real, she learned all these questions I couldn't even answer. "Hemingway's house in Oak Park...this is same Oak Park where Audra live? What about Maxwell Street Market, why they close down? Endee, why Berwyn have most banks in whole world? You never say about banks." One of them guidebooks showed *The Berwyn Spindle*, like this stupid pole with five cars stuck on it, kinda like a *shush likas* made from cars. Dana totally wanted to check it out.

The thing is, I kept sayin' my boss would never give me no week off, plus it was too expensive for us to go. So Dana got sick of my ass one day and just frickin' went on the internet, bought cheap tickets for Megabus. "We need holiday, Endee. And finally we meet your family." I said stuff about my boss and job, but she said, "Fuck that *debilas*. I hate so much you work that place. Who cares, because we have money or my mama will send. After holiday, you get better job. Call boss today, say him *fuck you*. Yes, because if not then I will call. Believe me, I will do."

Dude, it kinda came outta nowhere one day when I quit and we were goin' up to Chicago, like late March, 2007, the Megabus goin' up frickin' I-65. I thought I would be pissed off and scared, but it totally felt like freedom. A surprise for me cauze I was seein' stuff totally different from ever before in my life, more the way Dana seen it where it was brand new. When the bus went up the Skyway and Lake Shore Drive, Lake Michigan was this awesome thing...a couple ice chunks still floatin' out by the lighthouses and the sun makin' white and blue shimmers. Then we drove in downtown by all them tall buildings and the river with drawbridges. People were walkin' so fast all around in the cold day and a million cars went drivin' all over. I totally forgot the rush and the noise in Chicago, the hard ass wind when you go around a building.

Me and Dana got beds at this youth hostel on Wabash. At first it was kinda weird cauze Dana was showin' *me* around for a couple days with them guidebooks. She totally fell in love with the city...like the harbor and Museum Campus...the John Hancock and Union Station. The el went rumblin' over our heads and she thought it sounded totally hardcore. Even though we didn't get no opera tickets, we found the company and seen the building. I showed her The 3rd Coast, that cafe where me and Audra ate cheese for a ripoff. Drinkin' strong coffee, Dana almost got pissed at me, "Why you never say your city so beautiful? *Look* this cafe. Why you never say?"

"Dude, this ain't really my city. Cauze Berwyn's real different."

"*Nu*, we go tomorrow. You call your mom today."

I was real quiet. "It's better we don't call, Dana. If you wanna go."

"Why?"

I shaked my head. "Cauze I don't want no guilt trip. It's better we just show up."

"But she must to get ready."

I just shaked my head. "Trust me on it, Dana. It's simple, but also it's real complicated."

The next day we took the Metra train down the Burlington Northern, sat up on top the double decker by the green windows. The train passed the West Side where I know Dana never seen nothing like it, all the busted up houses and them back yards filled up with wood and tires or other junk...frickin' factories, some land trashed with car parts and metal. She watched it all dead quiet, sometimes her eyes goin' real big. But then we got by Cicero where it's a huge train yard, then little bungalows or two-flats. We passed MacNeal hospital and the shack by the tracks in Berwyn. Me and Dana got off at Harlem Avenue, walked by the same restaurant where Audra bought me Long Island Iced Teas. And I showed the way down to my mom's house.

All the houses looked like castles for her. "Bigger like in Bloomington. This one is only one family?" Her mouth opened up when she seen my mom's house...like I never thought about it, but the frickin' porch was almost bigger than her whole cabin in Nida.

And I could feel how she got edged. "How much money she get in bakery?"

I told her, "The house is real different on the inside, Dana."

Gram was totally home like always. She was watchin' *The Price is Right* in the front room and drinkin' hot tea with sugar and Clan McGreggor. Dana got a little pink to meet her even though gram didn't make no big deal that I'm home. She just said, "Welcome along. Look who's back with the wind." Dana didn't know where to sit or really how to move cauze the place was a mess. Greasy plates and nasty cups with fingerprints, dust on the tables...newspapers all over and the old cigarette smell. The coffee table had a pile of butts in mom's big ass ashtray and right by that was a can of peanuts. The carpet didn't get vacuumed and somebody left a pizza box on the floor with dry crusts. Lots of furniture got pushed crooked, like one chair knocked sideways. When it was commercials, grandma finished her tea and said, "Who's the princess?"

I told her, "This is Dana, gram. She's...like me and her got married."

"Oh yeah? Well that's news. Low and hello to you." Gram held out a hand and Dana squeezed it. Then gram cleaned her eye glasses a little with a sleeve. "Now what's your name?"

"Dana."

"Well. A real pretty one." Gram looked at her for a good while. "But where you meet Andrew?"

"In Vilnius."

"Hm, where?"

"Vilnius."

"Yeh? And where's at?"

"In my country. In Lithuania."

"Oh, where?"

Dude, grandma didn't know where I was gone for like nine months and she gave a hoot's ass. We sat around with the TV blastin' and heard her tell the story how Jen ran away from Gunther's place and got put in rehab. She wasn't takin' no speed typing or GED classes at Sterling College. I asked, but gram didn't know no stories about handguns or if Jen got a Glock. I said "Where's mom?"

"Works different job now. Walgreen's. Took the car to change oil, though should be back soon."

Dana was real uncomfortable sittin' on the edge of the sofa where it was totally covered with cat hair. And she kept tryin' not to look around even though her eyes were flyin' all over the place. Never ever *ever* in all her most wildass dreams could she figure two women lived someplace without never cleanin' up. She just kinda whispered to me, "*Nu blet.*"

Gram said, "Be a dear, Andrew. Boil water and make tea my way, yeah? Just bring me the sugar. And Diana, you wanna high ball? Or Irish cream?"

"No, thank you. No, really really, thank you."

"Mm, fine fine. Won't force nothin'."

I was in the kitchen tryin' to find the tea bags. It took me a while to boil the water and Dana was talkin' to gram about weather, like how long till Chicago gets spring. When the water was already near boiled I heard the door close and a long pause when mom came home. She was breathin' pretty hard. "Oh...yeah, hello. Who're you?"

"Hello. I'm Dana."

"You from them new neighbors?"

Grandma said, "We gotta visitor, Betty."

I came in holdin' grandma's drink and the sugar bowl. There was a place by gram's arm where I put the drink. Mom was sweaty and still breathin' pretty hard, dressed with real huge sweat pants and a yellow hoodie. Her face was red and shakin' a little, but when she seen me she got still and said, "Well...well, will ya lookit that?" Mom kinda kicked her boots off by one of them rubber mats. "Will *you* lookit *that?*"

"Hi, mom," I said. "It's...I'm here. I come back."

"Won't you bet it? Won't you bet your sweet ass? Cauze the cat stopped draggin' in maybe a year ago."

Dana came over by me. "This is Dana," I said. "Since September. She's my wife."

"Your what?"

"My wife."

Mom laughed real sick with a knuckle on her mouth and her eyes kinda watered. Dana said, "Please to meet you," but mama stared at her like it's all a big joke. She said, "You meet her out there, Drew? 'Nother Lugan?"

I nodded.

"So what you want here, Drew?"

"I come back. Just come back..."

Mom interrupted, "Your not livin' here. Not no couple people extra. Better get that crap outta your head straight." She looked through her purse for smokes. "And forget stayin' with Jen cauze she ain't at Gunther's no more." It took her maybe four tries to light the lighter. "Where you livin'?"

I said, "We got a place."

"Where?"

"Indiana."

"Oh...*Indiana*, oh? Where's the other one? Where's rich missy? You dump the rich one for *her*?"

Dude, right there Dana got talkin'. She started out real slow, "*Oi*...no. Not Endee dump, no. The another one, you mean Audra...yes? Yes, because first she *my* girlfriend, like old girlfriend. But becomes boring for me, so I dump. Yes, dump for *him*." Dana smiled kinda sneaky, shruggin' a little.

"Well, that's a wise cracker. He brung a wise cracker. Sweetie, look who's gonna be laughin' last. Cauze you don't know even what your talkin'. Know where your hubby's been? The kid's lied to you. What you tryin' to get from him anyways?"

"Get?"

"What's he tellin' you?"

"Tell?" She gave me this confused look. "But this mistake, because not tell. No, I see myself. Yes, woh, like this," she made a fist. "Yes, so big. Yes Hancock. John Han*cock*. Top so high. Because all my life I never see so big like this one."

I had no idea what the hell to do and just bit inside my mouth. Mom said, "Oh...ain't you brung me a treat, Drew? And ain't you just a sweet Dairy Queen?" Mom kinda slumped down on the sofa with her Basic 100. Like usual when she got pissed, the smoke came out from her whole face. "You gotta job, Drew?"

"Not no more."

"Mm, hm mm," she was smokin'. "Not no more?"

"Who cares what I got, mom? I came so you could meet Dana. I ain't gonna take nothin' away from you."

"No. But your sweetie here's got shit to give." Mom ashed. "You know Jen's in rehab?"

Gram said, "I tell 'em." She was lookin' at the blarin' tube, kinda leanin' on one side. Mom looked at me for a real long time and shaked her head a little. She said, "Ain't gonna be cheap." She was holdin' the cig stickin' out by her temple, like her whole hand on a cheek.

Gram coughed real loud and totally fake.

Mom asked, "Who'd you invite to your weddin'?"

Dana said, "*Nu* small, very small. Like this, on table, like peanut. Really, small little *pea*nut wedding. Without salt."

I kinda pinched Dana's pinky. "Mom, it was just at the justice of the peace."

"You did it out there?"

"Oh yes," said Dana. "We did. Because I like to do."

Everybody was quiet with me bitin' my mouth even harder and grandma slurpin' her tea pretty damn loud. On TV some guy was tryin' to guess the showcase and all his friends were jumpin' up and down. Mom said, "You know what's waitin' for you, Drew? Cauze this little wise cracker knows it. You sign a 'nuptual?"

"No, mom. We didn't sign nothin'. Cauze we ain't gettin' divorced."

"No!" She wiped her mouth with her hand. "No no, cauze you *never* mess nothin' up. Never wet your bed, not once. You wait. Just wait. Cauze when she gets her green card, then we'll see, and it ain't gonna be your decision. Sweetie gets her green card, she'll be gone. Your naive, Drew. This one here knows it...the only reason she's with a nobody." Mom finished her smoke. "If you'd listen for once, you'd be somethin', at least with a job. But you just keep wettin' your bed, Drew." She went by the bathroom and we heard the shower go runnin' in there.

I didn't really have no time to feel them words cauze grandma put her tea down. And for the first time since I can frickin' remember, she picked up the remote and shut the tube. Gram poured a little more Clan in her tea, took a sip and stood up real difficult. But then she came up and grabbed our wrists, whisperin' a little closer to me, "Andrew." She was kinda smilin'. "And Diana. Between you guys and me. Shh, shh, cauze lemme say it."

I leaned toward her.

"Andrew, your ma's a bitch." She shaked her head. "Wishes she ain't. But Betty's been wishin' since kindergarten, will keep right on wishin' till she's pushin' daisies." Right there she pressed my hand real hard...I didn't even know she was that strong. She looked at Dana. "But you, Diane, your a star. That was quality. You got me on your side...don't never let nobody give you shit. Maybe teach Andrew about that since he needs backbone."

Now she bent down and took the sugar bowl. She waited a bit, almost like she got unsure about an idea. But real fast I seen her turn soft and quiet, just starin' at the thing kinda sad. "I wanna give you somethin'," she said and winked at me. "You guys in a hurry someplace?"

"No, gram."

She pinched her chin real hard. "Make more tea my way. Then come back at seven cauze your ma's gonna be gone. And I wanna show you some things."

Small World

I won't never forget the way gram looked at that bowl right there. It's like one of them moments you get when somebody you know real good kinda changes in front of your face. They show they got something inside and it's gonna come out soon if your ready for it. For real, that's kind of exciting though also you get worried.

Me and Dana went for a walk around Berwyn, like down Proksa Park, then back to Windsor where they got a place to get coffee. Dana already knew the story, how I used to pee. And we talked about it real easy in my normal voice, like people at the next seat would of heard if they cared. Cauze all of a sudden that shit wasn't even important no more, just one more story from my life. The same like meetin' Tepti under a bridge or gettin' my ass kicked at the dance bar. Like meetin' Audra in the laundry or sellin' weed to Big Beard.

Gram was real mellowed out when we came back at seven...maybe she forgot to expect us. But so soon when we came in she turned off the tube and made sure me and Dana had some Clan and Lipton. Without wastin' no time with smalltalk, she said "Who's got the locket?"

"*Your* locket, gram?"

"My locket. Where's it at?"

"Probably still in the bowl."

"Well...fish it out. Diane, your hands are smaller."

All my life since I was a kid, I knew gram's sugar bowl had them two things in there...a diamond ring from her wedding and a gold locket. The ring didn't fit her no more since her hands got swelled, and the diamond was real small, worth maybe a couple hundred bucks. In the locket she only had my grandad's picture. Gram said, "Drew, open it. Open it total, cauze you gotta take out that pic."

I was maybe nine or ten years old the last time I seen that photo. It shows my grandad wearin' one of them old school White Sox caps, like a real mellow smile on his face. When Dana seen it, she said, "Endee, he look like you." It was kinda true...I had a thin nose like him and light brown eyes.

Openin' the locket was real hard, but grandma wasn't gonna touch it...she barely even looked at me. We finally got the little pic out and it fluttered down by the coffee table. "Look on back there, Andrew." Dana looked first and seen three numbers in handwriting...31-7-27. "Is that a date or something, gram?"

"No, Drew. It's a combination."

Right there I totally felt this electric buzz go up my neck. Cauze I frickin' knew exactly what the combination was for. Gram must of seen the look on my face cauze she didn't need to explain, just said, "Andrew, go up there and bring it down." Me and Dana went up the dustyass and stuffy attic, all the way to the back where it was an old dresser with a broke mirror. That's where gram had a box stashed in a drawer that screeched real loud. The box was real rough wood, a brass latch with a padlock. Lots of times when I was little I wondered what was in there and would ask gram about it. But she always said, "It's empty in there."

"So how come it's locked?"

"In case somebody tries puttin' a thing where it don't belong. Or wants to see what's empty in there."

The box wasn't that heavy but Dana wanted to help carry it down. When we opened it up gram touched all the things like they could break. Her box was full of family stuff, like a small photo album with her relatives, plus grandad's things from back in the day. An old stamp collection, two boxes of baseball cards...1965 and 1967, then a pile of collected things...a 35mm camera, this real smooth harmonica, a money clip and cuff links. All the way on the bottom of the box something was folded up in cloth...it was a big frame photo with gram and grandad sittin' by a tree. They were real young, like she was younger than Dana. You couldn't tell in the picture, but she was already pregnant with mom and wore a real pretty dress with yellow flowers. Grandad had his soldier uniform, probably a real short time before gettin' shipped to Vietnam.

Way at the bottom of the box grandma stashed some letters he sent home when he was gone. She made sure I didn't let her see them letters. "You read later...just keep all of 'em in there now and don't rustle. Don't make no noise with it." It was a good stack, maybe 25 or 30 letters tied up with fishing line. Gram said, "Just tuck it back in there and look later. It's a wedding present for you. From me to you so you keep it. And the locket and my ring too. Only leave the sugar bowl for me. Cauze a lady needs her fix."

The rest of the night was real weird. Drinkin' hot tea with just a little Clan gets you buzzed quick, and gram was sippin' away already for like 8 hours (and 20 years). I seen her get some trouble movin' to lift the cup cauze her one hand got the shivers pretty bad. But she kept takin' off her glasses and wipin' her eyes...a couple of times she tried to talk. "Andrew." Gram was quiet for a couple minutes. "Diana..." We nodded or inched a little more near by her. "Andrew and Diana, I ain't handin' over this just for a burden on you. Not no hard feelings or to force some shit. Won't pretend it's an easy thing I'm sharin' along. Just I want you to know what it is, cauze it's somethin' real." She sat way back in her chair and hid the shakin' hand under her sweatshirt. "You listen to me. Cauze if you get kids. At the right time...you should get some. Not right away, not now...but I can tell your smart, Diane. And later on when them kids get ready and wise up, you should let them see in the box. So they know what can happen to somebody. And so Kenny don't die total."

Me and Dana peeked in them letters the first time at the Metra station. We were totally like a couple kids tearin' a hole in a

Christmas present. Readin' the first letter, that thing sucked our asses in so we almost missed the train. We were readin' in the youth hostel and the Megabus to Bloomington...for three or four days it was just them letters...some I read over and over and over till they were almost memorized. Lots of times me and Dana couldn't even talk after we read them. Just sat on the balcony with herb tea and looked at cars tankin' up.

The same way like I organized Audra's notebooks, the numbers here don't mean nothing. The only thing you gotta know, they got wrote from around May 1970 to September 1971. Also I had to change one name to "Larry" or "Lawrence." You'll understand why when you get to the end.

1

Ellyn, so damn beautiful out here. It's a pressure cooker by day, but at night the temperture gets down about 60° for a little relief. The white moonlight's making the paper glow and there's a low thick fog about knee-high, very eerie. The jungle sounds with birds and insects you never heard before, but some of the guys say it's cats. All together it's very special and fits somehow.

Sorry to hear your back keeps hurting. And your ankles have swollen more–I believe that. I think Betty is a wild gorgeous name for a girl. Beatrice. Make sure you tell them, put Beatrice on the birth certificate, not just Betty. But if we have a boy, I changed my mind about "Lawrence". There's a guy here (Larry) with that name and I hope I don't remember him when I meet my baby. Wish I could be there in the waiting room, wish with all my heart. It's weird because I'm nervous just writing. Smoked more cigarettes than normal. Maybe when you get this letter the baby's already born.

I know you will laugh, but I always liked the name Felix. Felix the cat, the wonderful wonderful cat. Something something magic tricks and something something kicks the sticks. Can you believe it? Just a month in Vietnam and already I forgot that song!

2

You remember how I wrote about Larry. After all the fines and extra duty, now he's been busted down to Private. If he got a dishonorable discharge he wouldn't even care, because his family is rich, his dad owns real estate all around Chicago. He gets extreme drunk and I think he might be on dope. Lots of guys are, it seems pretty normal, although one day they made a surprise inspection. Didn't find nothing which makes me think it's only charades. Doped up or busted down, it's all the same. When they need men they send them out to fight.

We've seen some crazy things in these months, worse than the last time I told you about. I'm definitely more jumpy and very very tired very often, and I've lost a ton of weight. Right now the worst is I'm constantly dirty and can't get clean. Either it's the rain or the mud or dust or the unbearable heat when you sweat and everything sticks to you. To your skin with chiggers.

I want you to send some newspaper clips about Kent State. A shock to hear about it, but I don't think we got the whole story out here. That's not what I'm fighting for. I don't know one single guy out here who's fighting for that. Nixon is crazy. That's what I'm fighting for. The freedom to say Nixon is crazy. NIXON IS CRAZY!!!

3

I got the pictures of Betty. All the guys think she's the sweetest thing, especially the picture on the rocking chair. That chair seems so large. She's starting to get your face. You should be pleased because that's the most beautiful face around. Don't think it's hard on me to get pictures sent. It's the opposite—you should keep a camera around all the time and send more.

I'm getting to know the people here, the Vietnamese Army. They are not paid very well, a little more than $30/month. We had Captain Brose go in with them and they did everything he said, followed all his orders, fought brave. But he got shot right through the collarbone and guts. The Vietnamese Army fought the NVA off—they dragged the Captain out, but not without first taking his watch and chain, going through every pocket. They took his rifle, pistol and boots, even his belt, all of that to sell. I got so full of rage I could have killed the next gook I saw. If I see one with his pistol. I'll know that pistol.

I do hate sometimes. Larry and I talk about it more and more–it's easier to talk with him than the others sometimes. In a way, he's realistic. He says hate is beautiful, hate keeps him awake on guard duty. There's no difference between hating the war and hating the people because war is their baby. Of course, we didn't make this war. We're trying to help. And they strip us once we're dead.

4

Something strange and very different now. I have to tell you. After you wrote with Betty's first birthday, when you helped her blow the candle. For two days I was thinking about this: how it would be great to count to three and blow. I could see it like a photo on the fridge and remember the cake like I was there even though I was here. Told Sean because he knows–he has two boys. We were talking about that just before going in a village today.

There were 2 VC in there, we knew about it for sure and went to get them. But it was me and Craig and Sean when we heard sounds from a little boat. We found a girl about 16 or 17, had only one leg. She was in labor with a shirt clumped in her mouth to muffle the noise, and to bite from the pain. We had a medic close by, so it was four guys, me and the medic and Sean and Craig and this scared girl who can't talk to us, can't understand us. We carried her and put her down better. You don't need 4 guys to deliver a baby but all of us stayed. It happened, she gave birth to a girl covered in slime and giving this crying scream. Very different from the scream when a guy's less than a minute from it, that's it...when he's gone and he knows it. But the baby doesn't know it yet. She didn't do wrong, not one single thing yet, but already she got born in hell.

Do you know what I thought? I saw the girl holding the kid. And I thought if you have any mercy in your blood you'll put a bullet in the baby's head, then the mom's. Because. because Because because because that's as close to painless as it ever gets. Ellyn, in your next letter please promise you won't ever hate me. Because I love you and Betty so very very much.

5

Yesterday for the first time ever in my life I prayed. It came out my chest like a shell through a wall. Mortar rounds and artillery, the sound, it can land anywhere. Anywhere anywhere, where's the next one? A shell went through the wall, through four feet and landed right across me, a dud, pure luck. Craig says don't write about it to your wife if you have any sense. When I saw a huge fireball I thought they hit our ammo dump. The VC are accurate with mortars. They don't have as many and each one has to count...

...You asked me to tell you something positive to help you believe. There are many men here, for example Craig is still a nationalist and a Christian, and Sean died believing in this war– Communism must not be allowed to spread–Jesus is Lord (He believed Buddhists in saffron robes go to hell)–America is the greatest country in the world. But Sean had never gone anywhere except the Philippines and here in Vietnam. When I said the South China Sea is more beautiful than Lake Michigan he called me all sorts of things I won't tell you. But he didn't ever see Lake Michigan. Sean didn't need to see, he only needed to believe. I know many people believe about the progress they read in the press. When people want to believe something, it's easy to convince them.

I want to believe Sean will rise three days from now. But he's been dead three weeks.

Right now, sweating here, the most postive thing I can tell you is that this war will end. And with some luck or Fate I'll be home with you and Betty. But Larry told me something I believe. He calls them "rich septic tanks" who figure how to profit from all this. After this war, they'll make another one just like it. When it comes to war, I won't believe any big difference between all the important ideologies. Every side has septic tanks. And everybody believes his country's the greatest in the world.

6

I wish I could write about the pound cake you sent. I shared it. Betty's such a pumpkin now. Actually, me and Larry devoured the cake in the pouring rain. We knew it wouldn't give us dysentery. *There's disease everywhere, anything you touch, everything's filthy. Craig's dead. I don't want to make you sad or sicken you. I won't send this out, though, so don't worry. We were in an ambush. It got so crazy you didn't know which way was back or forth. A lot of casualties, carry them out and thankfully it started getting dark. The problem is everyone's human, with costly mistakes. One day pan for gold in a river, the other day run through a whole village looking for 5 VC. The next day after that, an ambush has us pinned down for hours. We called in artillery, 105 mm howitzers. One of the rounds hit us right in the middle, guys in front and guys behind me and Larry. Shrapnel. Screaming and pieces of men, Craig fucked up bad but not a scratch on me and Larry.*

He used to say don't write about it to your wife if you have any sense. Write sensible. I want to make my own hammock by the garage. I'll teach Bet how to ride a bike in the alley. We'll have more kids, 15 or 20 and raise them good, read stories about a princess got saved by the hero and the Hardy Boys always solve the crime. But really what I want to do, I'll get a typewriter out on the back porch. To write a book. I already know the first sentence: My name is Kenny Briggs and let me promise you right now that everything in these pages is a lie. Except for one thing, if you saw what's true inside this man you'd only ever hate him. I was in the middle of it without a scratch. And up till now I haven't saved anyone or solved any crimes.

At the bottom of the stack we found a telegram. Real wrinkled up with a rip in the corner.

The Secretary of the Army has asked me to express his deep regret that your husband, Private First Class Kenneth O. Briggs was wounded in action...He received multiple wounds to the eyes and face, the chest, the abdomen and both arms. He is in a coma. He has been placed on the very seriously ill list and in the judgment of the attending physician his condition is of such severity that there is cause for concern...

Grandpa died not even two days after that telegram got sent, Sept 6, 1971. But that wasn't the thing that blew me through a wall. Sealed up real weird in a plastic bag was one more letter...it was from that guy "Larry". He typed up a real short note for grandma, just a few words. *Dear Mrs. Ellyn Briggs, I knew Ken back in 'Nam and remember stories about Ellyn and Betty.* Larry put his address and phone number in there, said *I would be very happy if you contacted me.* His letter got wrote in March 1982 with the war already done for like ten years. It had a pic stuck in there, grandad and Larry standin' by crates covered with some cloths and a couple tents behind them.

The first time I seen that picture, maybe I paid more attention to grandad. Cauze Dana noticed it first. "Endee...he look like my cousin." Like Big Head. Only younger with a super fat cowboy stash. I looked a little closer and said "Yeah, a bit. Real thin compared." But that was all, just some similar guy. Cauze there ain't no frickin' way in hell, no damn way on earth it can be anything different from that.

But the ice bucket hit me square in the face with all the hard cubes. I looked at the picture real close, checked the return address from Oak Park...it was somewhere on LeMoyne. And the real name on the letter...that was how Audra called him. It was the name I used to have in my cell phone, the name I called the guy when I sold him grass. Gram didn't even know it, she didn't know what she was givin' us. Cauze it was a picture of Big Beard in there, August 1971, like a month before grandad got wounded and died. Him standin' in Vietnam with Big Beard.

Larry

Here's the thing, I didn't know nothing about Vietnam. Gram didn't talk too much, just how grandad fought in a jungle and got killed over there, but nobody made no big deal about it. Gram told Jen she had pictures from Vietnam, and one time she told me I should never join the army...she didn't like nothing with war in it or no army movies, not even toy soldiers. Me and gram would watch DVD's a lot, though one time when I got *Full Metal Jacket* she couldn't watch it, just got up quiet and went to bed early. "That's not my cup of tea, Andrew."

I seen some of them movies like *Apocalypse Now* and *Platoon*, plus a couple more where I forgot the names. Even though I knew them movies were about a real war that happened, it never hit me clean. In school they kinda told us how the USA lost. But they never said about Ho Chi Minh or Saigon, the Gulf of Tonkin or Richard Nixon. For real, I didn't know nothing about Nixon, maybe just heard his name, that's all. Dana had to tell me about him cauze she learned in high school how he got fired from president. In my high school, we debated stuff like *Should Walgreen's keep the rubbers behind locked glass?* But Dana was hearin' about Henry Kissenger and Linda Johnson, and that's in damn ass Vilnius. Where she went to a frickin' MUSIC SCHOOL.

Dana wanted to know what we were gonna do. But I didn't even have no idea. For a while I just put Big Beard's picture away in the box, said there ain't no point meetin' with him or callin' him up. Maybe he already knew about me and Audra and would get revenge. You can't fuck with rich dudes cauze they totally use connections to mess you up. And they totally know how to get away with it.

But I couldn't forget about it or pretend it don't matter. Anytime I went lookin' for a job in the library I would google stuff like Nixon or Kent State, frickin' NVA and other things grandad wrote, the South China Sea and Saigon. So I read a lot about it and learned important things. (For real, how come they don't teach this stuff to everybody in school where it's important to know? Way more important compared with *Should they give rubbers on prom night?*)

On top of all this, I was also gettin' real worried about Jen. Like I wrote her a couple e-mails just to say hi, told her gram said she was in rehab. But I didn't say nothing about no letters, just how I had news with a surprise. I called her phone maybe three times, though her clinic probably didn't let her keep no cell.

Around the middle of May I got a job in this camping store, a real swanko place in downtown Bloomington. My job was to stock deliveries and dust off the canoes, plus I was doin' the register and makin' sure all the fly rods, hats and coats were hung up neat. That store was real mellow with the owner like a normal guy...sometimes nobody would come in the store before noon. And if I was done dustin' the canoes, I could google stuff on the computer. For real, I read about Vietnam almost every day, then later I got a book at the library.

Dana thought I should write Big Beard a letter. Make a copy of the picture with grandad and give my e-mail, tell Larry to write if he wants. That would of been a good move probably, though still it gave bad vibes. Cauze one day I googled Larry and stuff came up about apartments for rent in Berwyn and Cicero...but also I found his art website, one of them pages with all his clay statues and paintings for sale. Pictures with dudes fishin' and ridin' horseback, one with a guy lookin' down a field. Another painting was a blonde lady drinkin' red wine by a window, her shoulders real tired even though she tried to smile. That painting was Audra.

It made me unsure, so I didn't write Larry nothing even though the website had his e-mail on it.

Jen sent me a message around the end of May. It was all chopped up and weird, hard to read. She was stayin' with Gunther's mom in Berwyn. Me and Dana found out frickin' Mama Bullets was the one who made Jen take rehab, paid for the whole thing and also tried to make Gunther go. Right here is the end of Jen's message, the same way how she wrote it.

gram told how you made a visit. i knew you would end up with a hard chick drew, tough blood. though its better with somebody probably. where she dont care what she tell's no one so you know where you stand. i guess i dont hate myself so bad right now though still don't know if you should come by. only if you can afford the gas to come up. only you cant stay here cos she said no overnites. but maybe by diego he has room. or if you got a car since its warmin up now. but call first, say when its better for you cos for me any times good. since I dont got nothin to do.

Me and Dana called to say we're comin'. Made reservations at the youth hostel, rode the Megabus on a Friday. I kinda knew where Mama Bullets lived on Riverside Drive in Berwyn, probably the most pretty part of the whole town, a curved road with big houses. We rang the doorbell and Jen answered the door like it was a surprise. "Hey...wow, you made it?"

In two seconds I could see Jen was on hardcore meds, spaced out and movin' weird, like *way* slow. But she didn't look too bad...kinda skinny, though not like I seen some super thin tweakers. At first Jen sat in the kitchen and we watched how she did her nails with silver polish. She said the smell from that polish reminded her about Wilson, though I didn't know no dude named Wilson. Sometimes she smiled without no reason, real sad smiles that didn't show no happy feelings. She couldn't talk about nothing, just looked at us or the floor, then sometimes her hands.

I asked a couple questions, "Where's Gunther?" But Jen kinda shrugged, tappin' her nails together. She said, "I ain't goin' back to Wisconsin no more." I wanted to know what kind of meds they gave her and she pointed by the kitchen window where I seen some orange bottles. She said, "They make it hard to open them bottles, hard for your hands." I tried to start some conversations about stuff she liked, the White Sox and Simpsons, and to say more positive stuff. "It's cool Mama Bullets lets you stay with her. Could we meet her?" But Jen only shrugged. She looked at her hands and blew on them nails even though they were already dry. Then she stared at Dana real spaced out.

When I said it's time for us to go, Jen kinda perked up. "Drew, your gonna call me sometimes, right? Or I'll call you sometimes?" She took my cell phone to make sure her number was in there. "The old lady said I can get my own phone back pretty soon if I don't fuck up. But it would be later on." We left real awkward without no real goodbye. And Jen didn't really show us out, just turned on the tube by the front door, one of them shows about models.

Me and Dana had our ponchos to go walkin' in the drizzle like a couple school kids. For real, I kinda felt baked after talkin' to Jen. And me and Dana couldn't know...was it a good or bad thing we just seen? Dana kinda took over when I found the Oak Park Ave bus stop. She said, "Endee...do you want to go there?"

I was quiet. "Dana. I don't frickin' know."

"For example, where is laundry? Laundry where you meet her. Because I like to see."

That was maybe a 10 minute bus ride. Before I could think clean what to do, I seen the bus was comin'. "Guess we could take it down." The ride went past the Buona Beef on Roosevelt and the bridge over the Ike, dropped us off right on the corner by the laundry, Oak Park Avenue and South Boulevard. Them streets were real busy with people...the el was makin' noise and some Metra trains went flyin' by. For real, it was totally a time warp cauze that neighborhood looked frickin' the same. But I got real surprised when I seen the laundry got shut down, black spraypaint on the windows. Some kids glued flyers on the door, like rock bands with freaked out names...*Thrash Wednesday* and *Busted Faces*. For a while me and Dana just looked at that black spray paint to see our reflections. I told her, "This is a bad idea."

She got crosseyed. "Why? Just because they close laundry?"

"If Larry's home...what the hell we say to him?"

"*Nu*...what? You say...just *say*. What people say in visit?"

I stared up and down the street like maybe an answer was hangin' on a tree. Then me and Dana started walkin' north down Oak Park avenue, the way toward Larry's house. I told her it was a real long walk, but me and Dana needed some time to think it through and make a plan.

"We can't say nothing about no Lithuania, Dana. It might splut out by accident, so be careful. Definitely never no words about Audra or Vilnius."

"Endee, we *must* to ask this. Because this most important to know."

"Know what? There ain't nothin' to know...you crazy, Dana? Nobody does that..."

"*Blet*, he will ask *Nate, where you meet your wife?* *Nu*, where? In airport? No, because I don't lie."

"No one says lyin'. Just don't mention about no wife. That's all."

"Larry never like Audra anyway. For him she is who cares."

"I say we call first. Cauze we need a better plan than this. We gotta agree on the strategy or it's all messed up."

But we never settled on no good plan. And pretty soon I found where Big Beard had his frickin' house on LeMoyne. The place looked the same, them little bushes just how Audra drew in her notebook. The Navigator was in the driveway and I was totally rememberin' it. But then Dana went real brave up them front stairs so I had to follow to make sure she don't bang on the window or do something nuts. When I came up, she just went whisperin', "Okay, Endee, try."

"Try what?"

"Bell. Or...no...look in postbox. It has room?"

"That's a bigass mailbox."

"Because I write letter. You have pen?"

"No, Dana. I'll write it."

Right there we heard the door unlockin'. It was serious panic with electric stuff up my neck and all through all my teeth. That huge wood door was openin' like *ch-shhhhh shh* so everything went slow motion. And when the Mexican lady peeked at us, me and Dana just got froze. We seen how the lady was real curious and unsure.

Dude, I didn't even know Dana could talk some Spanish, but she busted it out. "*Oh la, Usted. Ci, porque Larry mi amigo. ¿Hoy su casa?*" The lady talked back to us in the best English, her voice like a lady on a radio show. "Larry's sculpting right now. Do you have business?"

I said, "Kinda. He sorta knew me before. I'm Nate. I mean...yeah, you can tell him Nate. Only hold on...you should also show the picture with the name. Dana, where's it at?"

"I don't *have*."

"But where is it?"

"Where? *You* have. In backpack, in notebook."

"I seen you take it."

"*Nu, blet.* You have."

I told the lady, "Excuse me." Then I was messin' in my backpack. "It's kind of a long story. But I'll try findin' it."

The lady let us in Big Beard's front room where the place was cleaned out without no furniture. He only had some cardboard boxes and a huge metal suitcase by a wall, then some grocery bags and fruit crates by a door. I kept lookin' through my notebook and the picture kinda fluttered out, so I gave it to the lady. "He'll know if you show him that."

"You said your name's Nate?"

"Yeah, Nate. But my real name's Andrew Nowak. Probably tell him both of them names together."

She made us wait in that room. It didn't have no chairs for us to sit down and the whole place smelled like plaster and cardboard. For real, everything in there started feelin' lonely. I kinda looked over them groceries and by accident I seen a whole mango crate. Dude, right there it frickin' hit me like a brick in the head, cauze I remembered the exact same Mexican lady *cuttin'*

mangoes when she seen me with Audra. A damn blender totally
went off in my guts and I whispered, "Dana, frickin' look."

She was confused.

"Makin' mangoes. Did I tell you...that lady seen me that day.
With Audra that day! She seen me!"

"*Same* lady?"

"She was usin' fuckin' mangoes for a blender."

"You ate?"

"No, dude! We gotta get outta here." I tried the front door,
but the lock was one of them where you need a key from inside.
"Fuck."

Dana said, "I hear coming."

"Dude, act regular."

We could hear Big Beard's steps creakin' the floor before we
seen him. Then it was that huge ass beard, only even bigger now.
His hands were all dried up with clay and he was wearin' one of
them gray smocks. The lady gave me the picture and took away
some of them grocery bags. Then the little mophead dog came
around to sniff my shoes. I just said, "Hey. Remember me?"

"You damn right," he said. His voice was raspy dry and he
coughed to get it back. "Remember you damn well." You should
of seen the guy's face. He was waitin' his whole life for aliens and
now they finally come in his house, only it was the wrong aliens,
like a buzz kill. His eyes got like spotlights steamed in the rain,
cauze Larry was frickin' stoned. He went countin' some shit on his
fingers   and   finally   said,   "Ellyn?"   kinda   surprised   from
rememberin' it. He looked me through real deep. "It's her name,
right? But not...she's not your *mother*. Maybe your grandmother?
Still alive?"

"Ellyn's my grandma. She gave the picture. For our wedding."

Dana came up. "*Nu*, I am Dana." Larry's messy hand took
just her fingertips. "I am wife. Endee say to me about you."

"So sweet t'meet you. That's really sweet to meet you." He
sat down on one stack of boxes and all this dust went flyin' from
his huge ass. Larry asked Dana, "Ellyn? She's well?"

I said, "A bit sick. Though okay, mostly."

Big Beard kinda spaced out again. "Kenny's daughter? A short name, right...name's short."

"My mom? Her name's Betty."

"Right, right. Betty. Dammit, your mother..." All of a sudden he got real buzzed up and started rubbin' his face kinda fast. "Holy mack...damn unexpected. Not in my...not *today*! Priscilla, my housekeeper. She thought you're the people come to buy the Navigator. Come a few hours early."

Dana said, "No, we don't buy."

"But it's fucking Ken's grandson. Jesus Christ." Larry got full of feelings. He came up real close by me so I could smell his garlic lunch. The dude went lookin' so deep in my face, totally like I'm a piece of clay he wants to squeeze and cut. "That's a *lot* like Ken. A lot alike, yes...only no. But my god, my god, a *lot* like Ken. More hair. You have more hair, thicker hair." Them stoned eyes and nasty breath got real uncomfortable, plus that beard so huge you could stash a chicken in there. He rubbed his mouth pretty hard. I said, "What you think we should do?"

Big Beard sighed out real long and heavy. Then he squeezed his pinky tip real tight. "You should. You should go in there." His chin went shootin' down the hall. "It's my office. Some furniture left, not much, but enough. I'll be a minute to change." He backed down another way. "You help yourself, whatever you find in there. Some booze, make a drink. But wait for me. Don't leave. Just a minute for me to change."

Me and Dana walked kinda careful down that hall where all the rooms already got packed away. Larry's office was real trashed, the chairs and some desks from a garage sale. His plastic shelves all got curved down from way too many books, and the guy left frickin' gadgets layin' around...a couple digital cameras and hard drives, some computer parts and wires tangled up on the floor. One corner had a coffee table with Gordon's gin and a liter of tonic, them bottles kinda dirty from clay fingerprints. Dana whispered, "I knew it. Look this room. He is pig."

"He's loaded. So it don't matter to him."

"But whole house empty. I know, because he lose all money. Yes, men like this with beard, they like roulette." Dana seen a couple beer cans on the floor. "How can he stay so dirty with slave in house?"

"*Jesus!* Frickin' whisper, Dana. Not no slave. She's a *maid*."

"Where...what she made? No, Endee. Because you *see* her? Look in face, I can tell. She not happy, don't like work here. And she don't remember you. Or if she remember then she don't care." Dana made gin and tonic without no ice. And she wanted to see Larry's books.

Them shelves were kinda organized. One shelf was only war books, like Vietnam, Afghanistan and Iraq. The middle shelf had Global Warming books, plus folders with DVD's and some scientific mags. But Larry's biggest shelf was all about money and business, stuff like Marketing, Economy and Real Estate. Real weird, on the bottom Dana found one of them Marilyn Monroe Playboys. "Look. Monroe sign her name."

"Dude, that's mint. Don't touch it."

"He say help self. So I help."

Larry came in right there and said, "Yeah, you like that? Got it from eBay." Then he sat by the computer to put some iTunes, messin' over there with his back turned so he couldn't see Dana's face all pink.

The dude smelled like shampoo and his hair was still wet. He changed in a Blackhawks jersey with number 19 and some real loose sweatpants. For a while Larry kept messin' with iTunes. Priscilla brung a tea pot, some cups and a plate with real thin wafer cookies. She sorta talked like a waitress, "Would you like something else?" The way she looked at me, I thought Dana was right...she didn't recognize me at all.

Big Beard finished his song list, like all this Spanish stuff, guitars and some drums put on real quiet. There was a fridge under his desk...in there he had nuggs stashed in tupperware, then a six inch bong in the freezer. The whole room smelled like strong minty weed when he packed the bong. And he put that thing right by me, "Start it up, Andrew."

Holy crap, seein' that Graffix made me know it's a bad idea. Like opera cymbals went crashin' in my brain when I knew what kind of hit I'd get. What kind of shit would I talk if I got ripped...probably I would fuck up for sure. I went, "Larry, that's a real nice bong. Sorry, though. Cauze smokin' up ain't really what we come for."

"It's packed. The thing's packed."

"Not right now."

Dana said, "Very large pipe."

"Well...for the petunia patch...I can roll a joint. I got some other pipes. But most are dirty right now."

I said, "You smoke if you want. But I'm cool. Gin and tonic is alright."

Larry just shrugged and took the bong. The old man ripped it like a rock star, the whole tube fillin' up with thick smoke, then he hit it BOOM so the whole room was a cloud. He didn't cough too much, just took a sip from that hot tea. And his eyes turned like wet marbles, his whole face real flabby.

Right there the dude rubbed his stash a couple times and just started talkin'. Cauze in the shower he already planned a big ass speech, only no way in hell can I write THE WHOLE stuff he babbled. For real, I can't even remember most of it cauze he didn't take no break for twenty minutes. The shit he talked went round and round with lots of details and numbers, stuff like mortgage percents and all them tenants who don't pay rent, how the laws don't let him evict nobody. When he finally took a small break to drink some tea, Dana asked, "Where you are moving?"

Larry's whole forehead got deep wrinkles and his eyes turned kinda wide. He tapped his thumb real nervous on the tea cup. "You know Costa Rica?"

"Center America."

"Cen*tral*. Cen*tral* America." He nodded and kinda took a sip, then he kicked up another speech. This time it was all about danger and terrorism, the government and information. For real, he talked real intense. "The rich people keep *us* weak, make sure *we* can't make money." For him rich people were already making

World War III on purpose with Iran, so after that it would be even more terrorism. That's why Larry was gonna buy gold, plus a house in Costa Rica. He made Costa Rica sound real cool with pretty girls, nice beaches, good weed and nobody wanted to attack over there. But Larry talked like me and Dana could afford gold and a beach house.

Dude, he totally kept goin' about the environment and World War III. Larry knew lots of secrets from the internet and books. And his favorite word was *information*. All the problems...the environment, the Iraq war, religion, terrorism and the reason everybody's poor, "It's made by rich people. On purpose. To keep you out of it so you'll never crack through, so that you'd die or fuck up. They've set us up to fail. If you had the information I have, there'd be no doubt in your mind. None." I thought maybe he ain't healthy, like there's a chance he hears shit in his head. Voices that talked secret plans with *information*.

Them Spanish songs stopped playin'. Larry took some wafers and sat chewin' to think more stuff he could tell us. All of a sudden I seen some real sad feelings come strong in his face, kinda like he remembered a story by accident. He said, "You won't believe me," and his chin shot to Dana. "Especially *you*, girl. What are you, twenty-two, give or take? Just a pup? *You* won't believe me." The way he said *you* talked down real bad. Though Dana just stared at him.

Larry went, "I'll get to it without any time wasted, a lesson for you kids. Because long after it was already finished, long after '73. After they had lined up *children*...because that's what they were, nothing more than children, younger even than you. Kenny was right around your age, Andy. Today you worry about your iPod, your horseshit text messaging. Well...he worried about booby traps. I won't ask *you* to know things...if you didn't witness something then what can you know? The rich bastards help themselves and *damn* the rest. *You* two might not know about it, the bullshit they fill you with. But time's pretty much up. And we're all on the rack.

"I know what you came to find out. And I can tell your bored with me. I'll admit I don't get too many visitors too often. And when I'm high I can get carried away. You want to know about the letter, why I wrote to your grandmother. So I'll tell you." He was quiet for a while and ate one more wafer. Then he finished his tea in a couple big gulps.

"Your grandfather, Kenny. He showed me every single picture Ellyn ever sent. *Every. Single. One.* She's standing with a fly swatter by the stove. And then watering plants and smiling on a porch. My favorite was this big one, 4 x 6...she's got yellow polka dots, a modest dress. Ken would hand those pictures to me, show them. Talk about her. Describe her."

Dana sighed.

"I knew things about Ken nobody else knew. Not you, or *you*. Not even Ellyn. After the war, I kept wanting...I kept thinking, well *maybe*...maybe. For some of us it's easier to shoot a man than to write a woman. Ellyn knew who I was. I saw the letters Ken wrote her...he mentioned me all the time." Big Beard coughed a little. "And one day I found the guts to do it, to write her. My letter was very polite and simple. Straightforward...not any hint of anything. Not a *hint*. But Ellyn never returned it. She may never have even read it twice before passing it along. To some kids. To *you* two."

Dana asked, "Why you say this *you*? Every time with nose in air. Why?"

Larry totally ignored her. "I've tried a variety of things in my life. Letters. Have gone on the internet...I've explained myself on Craigslist in every single detail. Women wish for what they dream up, but refuse what you have to offer. They expect everything of us, but little of themselves. So why bother writing back? Or tell me this, Andy. She's your relative. Why'd she pass that letter off? Why that picture?"

Dana jumped in. "No...because woman don't expect *little*. She must to expect even more. Very good for you, all life you don't even work. Don't even clean up room. For example, I go university."

"God dammit, how's it possible?" Larry looked way down on Dana. "The guy sitting here, Andrew Nate Nowak, a guy like him. Doesn't have a single marketable skill. But little child, to *you* he's endlessly better than anything you can have out in *your* country. So please, pick a fucking number. Tell him *I do.* Then raise your nose to tell me I raise mine."

Everybody was quiet.

Larry looked at me. "Andy, I want to know. Did Ellyn tell you anything at all about me? Or about Ken, what he thought? Because it doesn't matter anymore...we're out of time. The rich and the poor..."

Now Dana was pissed. "Why you say rich? Like this...*rich.* What you think, you not rich?"

"You're asking me?"

"*Blet,* I asking, *yes.* Because you more rich like anybody I know."

"Romper room, romper room. You won't know the first thing about it. Because Russia is *full* of rich people right now. Some of the wealthiest people are in Russia. And they're pulling strings."

"What place Russia? Why you talk Russia?"

"Because in your country..."

"Fuck you, *my* country. Russia fuck up my country. My uncle to Siberia."

"Well...excuse *me.* You're a different one, Ukrainian, Polish. There's people pulling strings out there as well. They pull strings all over the world. My strings and yours."

"But also *you* pull. You *pull!*"

"Excuse me?"

"Not excuse!" Now Dana was standin' up. "Yes, this true. Because you think whole world should be for you slave. You bring here lady, bring in this house so dirty."

"You'll need to calm–"

"No, I don't need! Because you take lady. Lady has educa-tion. Yes, Audra, your wife. Me and Endee, we know her very good. And you want only show how she is like prize. Must to do exactly everything...everything everything *exactly* how you say. Audra can't have baby. *Yes*, she can't *have*. This don't mean you throw human in garbage. Alone in street."

"Who the hell..."

"Audra say to me. You think world very bad place because Larry not king. But she want husband, not king. She tell me how you buy whore. Wait on purpose so she come home, find you with whore. Do like this on purpose so she can see King."

"That fucking lunatic told you this bullshit? She was coked up, a liar. A fucking thief. Got her passport and left."

"Because her father dying."

"How convenient, sister Christian, you know everything!" He leaned way back and grabbed his forehead. "Audra filled you up with sunshine, girl. Her father was boozed up for years...cancer for years. Dying when we got married, dying while she was stringin' me along. But daddy's health didn't bother her then." Larry grabbed his tea cup real tight. "I *said*. I told her a thousand fucking times I'd *pay* for his operation. But she didn't want the operation paid for...she wanted a passport and hard cash in her pocket. I was honest with her. Audra knew what she got herself into. Ahead of time. She pretended it was enough...fooled *herself* it would be enough. But it wasn't enough for her. Because she lies even to herself."

"What money she need from you? Nothing. You make her crazy."

"She *was* crazy."

"Yes, because you make her."

"Fuck, she *knew*." Larry was shoutin'. And he was startin' to wig so his face was gettin' red. "I outlined it. Ahead of time, disclosed myself *ahead* of time. Before any deal, any wedding, before anything was signed. And she lied, she *lied*! Right to my face...I told her, 'You're never coming back.' And you tell me, where the hell is she now? Wanted me to chase her? Humiliate me...humiliate me. But I have pride."

Holy shit, Larry was totally wiggin' out. He kept lookin' at the door like somebody was gonna bust in, and his stoned eyes got real wild. The guy was grippin' that tea cup tight, stickin' his fingers inside like he wanted to break it. It kinda worried Dana a little, but still she told him one more thing. "Also, Audra have pride. She want husband, not king. So she go home."

Now Big Beard kinda laughed out this little puff of hurt. He let the tea cup fall on the floor and then he grabbed the back of his head real tight. The guy mumbled some shit and stared Dana down with real bad pain and hate. I thought maybe he was gonna throw some crap, yell or call her names. That would of been better cauze no way was anybody ready for his next move.

Frickin' Larry stood up. I watched him do it with his hands and I was thinkin' *No way, there's no way.* He kept on messin' with the knot on his sweat pants. *No frickin' way.* But Larry did it. He showed us, a little shiver when he held the hockey shirt and pulled down the sweats.

It was where he got wounded. The scar started by his stomach and went all the way down below, just some thicker scars with hair, some skin left from an operation when they were tryin' to put remains back. Me and Dana felt like *don't look away, don't be mean,* but also Larry was forcin' it on us, showin' when we were shocked and sick and totally sorry. He spaced out and wasn't gonna lift them pants back up. But then the doorbell rang and Big Beard covered up to hide all them scars. He rubbed his face real hard and went out from the office.

Me and Dana couldn't barely move, just felt real heavy and wrong. After a while I kinda stood up and seen Priscilla in the doorway. Real polite she said, "If you come this way, I'll show you out." Without makin' no big deal, she led us by a side door. Then she held it open and said, "Thank you for coming. And a very good night."

Audra

Oak Park gets real dark at night, just a couple street lamps between all them big trees. Without no cars you can hear the drizzle real easy, the mansion gutters tricklin' water on the ground. I never seen Dana lookin' so ashamed, her eyebrows dark and face real white like Elmer's glue. We went by North Avenue to wait for the bus and she just moped around, sat real glum and quiet. Ridin' the bus and the Blue Line, I thought a couple times she was gonna say some things to me. But for the whole ride she only looked in the dark window.

The hostel gave us one of them dorms where the el makes earthquakes all night long...you feel it in the bed and the walls. I laid right by her on the bottom bunk and we got real close in the small bed. Them trains kept makin' real bright electricity flashes almost the same like a storm, so I thought there's no way Dana would crash. But pretty soon I seen she was totally passed out, even snorin' a little.

Dude, I tried to crash just like her, but it didn't work out. You don't know how many crazy thoughts I had goin' in my head...like hot shrapnel shot below my belt where it was burnin' up my guts. It was that feeling when you know nobody can help you, something's already done and nobody can change it, so it's gonna stay that way forever. But also I kept hearin' Larry tell me...it was like an echo goin' over and over again, *you don't have a single marketable skill*. Like I could imagine all them important people at Jacob's Music School...frickin' opera teachers and smart people. All them people would talk gossip behind Dana's back, "A shame about her. Such a talented girl. But she married that fool without a single marketable skill."

I knew it wasn't no use to try crashin'. So I got up from the bed real quiet and went down by the lobby. The hostel puts internet and soda machines over there and I got a ginger ale to google shit. Like Costa Rica...I seen pictures with brown rivers like cream coffee, then frogs and different color birds, lots of sunset beaches with black sand. That country was a real nice place Larry picked to live, though I didn't get jealous or feel no connection at all. It was kinda autopilot when I googled *community college for Bloomington Indiana*. And in the youth hostel was the first time I found out about Ivy Tech, a real swank college maybe three miles from our house. Not even a 20 minute bike ride, or I could walk there if I wanted.

I went lookin' through my e-mail and seen there was one old message from Varna, maybe a week or five days old, though I never opened it. He would write me pretty often and I got used to his messages bein' kinda sick, like messed up pics from emergency rooms and doctor examples. Sometimes he would send drunk dudes passed out in the farms, then frickin' weird porn from Germany. But this time his message was a regular one just with some news. He said he was walkin' down *Vokiečių Gatvė* with Raimis after he got off work, and by accident they seen Audra drinkin' red wine at some cafe. Them dudes didn't talk with her, but Varna said she looked more thin and was wearin' regular clothes, nothing too fancy.

Dude, even though it was weird to get a message like that after our night, I didn't feel shit about it. Like Audra was out from the hospital for sure now, but when I thought about it I barely even cared. I wrote Raimis and Varna a longass message, put all the details about what happened at Larry's place. That message cost me $3.50 to print, but I wanted to glue it in my notebook. And Dana read it on the Megabus down to Indy, said she felt like a longass story was finally over. "Thank you for coming. And a very good night." When we got back to Bloomington, I shoved that whole notebook next to gram's box way under our bed and covered all that stuff with a crap towel. Dana said, "Now we don't look at it again. Maybe when we are old, more than 30, but that's all." It was kinda true...I never had no more temptation to look in that stuff or flip through pictures. The only thing, sometimes I wondered if I should show them letters to Jen.

The first time she called me, I was down by Ivy Tech to see the place. A front desk girl gave me this one pamphlet about the placement test and all the rules. Jen called me when I was lookin' through information in the cafeteria. She had a real weird question for me..."Drew, where's a place around Berwyn to get a raincoat?" I didn't really know, but I said North Riverside Park or maybe Marshall's. Jen said thanks and hung up real fast, didn't call me back till me and Dana were eatin' some pizza at home. She said, "Drew, I totally got a raincoat at Marshall's. So that was good advice."

"That's cool, Jen."

"Holy crap, it's *pourin'* up here. First time I go outside without the old lady and it's buckets. Though I went walkin' around anyway, I didn't give a care. Frickin' now with a raincoat it's way better to walk around." She stopped talkin' and got totally quiet, kinda waitin' for me to talk something, though I couldn't think what to say about the coat. She went, "Drew, you havin' dinner?"

"Me and Dana. Just eatin' some pizza."

"That pizza probably sucks down there. Not like Salerno's."

"We don't got nothin' like Salerno's down here."

"Then I won't bother you guys. Though you can call me if you want later. Like after dinner, if you get bored'n shit."

But anytime I tried callin' Jen she wouldn't pick up. I would leave some messages or ask questions just for small talk, but she never answered them direct. Instead she would call me with unexpected stuff. "Drew, what's your favorite website?" or "Hey, if a car's burnin' oil, then how far can you drive it?" One time she called and stayed totally quiet, then frickin' got grumpy with me. "You don't even wanna talk?"

"It's hard, Jen. I don't know what you wanna talk about."

"Well, you should pick a topic."

"Okay. Like...maybe you seen the scores today? How about them Sox?"

"No, Drew. Not no sports."

"No?" I was lookin' at my Ivy Tech schedule where I left it on the table. "Tomorrow's like my first day in class."

"What class?"

"Just one class is all I can do. English 025. That's like writing for beginners."

"For writing?" She turned real quiet for a while. Jen didn't talk for maybe three minutes so it got real awkward. She said, "It's cauze Dana said to do it, right? She wants you to take college?"

"No. I found out on the internet and just signed up."

I could hear Jen make taps on something. "But what would you think...like if I asked her about that makeup she had? You think she would tell me about it? Or no?"

"What makeup?"

"That makeup she had when you came by. Where's she from again? Cauze probably it's from her country."

"She's from Lithuania," I said. "But I don't know about makeup. Dana don't really wear none, Jen."

"No, *Drew*. Cauze I can tell when it's frickin' makeup. Not some crap from Penny's, probably a way better store." Jen kept on tappin' something...it sounded like a fork or a knife on a plate. Then she hung up.

After that Jen didn't call for a long time. And she wouldn't pick up if I tried...sometimes her phone was just turned off. I wrote a couple e-mails, said Dana's makeup was *Lancome* from the London duty free. But Jen didn't answer none of them messages and totally gave me the silent treatment. So I gave up tryin' to reach her.

For real, things got busy real fast when my class started. Pretty much the only stuff I did was work the camping store, do my homework and go to my class Tuesday and Thursday nights, like six hours each week. The teacher gave homework every day, a book to read called *Collected Essays* and complicated papers to write...*Think about a decision you made in the past that had both negative and positive consequences.* Dude, the class got me real surprised cauze I totally got into it, like sometimes I frickin' wanted to go. The teacher said he wouldn't make no censorship or report my ass for anything I said in a paper. So on my first one I wrote how I met Audra, almost the same like *That Fateful Saturday*, only real different. And when the professor read it he didn't make me talk with no counselor or take no abstinence pledge. I got a D on it, which showed me I could pass. Stuff just kept gettin' improved, cauze any grade I got was always D+ or C–, never nothing lower than that.

On this one night in June I came out from class real jacked up. The teacher gave a reading test and I got 78%, like the highest grade I got since maybe fourth grade. Walkin' to the bike rack, I turned on my phone to call Dana, maybe set up a place where we could meet and get some Jameson. But then I seen my phone said *five missed calls*, all them lights blinkin' all over the place.

One call was Dana, but all the rest was Jen. She also sent a text message *Call me asap* and left voice mail, "I'm totally lost, Drew. Where you at?" Her voice had some shake and edge since she was real wound up...for real, I got scared maybe she was tweakin' again. When she answered the phone I couldn't hear nothing she said...the whole thing sounded like this, "Drew, *mumble mumble,* store, Marsh. *Pshhh fffff kshhh* by a Marsh." Frickin' she was blastin' *Avenged Sevenfold* real loud in her car, then finally turned that crap off. "Drew, I don't even know. I'm lost. It's called Marsh. I'm by a Marsh."

"Hold on, Jen. Where you tryin' to go? What the hell's a *marsh*?"

"Like a store. Off Route 37 someplace. They got like a mall over here."

"Your in Bloomington?"

"I guess. A sign said Bloomington. The Indiana one, right...not the one for Illinois? Sorry, cauze I stopped in a rest area, fuckin' left my Yahoo directions in the rest area. Got off 37 and went some way, pulled over by a fuckin' store. Some big huge red letters, *Marsh*...it's a car dealer around here too. You guys don't mind it if I stay for the weekend?"

"It's Tuesday, Jen."

"Well...then just a couple more days, like two extra."

I told Dana I was gonna be gone for a while. Had to look up all the Marsh stores on the internet and it took me a frickin' hour to bike by the right one on the other side of town. You could hear Jen's suicide music blastin' across the parking lot. She was sittin' in her Honda hatchback bitin' her nails and drinkin' Citgo coffee.

The car was her Civic from high school, totally beat up and rusty with old duck tape still stuck on. The only stuff in the hatch was a big blanket and a backpack, so I threw my bike in there and left the hatch open. Drivin' with her, I seen how bad she was wired, though she pretended everything's regular...this is just one of them normal surprise visits. We came to a red light right near Jacob's school and Jen said, "I'm hungry, Drew. They got a place to stop somewhere?"

"You were waitin' by the grocery for hours."

"Hungry now, Drew. Wasn't fuckin' hungry back then."

In the BP by our house she bought Pringles and a hotdog, plus one of them real sick microwave burritos. Jen sat in our kitchen shovelin' that food and talkin' with her mouth full. For real, she couldn't stop babblin', only she looked mostly at Dana when she talked. "Gunther's up in Wisconsin still. It's for good now cauze we're broke up and I found out official. Like total divorce, we need to get that done. But it don't matter since he don't call me no more...all them tweakers in his crowd, he's way too busy. Though...you guys, you know? It's true how bad I'm cravin' it. They said it would get better, only for me it's gettin' worse." Jen almost finished the whole can of Pringles, leavin' just a little at the bottom. She seen the clock by my bed and said, "Drew, gimme my backpack." Her hands shaked a little when she was lookin' through for something. "Forgot it's an hour later out here. But I got some strong ones so we can go to bed." She busted out a little medicine case with these hardcore sleeping pills and one of them knocked her wired ass out in ten minutes.

The next day Jen was still passed out when I went to the camping store. She woke up around 11:00 and called to ask where's the best place to hang a wet towel. She said she was gonna clean the kitchen with Ajax and maybe cook some mac and cheese. But when I came home I found all the windows open with the balcony door swinged wide. It totally smelled like burning and Jen was wavin' a t-shirt around. "Fucked up real bad, Drew. Your pissed? Fuck, your pissed." She forgot some macaroni on the stove and burned it black, melted the plastic handle on the pot. "Left that. Went to the store. I totally promise I won't cook no more, just microwave. But we can still eat cauze I got salami and bread in this bag." She took that food out and started tryin' to fold the paper sack, rustlin' it real loud. But then she stopped and sat by the window to stare at the BP roof. After some quiet where she was bitin' her nails, Jen said, "I fucked up comin' out here, right?"

"You gotta chill, Jen."

"Should do the dishes."

"No. You should just hang out. Cauze your jacked on coffee. Did you ever drink this herb tea? Dana drinks it to mellow out."

"I'm mellow. Right now I'm mellow."

"You don't need to work around here. Since your on a visit, you can just chill."

"But I don't wanna eat none of your food." She was talkin' slow and way too quiet. "Like, I wasn't even hungry...just to cook dinner for you guys. Plus to keep busy since it's easier when I do stuff, not stare at walls all day." Jen took the window drape real light with two fingers and put it on her knee like a skirt. "Kinda went around town today, got a newspaper'n shit. You didn't say it's cheap to live down here compared with Berwyn. Rent's real cheap."

"That's cauze they got lots of students here."

For a while she was just lookin' at that drape. But then Jen gave me eye contact, stared me through real deep, lockin' it up on me totally intense. It was kind of a surprise how I seen her for real, exactly where she wanted to show me inside. And I wasn't ready for it so sudden when I could tell how hardcore she was depressed. Jen's eyes were like plastic without no shine left. And she was all ate up like one of them boards the termites finished so you could just kick it in half. For a while we were just lookin' at each other like that. But then she mumbled to me, "I'm fucked up, Drew."

"What's wrong?"

She was quiet. "Cauze there ain't no point."

"Don't think like that. Don't talk that shit, there's lots of stuff."

"Like what?"

"Like..." I was lookin' around the room. "Like when you take a trip. Or when you meet cool people. For me it helped...you should try gettin' a dog."

Her eyes went half closed. "Can't get no dog. To forget him in a car without no air?"

"Don't think that crap."

"I forget stuff, Drew." She was rubbin' her knees. "Them meds make me do it. That's why they make 'em look like erasers. It's probably on purpose for a joke on you, when they erase your brain."

"But you should take them meds. I mean...if they said to do it."

"Meds fuckin' suck, Drew." Jen went by the sink and ran hot water to wash her face with dish soap. She rubbed dry with a paper towel, though her face was still a little wet when she turned around. "Dana's comin' home?"

"Pretty soon."

Jen crossed her arms real tight. "You guys get along?"

"We're cool. I mean, she gets pissed. Or I get pissed. Not really, though."

"You gonna have kids with her?"

I shrugged.

"You love her a lot, right? Really a lot, right?"

I nodded, but Jen didn't see me. She was spaced out day-dreamin' and lookin' at the floor, pickin' inside her ear. An alarm rang in her phone and she got the medicine case to take one of them pills. When she poured water in a glass she almost started tellin' me something, but Jen only shaked her head. She drank the whole water with the pill and sat down by the drape one more time. "I fucked up."

"It don't matter..."

"No! Shh for a sec, cauze you gotta listen." Real mellow, she tore a piece from that paper bag and crumpled up a ball to squeeze it. "I can't love nobody."

"That ain't true."

Maybe Jen heard me. She was pinchin' her ear, lookin' down and rememberin' some stuff real clean. "I'm in deep shit, Drew," she said. "Like if Lake Michigan got made out of shit and I'm on the bottom."

"No you ain't. It just looks like that."

Jen kept pumpin' that paper ball.

I said, "Pretty soon you'll get better. If you take a class, it helps a lot. Like you can finish up your GED. Or when you said about speed typing classes...I thought that was a real good idea. A job for an office maybe."

"She kicked me out, Drew."

"Who?"

"The old lady. So I ain't there no more. Already two days ago...frickin' three."

"Where? Where you been?"

"In the car."

"Where?"

"Rest areas. First drove up by Wisconsin, all the way by Mars Cheese Castle. But then fuckin' turned around to come down here. I know you thought I was tweakin' on the phone, but fuckin' I only drank coffee...swear to god, only coffee. And ate Krispy Kremes. Cauze I didn't have cash."

"How come she kicked you out?"

Jen shoved her thumb real deep in that paper ball. "Found out what I did."

"But she knew that already. She don't know it was meth?"

Jen looked at me with them plastic eyes gettin' wet. I was supposed to understand some stuff she ain't tellin' me. "If your gonna hate me, I don't care. You just gotta know it from me before you hear them say lies."

"What lies?"

"When I found out about it, for sure how it was true. Like a real test from a doctor, not no Walgreen's. I found out about it true, so I went by a woman's clinic. That's what happened."

I seen Jen put that paper ball on the windowsill. Right there I totally understood what she was tryin' to say and I didn't ask nothing dumb to make it worse. Jen looked at me real mixed up...kinda soft but also tryin' to show she was hard and tough. I waited a little before talkin'. "The old lady. She told Gunther about it?"

"No, Drew, cauze fuckin' it was Gunther told *her*. Even though the motherfucker paid for it...he told me *keep it secret, keep it secret, none of it never happened.* But since I run away, since I'm tryin' to get cleaned up, he started seein' how I don't need him. The fucker knew his ma's against it, like real Christian. Frickin' blamed me, said I did it on my own, like I stole cash. So that showed me good, cauze now I don't got noplace to go. Just back to him."

I said, "Jen, you can't go back there no more."

She seen my Drum tobacco on top of the fridge and grabbed it. "That's why, Drew, cauze I turned around." She rolled a smoke real thin and went on the balcony. I seen she wanted to be alone and let her be there for maybe a half hour till Dana came home.

Me and Jen didn't talk no more about this stuff for maybe a couple days. She went with Dana to some cafes each night and Dana heard everything, way more than Jen told me, like stuff you don't tell your brother. I bought some grass from my landlord and it totally helped mellow her out. Later on, Dana made some herb tea with honey and Jameson, frickin' knocked Jen out cold so she slept better. Me and Dana were sittin' on the balcony real late one night when she told me, "No, Endee. Because she must to stay with us. We have room. Maybe she burn food, maybe she break glass. But we have bed for her, and that's all."

Dude, I totally agreed with her. But I don't know if anybody readin' this right now knows what it's like to live with an addicted person. Like a girl without no GED where she can apply for only three or five jobs in the paper. Jen said she was gonna find a job...she talked all the time how she would get a cool place with a porch. But anytime I showed her *Help Wanted* stuff she would get mood swings. "You know how many tweakers work in a gas station, Drew? Like the late shift, that's frickin' headquarters." She said the pizza joint also had tweakers, like all the drivers and managers. Also the Motel 6 was tweaker city. Dana seen a job in the paper for dog walkin', though the pay was real low. Seein' that made her depressed so she just smoked weed on the balcony.

For real, she could sit on the balcony for hours sometimes and drink chamomile tea with Jameson or smoke Drum. I told her that's almost the same like what gram drinks every day, so that kinda wigged Jen out with motivation. For a day she went lookin' through all the job papers, even got an interview at Kinko's and the university kitchen. But Jen didn't go to them interviews. "They won't give me no job. What's the point?" She went to sit on the balcony and blast her iPod.

It was like July when Dana started askin' me, "*Nu*...okay, Endee. What we going to do now?" Jen really liked talkin' with Dana in the evenings. But Dana told me, "Endee, because I can't listen anymore. She talk so much, she say so much about this terrible Wisconsin." Like me and Dana started stayin' away from the apartment sometimes. I would do my homework in this cafe called Soma, and Dana practiced her opera at Jacob's school. Jen told us, "Anytime you guys wanna get laid or somethin' like that, I'll just go for a walk." But she only went someplace if me or Dana also went. The rest of the time Jen just sat on the balcony to smoke my Drum or grass, or she would watch a DVD and space out.

Dude, one day I lost my shit finally. Every time at night I would pack a lunch for work, like a sandwich with a banana or an orange. I always put the sandwich in this little tupperware thing where it fit real good. But at lunchtime when I opened up the tupperware I seen Jen took a bite...probably she woke up hungry or had munchies. Right there I called her phone, though she didn't pick up. So that kept me pissed at work all day when we were busy with frat boys buyin' a kayak and ten hats. Comin' home around six, I found Jen rippin' a bowl and watchin' Judge Judy on the tube, the table a total mess with banana peels and cracker crumbs. And that made me go totally apeshit.

I called her dirtbag and a loser, frickin' garbage and other names. "Your worse like mom. At least she gets jobs. She pays a whole house and bills without no guy to help her."

"Yeah, Drew, cauze that's the exact same thing like mom would say. Gimme a guilt trip and put my ass down."

"No, just finally sayin' the truth to your face."

"That ain't no truth. Sure, I took some sandwich. Just a little bite, so what? That ain't shit compared. It ain't shit."

"It's fuckin' dirtbag. Total bum shit, like a homeless dude."

"Oh right, Drew. Cauze you got our own place right now. Real swank, holy shit, it's Drew's place...frickin' don't make no garbage, don't piss in the pot. Cauze that makes him cry by himself. Makes him piss a mattress."

"That's stupid, Jen! Fuck off...go tweak with Gunther. That's all you want anyways, so fuckin' admit it! Get your fix!"

That got Jen real sloppy. First she kinda sat in a chair, but then she threw a cup at me and broke it on the floor. I was pickin' up all them pieces and she went stormin' out the back. From the window I seen her walk down the alley and right there I thought *good, go*. I hit the pipe pretty hard, didn't go to my English class at all. Just sat on the balcony to look at the BP.

But maybe ten minutes later I was already feelin' guilty. I knew Jen wouldn't answer no phone, so I went bikin' around Bloomington to look for her, tried places she knew...the Kroger, Jiffy Treet and Copper Cup. But Jen was way smarter than me.

She was hid out behind a dumpster just to watch my bike and see when I left. Then she ran upstairs to pack her stuff, stole like forty bucks cauze I left my wallet on the table. When I seen all her stuff was gone, I called her phone. But the thing went ringin' right by our TV cauze Jen forgot it plugged in the wall.

I had a look around and seen she forgot other stuff. Some socks and her iPod headphones, small earrings and that warm blanket. I just sat around my place feelin' like a dumbass, thinkin' I should call gram to ask some advice. When Dana came home I babbled the whole story, thought for sure she would be pissed at me. But Dana only yawned and shrugged, kinda laughin'. "Endee, you think she go away? Where she go? Forty dollar and without phone, shit car with tape? No, Endee because she call back. Probably call in middle of night."

"You think we should tell cops?"

"Sure. Hello, policeman. Yes, because my sister, she is crazy. Driving around Honda and without money."

At first Dana kinda pissed me off, but then I seen she was right. So I didn't call nobody...just kept Jen's phone with me all the time, made sure it was charged up. I guess I kept an eye out for her, got kinda perked anytime I seen a red hatchback. But I pretty much accepted there's nothing I can do. If Jen don't call back by the end of the week, then I'll call gram to say what happened.

But here's the thing...Dana started wiggin' out. Without no call from Jen for a couple days, she woke me up one morning. "Endee, I have very bad dream. Yes, very bad."

"Dana, it don't mean nothing."

"No. Because we must to call police."

"Why?"

Dana said she dreamed Jen was turnin' tricks and makin' porno. I said, "Even if that's true, which it ain't...but if it's true, then cops can't help."

"They can make protection. Or they know which car to look. You must tell car number, say she missing."

"But I forgot her license."

"*Nu*, Endee. I was wrong, so stupid. Yes, she missing. For people when they missing you can call police because I see in television. Endee, you don't know how the men take Jen."

Dana wouldn't leave me alone about it. She went by the window and started mopin' around, gettin' all worked up to make me nervous. That was the first time she talked to me about dreams and how she thought they were real. Dana said Jen was totally turnin' tricks for meth and gas money just to keep drivin' so far like that car could go. Hearin' her talk so real about it, I kinda got worried. "But I can't call cops and say my wife had a bad dream, Dana."

"*Nu, blet*! You say she *missing*. She go missing without money, several days, what they will think? You must say car number. Endee, if you don't call, then yes I will call."

"We should call gram and mom first. Cauze Jen could of went back there."

"No...because Jen making money. I know this. Yes, I know for sure."

"I'll call gram. She knows advice. Also, mom probably ain't home now."

"*Nu*, call. But I know she will say, *Endee, call police.* Already it is time. You must to call."

Dude, Dana went to make some tea, like the last bag we had left. Jen's phone was on the table right in front of me, a blinkin' rhythm light flashin' red. The only thing I did was stare at it kinda hypnotized and tryin' to think what to tell gram and the cops. So it made me real startled when *my* frickin' phone rang super loud in my shirt pocket. Dana hopped up, "Look, Endee! Who is? Who?"

The caller ID said area code 708, which was usually the Chicago burbs. Maybe Jen was usin' a pay phone or she was by someone's house. I also thought it could be cops or the frickin' hospital where she had an overdose. So I answered real unsure, "Jen?"

"Andy."

It was a lady's voice. Real womanly, like from a shampoo commercial. I thought maybe it's a doctor or a nurse, though that lady knew my name. "Hello. Andy?"

"Yeah?"

"You know who this is?"

"Kinda. Though no...who's this?"

"It's me, Andy. It's Audra."

If you know what they call *that sinkin' feeling*, I had one of them right there, only more hardcore cauze the whole house sunk maybe three feet. Dana said, *Who, who?* and Audra did her little laugh, "Hi, Andy. Hello."

I could only think one thing to say. "Hey, how's your hand?"

"My hand's healed, Andy. How are you?"

"Okay, better. I mean...yeah *better*. Kinda the same shit around here, though. Got a job right now. How about you?"

Blet, Endee, who? Who?

Audra took this deep breath. "Oh, God...How *am* I, Andy? I'm well. I'm really well."

"That's cool, Audra. You around Chicago or the burbs?"

Dana's face went frickin' Red Lobster.

Audra said, "Chicago? No no. I have one of Larry's phones."

"Larry?" I made big eyes at Dana and went noddin'. "*The* Larry...like your husband Larry?"

"He told me you visited." Then she waited. "Andy, are you distracted up there by something?"

"No, just a big surprise..." Right there Dana grabbed the phone from me like lightning and went babblin' lightspeed *Alio, alio* over by the balcony. Dana only talked Lithuanian, *Keketeki cuss ir kur ir mekpetinku shmeeshmaishmeel.* But her whole talk was short, not even two minutes. She hung up and looked at me real shocked, her mouth kinda open. "Endee. Oh, fuck."

"What?"

"Crazy bitch. She is downstair, downstair on our porch."

Dude, I totally felt the hardcore magnet. And Dana knew it too cauze she was feelin' it. We both got super curious, but frickin' creeped out. Like I started whisperin', "It's stalker shit. Perved."

"What you think, what she want?"

"Just so we go down there."

"How she find us?"

I shrugged. "Phone book. Internet. Maybe Raimis told her."

"Varna?" Dana was pinchin' her chin. "No...no, Endee. *Vashoo mat*, no, you call her back." She handed me the phone. "No, tell her maybe tomorrow we make some drinks. Or in evening. Because right now...yes, we have big mess in house. Or we have right now police business."

I kinda squeezed my phone. My brain was so spun up like a wash machine and I didn't know no excuse to tell Audra. I was tryin' to think something so it would sound normal. But I didn't even have no chance cauze right there frickin' Jen's phone went ringin' on the table, vibratin' around a circle like bedspins. My head kinda fell in my hand and I said, "Hey, Jen. What's up?"

"Drew? Hey. Hi, Drew. Hello?"

"Jen...listen to me real good. You gotta tell me fast. Cauze me and Dana got a total situation over here. Where you at?"

"Sorry. Your pissed, right? Your real pissed?"

"Jen, not frickin' now with that. Ain't no time, just where you at?"

"It's like some road. With farms."

"Where?"

"Around Indiana. Like not even a town out here. Real small cauze I'm stuck. Ran outta gas."

Dude, Jen was callin' from a bait shop about ninety minutes outside Bloomington, kinda north from this town called Terra Haute. For three days the only thing she did was drive around circles and go through country, down some roads she didn't even know. The bait shop owner said he don't mind to wait for us, so I made sure to save that number. I told Jen I'll call back when I figure out a bunch of crap...she should just stay cool and hang with the old man. I called in sick at work and me and Dana went down on the front porch.

Audra was totally waitin' for us. She looked pretty much the same...smilin' real bright with her hair kinda long, and she was wearin' a black leather jacket with dark blue jeans. Me and Dana got hugged together, Audra's head between our cheeks and a hand on the back of my hair. I smelled that same perfume from the first time when I met her, so it reminded me real strong about that day. She said, "Well, it's true, isn't it?" Audra kinda smiled and shaked her head, crossed her arms real tight. "You crazy kids got married."

Dude, I'm not gonna waste no time tellin' all the talk she had about Bloomington's pretty streets and how it was great to see us. Or the way she kept takin' both our hands and squeezin' so hard, explainin' how she tracked us down (frickin' gram told her). We took Audra up to our place and gave her Folgers. She said she was gonna buy us lunch since she had all this real important stuff to tell. Then pretty soon we had one of them moments when nobody knew what the hell to talk about next and it was real awkward. So I told her my sister was stranded in the middle of some road.

"Well," said Audra. "I never met your sister. How would you get to her?"

"I mean. Probably rent a car."

"Oh, why spend? Andy, I have Larry's Audi. She's not far, is she? We'll take a ride and eat lunch later today."

"It might take a couple hours. There's cool places in town where you can wait for us. That's probably better, since it could be hassles."

"I don't mind a hassle. Really, I'm only here to see you and talk to you. What difference does it make where we do it? I have to be back in Chicago on Sunday. Please don't make me wait for you in my hotel lobby or some cafe."

Dude, even though she was smooth talkin' us and actin' real nice, still I had a real bad feeling. But I didn't argue to piss her off cauze I seen how she wanted to tell us something more serious, and me and Dana got curious to know what it could be. I just got a map at the gas station and called Jen, told her we're comin' in a silver Quattro.

The drive through them small roads outside Bloomington was kinda nice and mellow. Trees out there get real thick and green and some of them curved roads go by pretty farms with creeks and round hills. I just sat in the back seat lookin' at Audra's rear view mirror while she talked Lithuanian with Dana, them girls laughin' about stuff. For a while the drive was almost fun, though it didn't take long for shit to get weird.

Audra started *winkin'* at me. She was tryin' to show how me and her knew things together, or she agreed with me about something even though I barely even said no words from the back seat. Audra told the story about Post, how he only let *wink* a couple old ladies visit in the hospital the whole time she was in there. When Audra got out, she sold the Vilnius apartment *wink* cauze her brother died. One day she seen Raimis walkin' down the street with a real hot woman *wink*, probably his girlfriend. Audra asked me, "Andy, this is *really* far from your home. Why was your sister driving around out here?"

"She kinda wigged out."

"Why?"

"It's real complicated."

"Where was she heading? Is there a town out here?"

Dana said, "We have argument with her and she run away."

Audra was quiet, though her eyes got kinda tight, more thin. "Well...she should know. It's impossible to run away."

I asked, "Are you goin' to Costa Rica?"

"Where?"

Dana said stuff in Lithuanian, how Larry bought a house in Costa Rica.

Audra got kinda confused. "Well...no." She nodded at me, though I could tell she never heard nothing about Larry's house and all the gold he bought. For a while she only stared down the road and the car slowed down a little. But then she said, "You won't be a more specific about Jen?"

Dana told it in Lithuanian. And Audra nodded, then shaked her head. I seen her eyes in the mirror, "You should know it's hard to live with an addict, Andy."

"She ain't no addict. Cauze already she finished some real hard rehab. The reason she's pissed, some of that's my fault since I yelled at her."

"Can I tell you something, Andy?" She didn't look at me. "I know it's unfair to surprise you this way, to show up on your porch. But I was scared you wouldn't see me otherwise. And I've come to be honest with you. I really want to be honest with you both. Andy...to be blunt, this is one of your biggest problems. You bottle up feelings too often. And you blame yourself for being angry or confused when someone's taking advantage of you."

I just stared at all them fields goin' by. "Jen ain't got no advantage to take. Cauze right now I'm pretty much the only family she's got."

"But her life's not your responsibility."

"It ain't yours neither. Though your still helpin' out."

"I'm helping *you*." *Wink.* "Because no one ever does."

"That ain't true."

She kinda sighed. "I don't mean to start an argument. But I understand why your sensitive." Now Audra was tailgatin' behind this F-150. "The reason I've come. I wanted to tell both of you good-bye. To make sure we say it, and part ways peacefully. Because you were important people to me even if I had a bad way of showing it."

I said, "Where you goin'?"

She ignored me. "We didn't get a chance when I was ill. But I'm not ill anymore. My mind's as clear as it's been since childhood." She was like five inches from that truck's bumper. "The most important thing...I've forgiven everyone for all they've done to me. Believe me, it's so much easier that way. I've forgiven my father. Also Post...they helped me realize in the hospital that I had never forgiven him for the accident. I've even forgiven Larry. Dana knows the stories, Andy...she may have told you how he used to treat me."

"Yeah. It's real sad."

"Please don't look at me that way, Andy. I'm not pretending I'm an angel. I admitted to Larry that you and I were lovers."

Dana said, "And also me?"

Audra downshifted and hung a quick one round the F-150, passin' him and revvin' up past five, but stayin' totally smooth and in control. "I want to tell that I'm really very sorry. For everything, both of you, for the way I acted. But I've also forgiven you. For all of it."

Dude, me and Dana didn't know what the hell we did wrong to her. But we weren't gonna ask some questions to piss her off when she was drivin' Lithuanian style. I said, "No hard feelings," and Dana said stuff in Lithuanian, reachin' to squeeze Audra's knee. Audra looked at me kinda warm in the mirror, though also fake. We were quiet and goin' over some hills. Then Audra asked us, "Do you want children?"

Dana kinda shrugged. I said, "Lots of people ask us though we don't think about it too much."

"I don't want children anymore," Audra said. "I thought about adopting, but I've let go. I would have been a very good mother, but I've managed to let go." She slowed the car down a little on this tight curve. But then she took off high speed when the long and open road turned totally straight.

Pretty soon we went past Jen's Honda. It was a hundred yards from a small bridge, like two miles down from that bait shop. She was in there playin' checkers with a fat kid and chewin' her nails. The owner was like a retired trucker or something...I seen him finish sellin' hooks to a dude with blue thumbs. The old man said, "I tole your pretty sis, give ten bucks if she needs. Or give a ride down, bring back a gallon. Wouldn't be trouble, but she made you come out. Well...okay then." I just thanked him and he gave directions to a Family Express down the road.

Jen got real quiet and ashamed around Audra, like a boy when he gets a crush on his friend's mom. Probably she felt weird cauze her hair was greasy in a pony tail and you could see she was tired with real dark bags. Audra said, "Jen, I've heard a lot about you. Glad to finally meet." On the way to get a can of gas, Audra kept lookin' at me in the mirror like *now I understand.* Jen turned real shy and Audra really pissed me off right there.

I went to fill up one of them plastic emergency cans, like a red one. While doin' it, we all had this weird moment when they were watchin' me. I was kinda down on one knee and Audra gave a real intense look. Just with her eyes she was askin', *Andy, who's coming with me in my car?* It got awkward and nobody talked, but still we were havin' a conversation together just with eyes. Dana was wonderin' *me or you, Endee?* Jen didn't want to go alone in the Honda cauze that would prove how the whole world hates her for sure. I told Dana, "You guys follow us. Jen, here's your phone."

Dana said, "Maybe I go with Audra?"

"No...you go with Jen. It's cool."

Audra said, "Jen, we're going to eat something in Bloomington. My treat. You're invited, of course."

"Thank you."

I said, "Okay. It's full. Let's go back to Jen's car."

As soon as me and Audra sat alone in the Quattro she got more relaxed, kinda leanin' back in the seat. We got Jen's car totally tanked up full and all of us were goin' back to Bloomington, so Audra finally started talkin' the important stuff she wanted. "Andy, it was a very beautiful message you wrote for me. You know which one I'm talking about."

"I lied cauze I never paid you back. I should still do it."

"Quiet, Andy." She messed around with the air conditioner. "I'm sorry Post didn't let you in the hospital. It was probably for the better. Though I know you wanted to see me."

"Yeah."

"What did you want to say?"

"I didn't have no plan. Just to say bye. Cauze it was time for me to go."

"It's very important to say good-bye when you have our experience, Andy. Face to face, not just letters and messages. Otherwise things feel incomplete."

"That's true."

"I thought about you a lot," she said. "I want you to believe that."

"Me and Dana thought about you too. Probably the main reason we went by Larry's place. Cauze it wasn't finished for us. Like, some questions maybe. Though it backfired."

"What do you mean it backfired?"

"Got kicked out. He didn't tell you that?"

"No."

"Priscilla made me and Dana go out."

Audra kinda nodded. "Your little Dana..." She looked back at Jen's Honda and kept her speed mellow. "Larry kicked you out? Why do you let people trample all over you? Can't you see what people do?"

I was quiet.

"What did Larry tell about me?"

"Stuff I already knew. How you were coked up. And you left him. Then he had pride so he didn't follow you." For real, I almost said how he flashed us. "Also he said you told him lots of lies."

"Andy, I never lied to *you*. Yes, I lied to other liars and hypocrites. They were trying to destroy me, so I had to protect myself. But among them all you were the only one. Although I got weak and failed you."

"That ain't true."

"You know it is. You *know* it. It's not by accident that our paths crossed. You deserve peace, Andy, not an addicted sister and a wife like that...one who'll...you know, trust me...she doesn't understand you. On the top she's very bubbly. But Dana has no respect for others, she's impulsive and selfish. And Jen's transparent, she'll be back on drugs. Most likely she'll have some idiot's baby. You *know* that, Andy."

"Girls get pregnant sometimes, Audra."

"Girls like Jen, yes. She'll have four or five before it's over. Or she'll want to kill them, ask you for money. And you'll pay."

"She don't ask me to pay."

"She will."

"You want me to kick out my sister? Just cauze maybe she'll get pregnant?"

"Already she's stolen from you. Your letting people trample over you. She calls and you come running, pay for her gas. I'm telling you because I love you, Andy. Love you beautifully...as a beautiful human being. You let people trample over you."

We went around this big curve, down a little hill and then up kinda fast. I said, "Jen's messed up, but she's tryin' real hard to get better. And Dana's real good to me. She could get any dude. Don't talk no more shit about them or I'll get pissed. Cauze I love Dana really a lot."

When I said that I seen a reaction in Audra's face, like a twitch in her jaw. It surprised me cauze she had to hold some stuff back. "She will never love you completely, Andy. She'll two-time...with men and women, musicians on the road. You don't know their culture, classical musicians. Of course, you'll stay with her anyway, won't you? No matter how she tramples."

I didn't say shit.

"Truth hurts, right?" Audra sped up the car even more. I seen in the mirror how Jen was tryin' to keep up. "I've been forgiven, Andy," Audra said. "There's a place for me."

"What the fuck does that mean? Your just talkin' weird on purpose."

"We're similiar. It occurs to me now, we've had similar fates. Yes...you know, we were both born in the wrong place at the wrong time. In a great past, we could of had the possibility, find real meaning among these idiots. But in this new world...Jen and Dana are the kind of people who'll feel at home here. But not you."

"You totally had a home, Audra. For real, you had two frickin' homes, both of 'em way more nice than most people get. Only you wanted it different. Though nobody knows what that is cauze probably you don't even know yourself."

"A *home*, Andy. Not a building, a roof over my head. Home's a place where you feel completed."

"Dude, home's a place with relatives. Or people who get together to pull it together, that's all."

"That's not you talking, Andy. You're not a sinic. She's making you that way. Because she's unable to complete you."

I just sat there.

Audra said, "There isn't anyone who can complete me either. I've come to terms. It isn't my fault people are unable to understand what hurts and what doesn't. I have the freedom to call my siblings fools, Andy. But your not giving yourself freedom to call Jen a fool."

I kept on starin' hardcore out the window real tense.

"You know I'm right."

"Audra, your talkin' total horseshit just to piss me off. And your flyin' down the fuckin' road like a maniac."

"Don't take your anger out on me, Andy. In the end it's very simple. There are bright, warm people and there are dark idiots. The two sides won't ever get along. Of course, most of the world is dark, the rest of us feel isolated. Or we make excuses for them the way your doing now, the way I made excuses for Kovas and my father. But the truth is that they were dark idiots."

I was gettin' scared cauze she was really flyin' down the road kinda reckless. "Please, cauze you gotta slow down. Jen's car don't go so fast."

She totally ignored me. "Where's your value? Tell me. Your meaning?"

I put on my seatbelt. "Why you drivin' so fast?"

"It doesn't fit. Where's a place we can fit, Andy? Nowhere down here. You believe me."

"It's just a frickin' Honda."

"You believe me!"

"Yeah. Yeah, I believe you! Totally, just slow it down."

She kept flyin' around them roads, passin' a little Ford like it was standin' still. Audra said, "Tell me you forgive me, Andy."

"I forgive you." Jen was way behind us, but I could see she was flashin' her lights. Then Dana called my phone. "Endee, what the fuck?"

"She's flyin' down the fuckin' road."

Audra said, "Tell her good-bye."

Dana said, "Endee. Make her stop car. We can't so fast."

Audra took the phone. "Good-bye, Dana. We're leaving. Enjoy the mess." She threw the phone on the ground and I tried to get it, but Audra hit my chest. "Let go!" She was shoutin' at me, "Let it go. We're letting go. Right now."

I seen the road goin' in front and I knew what she was gonna do. It was straight ahead, but then a sharp curve, a little valley on the other side with big trees. Audra had it floored and I knew for sure I was gonna fuckin' die. "Stop, Audra!" That curve was comin' closer. "It ain't fair!" Audra just looked straight, her body real relaxed, and then she closed her eyes, holdin' the wheel real light with only two fingers.

So I decided it right there, just *boom* like a reaction. I grabbed the steering wheel real firm and frickin' jacked the whole car hard to the right...over there it was a field with farm bushes and some crops. In that split second when I grabbed the wheel I seen Audra's face, how she got surprised and scared to shit, totally freaked out. Cauze she would of never figured I had the guts to do it, to mess shit up for her so she couldn't get things perfect. So she didn't get it exactly the way she wanted it in the end.

To Apply Ointment

Even though it's like haze, I totally remember stuff from the accident. Like all the airbags went off with noise, hard bumps, rumbles and smashed glass. Dirt and leaves got all over the window and I had a feeling like a cliff's comin' so we're gonna fall. The whole thing went slow motion but also super fast...this real strong power all around where you can't control it. You just wait for something, though you don't want it to come. It's like *no please don't, no please no.*

Then all of a sudden the car stopped and everything went dead quiet. It was a surprise for me and I went lookin' around, seen the airbag like a huge used rubber, then another one by the window. Had that frickin' powder in my nose and mouth. But nothing hurt. For real, it was like a dream, though also panic to get out and I tried the door...didn't have no idea the whole car was upside down. For a while I went messin' with the handles and buttons, but then I remembered Audra. That's the last thing I remember, just gettin' confused. *Audra's in the car. What should I do? How do I do it?* It was andrenaline cauze I had bones broke in my whole body. Dana and Jen seen me tryin' to crawl out when I fainted.

I woke up in a hospital three days later. I don't remember nothing from it, but the girls said I looked at lamps and talked nonsense babbles. For a couple days I was comin' in and out all the time. I remember some voices, like mom sayin', "Them ugly robes," and then gram told somebody, "Just regular Lipton." The first face I can see clean is Dana when she stared at me and said, "Endee, it is crash. Very crazy crash." She was real sloppy

240

together with Jen and gram and mom so I thought probably something real bad happened.

Dude, it was messed up to see my whole body in that bed. A shock when I knew I'm a frickin' disaster. I seen a tube comin' out my chest and I couldn't barely move nothing except fingers, my left arm and a foot. Both my knees were trashed, plus a whole list of bones...four ribs, a collarbone, a dislocated wrist and a cracked hip. My right arm was busted in three places, like in the middle and by the shoulder. The tube was from a collapsed lung and the doctor said I lost some blood.

That doc kinda wigged me out cauze he looked exactly the same like Mitch Hedberg, frickin' even talked like him. One day he was showin' some x-rays to explain about a head fracture above my ear, how they made surgery to fix my eardrum. But then he told me, "Your very lucky, Andrew. No serious spinal injuries, no brain damage." I don't remember gettin' pissed, but Dana and Jen said I laughed in his face real dirty. "That's frickin' lotto, Mitch. Should gimme head by the window." Then I told Dana, "Don't smell no river. I don't smell no river no more."

Them girls said I was actin' weird for a couple weeks where amnesia got mixed up with imagination. I would talk like, "Your phone's in my safe place, Jen," and make a face at her...*duh, don't you know nothing*? I guess Dana kept tryin' to help me remember real life...she showed pictures and my White Sox cap, plus the ring from the train parts. Most of that stuff just made me sad and real confused. But then finally everything started comin' back super clean when she showed pics Dėdė Liudas took in Nida...the little cabin...Big Head and Ponia Grybienė sittin' by the stump table...then Tepti lookin' at me with one ear flopped over. Holy shit, right there it was like a flood and I could see my whole life in maybe 20 seconds. It was instant replay with them trees comin' right at me again, the Quattro haulin' ass down the road.

I didn't know what happened to Audra...maybe she was in another room. But Dana seen her body in the car right by me, something I don't want to describe right here. When Dana explained it, I knew it was true and stayed sloppy for an hour, real bad with pain in my ribs and head. Mom and gram didn't know why. They thought it was Mitch, since he said I would need a year to walk regular, like knee surgery after bones got healed. But Dana told them nurses more details about Audra and they totally brung me a shrink. I talked lots of stuff with her, though nothing about jackin' the car myself. For real, I got scared they would blame my ass or tell cops.

Especially since Dana got interviewed by a reporter (I was still passed out when that happened). His story ended up in one of them country newspapers, like a short article. It said Audra had a hotel room in the Bloomington Marriott and she left another notebook in there. She wrote her plan to make suicide after some visits with people around Chicago and Michigan. The thing is, she was havin' trouble...most people told her to fuck off and didn't want to talk with her no more. Her original plan was to crash the car in a wall by herself someplace, maybe in a bridge or a factory. It was a long list with all her reasons, most similar to stuff she said in the car, how she's smart and way too many people are dumb. That notebook probably got sent to Larry since they were still married legal. We found out he made creamation from her body and sold all them homes around Berwyn, Cicero and Oak Park, so different people live on LeMoyne now. Who knows where Larry moved, if that story about Costa Rica was true.

All the people from Lithuania went nuts when they heard what happened. Everyday I would get a picture from somebody and Dana would translate letters and messages. The pics with Tepti effected me real hard. I was rememberin' Lithuania, could smell the bathroom in ŠMC and see them drunks rubbin' up by kiosks, feel the long ass time it took the sun to go down out there. Sometimes I would wake up in the dark and feel panic...for real, I would think there's one more important thing to finish with Audra. But then it would be a shock cauze I would see my body and remember how bad I'm messed up. When your half-crashed on hardcore pain drugs and dreamin' about walkin' your dog by Proksa Park, wakin' up like that is a horrible feeling.

For sure, Jen was takin' everything the worst. Gram thought she might go deep end cauze she was blamin' herself and talkin' weird shit. But then outta nowhere Jen told everybody she got two jobs, a cashier at the hippy grocery and telemarketing. Even though she insulted some dude on the phone and telemarketing fired her ass, she got another one makin' beds at Motel 6. I don't think she did no meth the whole time since her rehab. She joined one of them circle groups where people talk for support and you can call somebody in the middle of the night.

Dana kept on workin' at the movies. Her semester started in August and she was crazy busy with opera classes. But she found a first floor apartment without no stairs or bumps between the rooms, cauze I would need a wheel chair and then a walker. Jen helped Dana set it up, this swank apartment with halogens and dimmers. A room with a TV and a wide table by a window where I could see one old timer's back yard, him sittin' out there with newspapers all the time.

That new apartment was higher rent, more than six hundred. I got shocked cauze mom paid the frickin' deposit (though we owe the whole thing back when we move). It was weird to see her change a little...talkin' with her is more easy now, just not for a long time. I was still on her medical insurance, but that company didn't pay all the surgery and rehab...you don't even know how high them bills are right now. The mortgage bank said mom can't do no more refinancing, so she put the Berwyn house for sale. Maybe she hangs some of that on me, though never to my face. One night in the hospital she got real sloppy, kinda hammered, babblin' all this stuff how I used to fit on her lap. Gram told her, "Bet, stop now cauze that's embarrassin' him," but mom didn't stop. She just sat sloppy, talkin' how she wished the whole life could be real different.

Jen got her divorce with Gunther right around February '08. It was real complicated and made her pissed with stress. But she scored money for a computer and a brand new Honda. She lived with me and Dana for almost a year, movin' in her own place around the middle of July '08. And for that whole year Jen totally helped Dana pay rent and bills cauze I couldn't work. Holy crap, I got so bored sittin' around the house with nothing to do. Like I would be laid down in bed and Jen would put a DVD for me, but I would space out and think real deep, way more than ever from my whole life. For a long time I was hearin' horror stories cauze the clinic said the worse case scenario...maybe I won't walk never again. I would have lots of pain in my hip and it would go through my leg and back. Or them muscle relaxers would haze my ass out and I would imagine my whole life in a wheel chair. If I didn't see the future then I kept *rememberin'* stuff over and over. Not just pictures in my head, cauze pretty much any memory would have a question with meanings, like regrets mixed up with wishes. *If none of this would of happened, then I never would of got married. But if I never would of married Dana, then I never would of killed nobody.* You can't look at it no other way. For real, I did it, though I never told nobody, only Dana. And right here.

For a long time I was *real* pissed off. I kinda wished I had somebody around to blame. If I seen anything happy, I would hate it...the geezer next door...frickin' joggers...anytime Jen laughed from a movie. In my body stuff was healin', only I didn't believe it...I thought they were tellin' me lies, cauze all the time the clinic said it helps if you get a better attitude. Dana was real patient with me, thought I just need time.

One day she brung a CD with songs she burned at Jacob's. Them songs were her favorite from childhood, totally happy songs her mom used to play. She put it on for me, Ella Fitzgerald, like a real famous singer I never heard about. "I don't wanna hear no old lady, Dana. Frickin' a song about a basket? Just sounds like a dumbass kid."

Holy shit, right there Dana snapped. At first she tried stayin' cool, but I seen her turnin' red till finally she went nuts and cracked the CD in half. I never seen nobody get sloppy like that, angry and sad...my mom never yelled at me like that. "You don't like song? Fuck, you don't like my favorite? Then what you like?

What you want?" It was a long speech. "Because crazy bitch kill you, Endee...yes, you are dead. Not in trees or crash, but still she kill you dead. What she wanted for us? She win! She want we have nothing, and now we have. Because you cannot see nothing good...like idiot, only negative and bad. Idiot who don't see nothing. Can't laugh. And I hate like this to live."

Dude, that kinda woke my ass up. It was like a 180 for me cauze I knew she was right. I seen stuff was healin', my wrist and arm, and my headaches were goin' away without no pills. I started doin' them workouts the clinic showed, weird ones where you pull a rubber band off a doorknob and twist a plastic ring. The therapist said I needed even more positive attitude, to try harder and get a hobby or do something with routine, not just movies and TV the whole time.

That was one of the main reasons I got writin' my story, startin' right around the time Jen got the computer. Even though already I'm sick of writin' this, I did it pretty much every day, takin' a small break after my knee operations. It totally helped me so I didn't go insane, plus it got easier around the house when I had something to do. And it made the time go quicker.

Right now it's already January '09 and I'm almost back to normal. I still need a walker if my hip gets bad, but at the gym yesterday I did treadmill for 25 minutes with good incline. Sometimes my one foot goes numb without no reason and I feel crap in my body before the rain, all them places where bones broke. My one wrist don't work the way it should and I can't lift too much heavy stuff with my right arm. The worst part, I lost about 70% hearing in one ear, something that won't never come back. But I'm workin' in the camping store already since November. And I signed up for twelve hours at Ivy Tech cauze I wanna try one of them Physical Therapy Assistant degrees. Lots of stuff has to go good for me to finish, since that job needs to massage people and bend over. But my assistant at the clinic got her degree after a car accident almost the same like mine.

I guess I don't worry too much about a job right now. I sorta figure I'll get the thing I'm supposed to get, cauze I seen how it happens with music people. Dana already met lots of opera singers and violin players, a French horn girl and this dude who plays triangle. That's all he does, just taps a triangle *ding ding ding* like windchimes and they totally gave his ass a scholarship. Hangin' around college, you figure out they got jobs pretty much for anybody. If you can't do the violin or sing them songs, for sure you can go *ding ding ding*. And the triangle dude gets to wear the same swanko tux just like a piano player.

I had a real important thing happen to me with that triangle guy, like a good place to finish my story so it can finally be done. He came over by our house one time with some other friends so we were drinkin' a couple beers. Right there I seen he couldn't hold no booze cauze one Heineken made him slur. The guy wanted to know how come I'm in a wheel chair, so Dana told the story, like a ten minute version. And the dude asked me a question, "So this crash...it make you feel more lucky or more unlucky?"

I just looked at Dana and Jen. And I bit inside my mouth. Maybe that dude didn't mean no harm...maybe he was just curious. But I didn't want no question like that...for real, I almost asked it right back to him. Cauze you don't need to be in a wheelchair to hear that question. Lucky or unlucky is a good question for anybody, especially a triangle player with a frickin' scholarship.

But I didn't say nothing. I just ditched the party and rolled back by my room to sit pissed. I knew I embarrassed Dana, so that got me even more pissed, like why would I do it? What's the point? I checked Skype to see if Raimis or Varna were on, but my friend list was just gray dots. My feelings inside didn't make no sense cauze I was like a steam pot. I could of took a moth with pliers to shove him in a candle. And I remembered Audra's story, how them brothers cut the serpent to make a blood wave.

For a while I was starin' at this radiator. And by accident I seen a spider web in the corner. The spider wasn't real big, but he had a belly and long brown legs. The web was only a couple feet from my desk and I could reach it real easy, didn't even need to move.

So you probably already know what I did. I totally grabbed the spider in my hand to squeeze so hard, a little surprised since it seemed pretty easy. The squeeze smeared the spider dead and I looked at the smuke to wipe on my jeans. Right there I frickin' thought I was hardcore, kinda proud since doin' this showed I changed real different. Stronger now with some good courage.

The thing is, I didn't know how bad the little dude got me. My hand was kinda numb so I didn't feel the bite, not no pinch or sting. But pretty soon I knew something was wrong...I got a cold sweat and wanted to puke. Then my hand swelled up red and stayed puffed up for a whole week...it hurt to push the chair around and to type. Frickin' I had to apply ointment in the morning and night, this greasy stuff that smelled like alcohol and gave a little sting. Totally like a reminder, like the little dude kept comin' back to ask how come I did it? How come I would get pissed off like that from only a question? And why would I take out my stupid feelings on something so small?

Andy Nowak

Bloomington, IN January 20, 2009

www.myspace.com/andrewberwynnowak

Acknowledgments

The completion of this novel would have been impossible without the support and love of Maria Storm, my wife and greatest inspiration. I also would have been quite lost without RP's steadfast and patient guidance. My former professors, primarily Michael Shapiro and Ben Marcus offered wisdom, ecouragement and important lessons. Mark Binelli, Dan Vyleta, Lisa Rosenthal, Helen Gallagher, Mark Litwicki, Christina Saraceno, Sean Robinson, Moacir P. de sa Pereira and Chantal Wright helped tremendously with feedback and advice. An *ačiū* goes to Janė Schrekengost, Rūta Kiverienė and Audra Mockaitytė for information about Lithuania.

The composition of Kenny Briggs' letters would have been impossible without stories shared by combat veterans I've met in trains, buses, bars and my Rhetoric classes. Two anthologies were indispensable: *War letters: extraordinary correspondence from American wars*, edited by Andrew Carrol with a forward by Douglas Brinkley; and *Letters from Vietnam*, edited by Bill Adler.

A very special acknowledgment goes to my students. So many of you have taught me more than any book or college class ever will. I can't list all your names here, but know that this book's for you!

Apologies to all the regulars at ŠMC still waiting for me to buy that promised round.

A shout out to Igor Lumpert whose CD *Minerali* does wonders for writer's block. (Hand picked love lights all around, dude!)

And, *pagaliau...Kaimiečiams KLAK!*